# "You coming to my lecture tonight?"

Joe leaned closer, drawing in the scent of her, the nearness of her, the warmth of her.

"You inviting me?" Dani said, concentrating on the plate she was drying.

She was smart and beautiful and sexy—and for some reason very peeved at him.

"I think you might find it very informative and educational."

"Really," she commented with complete indifference, adding the dried plate to the stack on the counter and taking the washed and rinsed plate he handed her. "You must think very highly of yourself, Detective."

"I do," he said, thinking that the sweet smell of her hair was like the elixir of life. "And if it scores me some points, I think very highly of you, too, Counselor."

"Really," she repeated in that same monotone. She added another dried dessert plate to the stack.

"I do."

"Enough to stick around for a while?"

"Maybe."

She glanced up at him, eyebrows raised. "Really?"

Dear Reader,

*Montana Unbranded* explores today's wild mustangs, and takes us back to the Bow and Arrow Ranch in Park County, Montana, and to the cast of characters who brought this historic ranch to life in *Montana Dreaming, Buffalo Summer* and *Montana Standoff*.

No other animal embodies the untamed spirit of the West as much as the iconic mustang. In our hearts they will always gallop free, manes and tails streaming behind them. Unfortunately, their reality is far different. Today, wild horses roam an ever-shrinking habitat that also plays host to ranchers and farmers whose survival is driven by the bottom line. Unbranded horses are protected by the Wild and Free-Roaming Horses and Burros Act of 1971, which states they are to be "protected from capture, branding, harassment, or death; and to accomplish this they are to be considered in the area where presently found, as an integral part of the natural system of the public lands." However, they are also subject to management by the secretary of the interior, and can be removed from their range by the Bureau of Land Management "to preserve and maintain a thriving natural ecological balance and multiple-use relationship in that area." The conflicts are obvious.

While writing this story, news flashed across major media outlets that the BLM was planning to slaughter forty-five thousand wild horses being held in BLM holding facilities. Public outcry prevented this from happening, but the problem remains. Enter the Mustang Heritage Foundation. Their mission is to get these horses out of holding pens and into adoptive homes. To learn more, go to www.mustangheritagefoundation.org.

It was Virginia Woolf who wrote, "Blame it or praise it, there is no denying the wild horse in us." I know it's in me, and I bet it's in you, too. Enjoy the ride!

*Nadia Nichols*

# NADIA NICHOLS

—

## Montana Unbranded

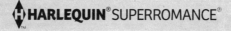

HARLEQUIN® SUPERROMANCE®

Recycling programs
for this product may
not exist in your area.

ISBN-13: 978-0-373-64042-3

Montana Unbranded

Copyright © 2017 by Penny R. Gray

Printed in U.S.A.

**Nadia Nichols** went to the dogs at the age of twenty-nine and currently operates a kennel of twenty-eight Alaskan huskies. She has raced her sled dogs in northern New England and Canada, works at the family-owned Harraseeket Inn in Freeport, Maine, and is also a registered Master Maine Guide.

She began her writing career at the age of five, when she made her first sale, a short story called "The Bear" to her mother for twenty-five cents. This story was such a blockbuster that her mother bought every other story she wrote and kept her in ice-cream money throughout much of her childhood.

Now all her royalties go toward buying dog food. She lives on a remote solar-powered northern Maine homestead with her sled dogs, a Belgian draft horse named Dan, several cats, two goats and a flock of chickens. She can be reached at nadianichols@aol.com.

### Books by Nadia Nichols

#### HARLEQUIN SUPERROMANCE

*A Soldier's Pledge*
*From Out of the Blue*
*Everything to Prove*
*Sharing Spaces*
*Montana Standoff*
*A Full House*
*Buffalo Summer*
*Across a Thousand Miles*
*Montana Dreaming*

Visit the Author Profile page at Harlequin.com for more titles.

For Dan, my horse and my friend, who has the unbranded heart of a mustang.

# *PROLOGUE*

EVER SINCE THE SHOOTING, his nights had been fractured with brief moments of consciousness, coming up out of the darkness to remember things he'd rather forget. The awful struggle to breathe. Marconi's face bending over him. Marconi's voice, taunting him. The taste of copper in his mouth and the smell of rotting garbage. The cold pelt of rain washing his blood into the city gutter. Rico finding him, the sound of sirens. Darkness and pain… How long that lasted, he didn't know, but it felt like forever before the tormented struggle between life and death finally became a deep, healing sleep.

The ringing of the telephone brought him awake with an upward lunge, a movement that exploded in pain as his hand stabbed beneath his pillow for a weapon that wasn't there. The room was dim. Shades drawn. The illuminated hands on the bedside clock read nine a.m. He'd been sleeping for twelve straight hours. Not possible, not in a hospital. He reached for the phone, his voice hoarse from sleep. "Ferguson."

"Hey, it's Rico, hope I didn't wake you. I figured you'd have been up for hours, flirting with the nurses. Thought you'd want to know, the date's been set for the court hearing. June 23. Thought you'd also want to know, Cap said you should get out of town until the hearing. Thinks it'd be safer. So do I. We all do."

He moved his head on the pillow, back and forth, as if Rico were in the room. "I'm not running from those bastards."

"I wouldn't, either—I'd fly. A Boeing 747'd get you a whole lot farther a whole lot faster."

"They won't try anything now."

"No? You dusted three of Marconi's henchmen in that shoot-out, and it's your testimony that's going to put him away for life. You're messing with the Providence family here, Joe. This is serious stuff."

"Tell me about it. I'm the one lying here looking like a piece of Swiss cheese." The door swung inward. A nurse entered briskly, opened the shades and gave him a brief, professional smile as she lifted the plate cover on his breakfast tray. He hadn't heard breakfast being delivered. Slept right through it. Jesus, Marconi himself could've crept in here and smothered him with a pillow, except for the two badges stationed outside his door.

The nurse frowned at the untouched food before replacing the plate cover.

"What about that pretty red-haired sister of yours?" Rico pressed. "Stay with her."

The nurse was taking his vital signs, jotting them on the clipboard that hung at the foot of the bed. He waited until she left before responding. "Molly's busy planning her wedding. She doesn't need her big brother hanging out."

"Molly won't have a big brother and your son won't have a father if you don't wise up."

"Find Marconi."

"We will. Meantime, go visit your sister."

"I'll think about it."

"Time's up. Dead men don't make good witnesses. And, Joe? I mean it. Don't tell anyone where you're going, not even your mother. Cap's hand-delivering a new ID for you this morning. He's making the flight reservations and providing transportation to the airport."

Rico hung up. The nurse had returned with a syringe in her hand and was preparing to draw blood, something nurses did 24/7 and seemed to enjoy. She put a rubber tourniquet on his arm, swabbed briskly with an alcohol-drenched cotton ball, pinched him with the needle. Blood flowed into the tube, as if he hadn't lost enough already.

"Rumor has it I'm being discharged today," he said.

She tucked the syringe and vial of blood into a little tray. "Not if you don't eat your breakfast," she said with all the warmth of the military police, though she softened her words with a smile before departing the room. He lifted the plate cover to study the contents. Lowered it. Looked around the drab room he'd come to hate over the past two weeks. Rain streaked the window, blurring his view. It hadn't stopped raining since the night he was shot. He was sick of the rain. Sick of lying in a hospital bed and counting the holes in the ceiling tiles. Sick of this city.

Maybe Rico was right. A few weeks in Montana with his baby sister might not be such a bad idea. She was always asking him to visit, and he'd always wanted to see just how much wild was left in the West.

# CHAPTER ONE

"STOP YOUR FIDGETING, Molly. I promise I'm almost done."

Dani Jardine deftly inserted three more pins into the cream-colored fabric gathered at her friend's waistline, then rose to her feet and executed a slow walk-around, studying the drape of the gown. Molly Ferguson was standing with her arms obediently outstretched at shoulder height and had been for the past five minutes, but her patience was wearing thin. She met Dani's eyes in the mirror, tossed her shoulder-length mane of red hair, blew out an impatient breath and dropped her arms to her sides.

"Well? Can you fix it?"

"There might be just enough fabric for me to make the alterations."

"Will it look all right?"

"You're going to be the most beautiful bride ever."

"You don't think I look fat?"

"Molly, you couldn't possibly look fat."

"I've gained five pounds in the past two weeks."

"So stop eating all that corned beef and cabbage."

Molly gnawed on a fingernail, turning sideways and eyeing herself in the full-length mirror on her friend's bedroom door. "I wish it were that easy, but it's more than just food."

Dani met her friend's eyes in the mirror. Molly's were dark with unspoken pathos and shining with tears. For a few moments Dani wondered what could possibly be wrong, and then it clicked, and a big smile brightened her face. "You're pregnant! I don't believe it." Dani hugged her friend impulsively. "You're having a baby! Why didn't you tell me?"

"I only found out this morning. All winter we've been crazy busy with the fund-raiser for Madison Mountain and I was so afraid we wouldn't make Condor International's deadline to raise the money. I was sick to my stomach all the time and I thought it was from the stress of it all. Then we made the deadline, we raised the money, we did it. The mountain was saved from that huge mining operation. I should have felt better but I just kept feeling squeamish. Then this morning, because Steven insisted, I went to see my doctor and…" Molly drew a sharp breath and the three recently inserted pins popped out of the fabric. The tears spilled over and Molly wiped them from her cheeks. "It turns out, I'm *very* pregnant."

"That's wonderful news, Molly! You always wanted kids, and in a few weeks you're getting married to the man of your dreams. But you're acting like the doctor just gave you a death sentence. What's wrong?"

"Steven doesn't know yet, and when my mother finds out she'll disown me. She's *very* Catholic."

"Steven'll be tickled pink and so will your mother. How far along are you?"

"Dr. Phillips thinks almost two months. Eight weeks! And I didn't even notice missing my monthlies, that's how stressed out I've been."

"A December baby is perfect."

"Why?"

"Because a baby has to be the most perfect Christmas gift of all," Dani said, giving Molly another hug. "I'm so happy for you both."

"But the timing couldn't be worse—we don't have any money, the practice is struggling, we're living on a shoestring and…"

"You have each other and now you have a baby to celebrate. You're the two luckiest people in the whole world."

Molly wiped fresh tears from her cheeks and

tried for a smile. "I know you're right, Dani, but the baby part scares me. I'm not ready to be a mother and I don't know how I'll tell Steven. We agreed to wait a few years before starting a family."

"Unless I missed something in high school biology, Steven had something to do with all this."

Molly heaved another big sigh and more pins scattered to the floor. "Oh, Dani, I wish we still lived in the same town. I love Steven's place and it's close to our office, but I miss our talks over lunch. And right now I really, really miss those big, steady paychecks I got working for Skelton, Taintor and Abbot."

"You'd hate yourself if you were still working for those heartless corporate sharks. The law firm of Young Bear and Ferguson is going to be a great success, and who knows where I'll be in a year's time. I might just have to move south to be nearby when you need a babysitter or a third partner."

Hope illuminated Molly's face. "I'd love it if you moved to Bozeman, but what about your house? What about Jack?"

Dani picked the pins up off the floor, avoiding Molly's eyes. "Jack and I split up," she said with what she hoped was an offhand shrug. "It was bound to happen, Molly. He was gone ninety percent of the time with his job and surrounded by beautiful stewardesses."

Molly reached out and clamped on to her, all wild red hair and hazel eyes. "You mean, Jack's *gone*? When did this happen? How could he just walk out on you like that? What about the house? The dogs?"

"The house was mine to begin with and he left me his dogs. He walked in one night about two months ago, told me he was in love with another woman, said I could have everything, not that there was anything of his here except for the dogs, and that was that. It was all very civil. Too civil, really. I didn't cry or beg him to stay. I don't think we ever really loved each other, not the way you and Steven do."

"Let me get this straight. *He walked out on you two months ago, and you didn't tell me?*"

"I didn't want to upset you. Your wedding's coming up and you were working so hard on raising the money to save Madison Mountain and…"

"Oh, Dani." Molly embraced her fiercely, causing more pins to pop out. "How could he do that to you? You're the smartest, sweetest, most gorgeous girl on the face of the planet and he's the biggest idiot of all time. I'm so sorry it didn't work out. Or maybe I shouldn't be. You deserve a whole lot better and now you have the chance to find that person."

Dani shook her head with a rueful laugh. "Not me. I'm done with men. Come on. Get out of that dress, very carefully, and I'll buy you lunch."

"I can't eat for another month, remember?"

"You're eating for two now, and don't worry about your gown. I'll alter it this week, but you might want to think about bumping the wedding date up."

"I'd rather not," Molly said with a shake of her head. "The invitations are in the mail. But I'll think about it."

Molly's cell phone rang while she was in the midst of peeling out of the wedding dress, and in her haste the last of the pins scattered onto the floor. Dani rescued the gown and the pins while her friend rummaged in her purse for her cell phone. "Ferguson," she said. Then, a heartbeat later, she squealed, *"Joseph!"* and her face lit up so bright that even if she hadn't cried out his name, Dani would have known it was Molly's beloved older brother.

"Joseph, saints be praised. Mom told me this morning you were doing much better! When are they letting you out of the hospital?" She paced across the room, then stopped abruptly. "You mean, you're *here*? In Helena? At the airport?

*Here?* Right now? Jesus, Mary and… Oh, Joseph, you should have let me know you were coming!" Another pause. "Well, you're just lucky I'm in town because I don't even live in Helena anymore." After a brief pause, she continued. "Yeah, I'm only here because I'm visiting Dani. She took Friday off from work to alter my wedding gown." Molly caught her eye and made a face. "I live outside Bozeman now, with Steven, about two hours away. But don't tell Mom! She'll have a fit. You'll love Steven's place—it's really pretty and you'll have your own bedroom and private bath and you'll get to meet Steven and, oh, Joseph, it's so good to hear your voice! Are you sure you're really all right?" Another pause. "Well, you did the right thing, coming here. There's no place like Montana. We'll take good care of you. You'll love it, you'll see. You won't want to leave. Dani and I will pick you up and then take you to lunch before heading south. Sit tight, we'll be there in two shakes of a lamb's tail!"

She hung up and spun around with an incredulous laugh, beaming. "Joseph's *here*! His flight just got in. He was released from the hospital this morning and decided to come *here* for a visit! Can you believe it? Big-city cop from back east finally meets the Wild West!"

Dani held the discarded wedding dress in

her arms and watched while Molly shimmied into her skirt and pulled on her blouse, fingers flying down the buttons. She made another face as she zipped the skirt. "I won't be able to wear this much longer, either." She slipped her feet into her leather pumps and reached for her handbag. "Come on, Dani, you have to meet my big brother. He's the coolest, handsomest and nicest guy in the whole world."

"You told me Steven was the coolest, handsomest and nicest guy in the whole world."

Molly laughed. "They're the two coolest, handsomest, nicest guys in the whole world."

"He must have made a miraculous recovery. Just last week he was in critical condition and you were ready to hop a plane back east and hold his hand while he died."

"He's a Ferguson, tough as they come. It'll take more than a few bullets to keep Joseph down. Come on, he's waiting!"

Dani shook her head. "You two have a lot of catching up to do, and I should stay here and get to work on this gown."

Molly took the gown from her and tossed it over the nearest chair. "You've got a whole month to figure out how you're going to alter the dress. I want you to meet my brother. Now that Jack's out of the picture, I think Joseph would be perfect for you. You'll get along great.

And so you know, he's unbranded, just like those wild horses you dote on. Doesn't belong to anyone. Footloose and fancy-free. Let's take him to our favorite deli for lunch. Like you said, I'm eating for two now."

TEN MINUTES LATER Molly was circling her bright red Mercedes sedan past the terminal looking for a place to pull over and park. She huddled over the wheel, scowling with impatience. "I've never seen so much traffic at this airport. I can't double-park—I'll get a ticket for sure. Dani, jump out here, run inside the terminal and bring him out, would you? He'll be at the Delta gate and he already knows you look just like Julia Ormond in *Legends of the Fall*— I've told him a dozen times."

"What does Joseph look like?"

"He's tall, dark and handsome, a rugged Tom Cruise type, you can't miss him, and he always wears a dark leather jacket and looks a little dangerous."

"Does he have red hair like yours?"

"No, I'm the only one in the family who was cursed with that. Quick, get out, I'm holding up traffic. I'll drive around again and pick you up."

Dani obeyed reluctantly. She entered the terminal and headed toward the Delta gate, where she spotted Joseph easily, seated in a corner chair just outside the gate, back to the wall, forearms resting on denim-clad knees, hands holding a paperback. Head down, reading. Dark glossy hair. Dark leather jacket. Had to be him.

"Joseph?" He glanced up from the paperback and she felt a jolt clear to her soul. Dark eyes, sharp and wary, measured her in a split second and deemed her safe. "I'm Dani Jardine, Molly's friend. She sent me in to find you because she had to stay with the car—there's no place to park."

He stood and shoved the book into his jacket pocket. "The name's Joe," he said, extending his hand. "Molly's the only one in the family who calls me Joseph." His handshake was warm and firm.

"Do you have any luggage?"

He shook his head. "Spur of the moment trip."

They exited the terminal together and stood at the curb. Dani was relieved when the red Mercedes appeared almost instantly. Molly slowed as she drew abreast of them and then stopped abruptly with a chirp of brakes. She jumped out, leaving her door ajar and ignoring the driver behind who laid on his horn. She raced toward her brother. "Joseph! Sweet Mary, Mother of... What have they done to you? Oh, Joseph, you look like death warmed over." She plastered herself against him and burst into tears.

"I'll move the car," Dani offered, and beat a hasty retreat to the driver's side, slamming the door and pulling ahead of the stopped traffic. She drove around the circuit, and by the time she drew near the terminal again, Molly and her brother were ready and waiting. She double-parked, brother and sister climbed aboard and she drove off.

Molly sat in the back and made Joseph sit in the front. "There's more leg room," she explained, and she blew her nose as Dani pulled back into traffic. "I can't believe they let you out of the hospital, Joseph. Mom said you were much better. She lied!"

Joe hitched himself carefully sideways to look at his sister. "I'm just tired, that's all. It's a long flight to the Wild West. Where's this deli you were talking about?"

"I bought a rotisserie chicken for dinner last night. How about we go to my place and I'll fix us chicken sandwiches," Dani said, wondering just how much more activity Joe was up for, considering the injury he was still recovering from and the journey he'd just made.

Molly dabbed at her eyes and blew her nose again. "I think that's a much better idea, if you're sure it's no trouble, Dani."

But of course it turned out to be big trouble, because Dani hadn't considered the fact that she'd not done any real grocery shopping since Jack moved out. She had no bread, no lettuce, no mayonnaise and nothing to drink except tea, but Molly was too distraught to notice and her brother was too polite to do anything but thank her for the cup of hot tea she handed him, along with half the cold chicken sliced and arranged as artfully on the plate as she could manage, with a garnish of two dill pickles, one on each side of the plate. "Do you take sugar in your tea?" she asked.

"No, thanks, this is fine," he said. He sat at her kitchen table and deftly kept her two golden retrievers at bay while he ate. "Thank you, that was great, way better than hospital food," he said after finishing off all of the chicken, both pickles and his second cup of Earl Grey. "Eat up, Molly."

"I *am* eating." Molly's eyes were red-rimmed from crying.

"No, you're not. You haven't touched a thing," he chided. "What're your dog's names?" This he asked of Dani, who was nibbling on a chicken wing with about as much appetite as Molly.

"Winchester and Remington." She smiled at his expression. "Jack liked to duck hunt."

"Jack?"

"My ex. He left me his dogs when he moved out, but I'm not complaining. They're great company, better than Jack ever was."

He grinned at her words, and all at once Dani saw what Molly had been talking about. Take away the hospital pallor and the shadows beneath those wary eyes, add about ten pounds and Joseph Ferguson became the handsome brother Molly had bragged about. Not handsome the way Jack had been handsome. Not smooth, well-groomed, airline-captain handsome. More of a tough, streetwise and dangerous handsome. "I've heard dogs tend to be better company than most people," he said.

"They go everywhere with me, except to work. Jack got them as eight-week-old pups, siblings, after we moved in together, but he's an airline pilot and was gone most of the time. I think that's the only reason he hung around so long, because he loved the dogs."

"I find that a little hard to believe," he said, and Dani felt her cheeks warm.

"Molly tells me you live in Providence," she said, changing the subject. "That's a big city compared to here."

"It's bigger, all right, but not nearly as good-looking." He grinned that crooked grin again and Dani was completely disarmed.

"You'll love it here, Joseph. You won't want

to go back to that smelly old city," Molly said. "Besides, you can't, at least not for a while. My wedding's in less than a month, and from the looks of you, you'll need at least a month of Montana living to get you back on your feet. Maybe little Fergie can come out early and stay with you. I haven't seen him since last year and I bet he's growing like a weed. It would do the two of you good to spend some time together out here."

"I've never taken a month of vacation time all at once, but right about now that sounds pretty good." He pushed out of his chair. "Thanks for the lunch, Dani."

"You're welcome. It's nice to finally meet you, Joseph."

"Joe," he said, wandering into the living room, flanked by both dogs. "Did you take these photos?"

He was studying the gallery of prints she'd hung on her living room wall. "Yes," she replied.

"They're really good. You obviously like horses."

"These shots are of the wild horse band in the Arrow Root Mountains. I'm documenting them for the Wild Horse Foundation, so I camp there a lot. I'm actually going up this weekend for the first time this year. I think the snow's melted enough to hike to the forest service cabin I stay at."

"Molly tells me you've climbed every mountain west of the Missouri."

"Not quite, but I like to hike and mountain climb. How about you?"

"We don't have many mountains in Providence, but I wouldn't mind climbing a few of yours," he said, casting that grin in her direction. Dani wondered if he always flirted so blatantly, and she also wondered why she was blushing like a schoolgirl.

"Joseph," Molly scolded. "You're in no condition for that sort of thing. The mountains out here are tall."

"I'm sure we could find a short one," Dani said.

"Just as long as it's not Braveheart," Molly said.

Dani shook her head. "We'll leave that one for you and Steven, but you'd better climb it soon or Luther Makes Elk might not officiate at your wedding."

"Luther Makes Elk?" Joe said.

"He's a Crow holy man," Dani said. "You'll meet him at Molly's wedding, if not before. Luther Makes Elk saved Steven's life."

"This Montana story just gets better and better. My baby sister's been holding out some key information from her big brother."

Molly jumped up and grabbed her purse. "Come on, Joseph, we better hit the road. I told Steven I'd be home for supper."

Joe cast his sister a questioning look, and Molly sighed. "I promise to tell you all about Luther Makes Elk on the way to Bozeman. Thanks again for everything, Dani. I'll call you tonight."

"You'd better," Dani said. "In the meantime, don't worry about your wedding gown. It's going to be beautiful."

"It's not the gown I'm worried about," Molly confided as they hugged goodbye.

"Everything will be fine," Dani said.

Joe shook her hand once more upon leaving, and Dani watched them descend the porch steps and walk out to Molly's red Mercedes.

She waved them out of sight, then closed the door and leaned against it with a sigh. Her hand was still tingling.

So that was Molly's big brother, Joseph. *Wow.*

JOE WATCHED THE scenic vistas roll past his window as Molly pulled onto the highway heading south toward Bozeman. Mountains loomed in every direction, walling off the horizons. He'd never been west of New York before and, as exhausted as he was, he found himself captivated. He also found himself wondering about Dani Jardine. Attorney, great photographer, down-to-earth and drop-dead gorgeous. What sort of man would walk out on a woman like that?

"You're being mighty quiet for a Ferguson, Joseph," Molly prodded after a while.

"Just thinking."

After ten more minutes of silence his sister cast another sidelong glance and nodded sagely. "You're thinking about Dani. It's written all over your face."

"Not me, baby sister. I swore off women after my divorce."

"I might have believed that two hours ago, but Dani's smart, beautiful and has a heart of gold. I don't see how any red-blooded man could help falling in love with her, especially after she fed him lunch." Her teasing smile faded and her face grew serious. "Why are you *really* here, Joseph? You didn't come just to see me. You would've called first, and Mom would've told me you were coming when I spoke with her last night. She doesn't even know you're here, does she? Does this have anything to do with Marconi?"

He gave her a sharp look. "What do you know about it?"

"Honestly, I wasn't born yesterday. There's this thing called the internet. I have access to legal search engines, and I tend to dig a little deeper than your average newspaper reporter. And don't forget, I grew up with some of your friends. Rico always gives me the straight scoop."

"Do Mom and Dad know anything about Marconi?"

"If they do, they didn't get it from me." She cast him a curious glance. "What did you tell them?"

Joe shook his head. "Same thing the newspapers said, that I stumbled into the middle of a drug deal and stopped a few stray bullets."

"Have they caught him yet?"

"Not yet, but they've got him cornered. It's just a matter of time."

"You think you're safe here?"

"Marconi's too busy running from the cops to be running after me. Nobody knows I'm here, and I traveled under a false name. The hospital's keeping me on the patient list for the time being, stringing the press along with updates on my 'guarded' condition. I'm safe here."

"But, Joseph, we're talking the big time. Isn't Marconi one of the biggest cheeses on the East Coast, and aren't you the undercover cop and key witness whose testimony will be sending him to jail for a very long time when they catch him? Aren't we talking witness protection plan here?"

Joe gazed out the window. He'd forgotten how annoying his baby sister could be. "Stop worrying about nothing and tell me about Luther Makes Elk and how he saved Steven's life and why you've never told anyone in the family about this."

She drove in stony silence for a few minutes before responding. "Luther's a holy man and he's Steven's adopted grandfather and…" Molly blew out an exasperated breath. "I'll do better than tell you about him. I'll take you out there while you're here and introduce you to him. And if we go this weekend we might even run into Dani. She always takes Luther something when she camps in the Arrow Roots." Molly cast him a teasing glance. "Just so you know, I think it would be perfect to have Dani as my sister-in-law, and you'd make one cool cowboy."

## CHAPTER TWO

DANI LOVED THE utterly luxurious sensation of waking with a start, thinking she might have overslept and then realizing it was the weekend and she didn't have to jump out of bed and get ready for work. It wasn't that she didn't like her job. Estate planning was okay. Predictable. No courtroom drama, but she liked the law firm she worked for and got along well with her co-workers. Still, she loved her days off better. Loved planning her weekend adventures. Loved having the dogs pad into the bedroom while the sunlight laid banners of warmth across the bed.

She pulled the goose-down duvet up to her chin and peered over the edge of the bed at her dogs and their questioning eyes. "Good morning, boys. No doubt you're wondering why I'm lying here in bed when I should be up getting your breakfast, and no doubt you're also wondering what's on the docket today and what sort of grand adventures we'll have. We haven't been camping all winter, but I'm thinking today's the day. It's the end of May. The snow should be mostly gone in the mountains. We'll hike up to the forest service camp and see if we can find Custer's band."

She stretched like a cat under the covers and reached a hand to stroke the pair of retrievers, who laid their blocky heads on the edge of her bed and wagged their tails in unison. "You miss Jack, don't you?"

Their tails wagged faster at the mention of his name. She sighed. "I did, too, for a while, but I'm not sure why. He was hardly ever here. We were almost always alone, weren't we? Nothing much has changed. It's mainly been just the three of us since you were puppies. I know he really cared about you, and maybe he'll come visit you some day. But I can love you and take care of you and take you camping, and that'll just have to be enough."

The dogs heaved simultaneous sighs and Dani heaved another of her own.

She'd stayed up past midnight last night, redesigning Molly's wedding gown to compensate for the first trimester of her friend's unexpected pregnancy, the inspiration for the new design having struck her after Molly left with her brother. She'd also thought about Molly's brother a lot last night. Too much, truth be told, but it was the wedding gown that mattered, not Joe Ferguson. This would be no ordinary

wedding gown. This was going to be a grace-
ful sweep of elegance suitable for the red-haired
Scots/Irish goddess who was marrying Steven
Young Bear, the hard-hitting environmental attorney thought by many to be one of the rising
stars in Montana's political arena.

Molly's gown had to be perfect. She wouldn't
let her best friend down on such an important day, but creating the perfect gown for the
mother-to-be would require a big investment of
time. This weekend's excursion into the Arrow
Roots to photograph the wild horses might be
her last until after the June wedding. Which
meant she shouldn't be lying in bed, squander-
ing one precious moment of this fine spring day.

Dani pushed out of bed, reached for her robe
and wrapped it around her as she went downstairs to start the coffee. She'd lived in Helena
for five years in this comfortable house, built
in the late 1800s, with a big fenced yard for the
dogs and only five miles from her office, but
since Jack left she'd found herself wishing for
a piece of land to call her own, large enough
for a horse barn and pastures. It was no longer
important to live within a stone's throw of the
airport. So she'd taken the plunge and recently
listed the house with a real estate agent, who'd
called yesterday to arrange a showing for Saturday. Perfect timing, since Dani and the dogs

would be off hiking. Maybe now she should seriously start looking for that special place. A change would do her good.

She organized her camera gear while the coffee brewed. Stuffed her backpack with supplies while she sipped the first strong cup. Took a long, hot shower and dressed in comfortable, layered clothing. It got cold in the mountains when the sun went down. She plaited her long dark hair and laced up her well-worn leather hiking boots. The dogs watched all this preparation with increasing excitement. They knew she was taking them camping. They smelled the smoke of a hundred other campfires in her camping gear. They loved hiking with her, and she in turn felt safer in their company. Remmie and Win were well behaved, never roamed far from her side and their keen sense of smell and hearing had proved invaluable in finding the small band of wild horses that roamed the Arrow Roots.

She always stopped to see Luther Makes Elk when she crossed into the Crow reservation and today would be no different. She packed a jar of homemade raspberry jam for him and would pick up some Chinese food at the little restaurant in Bozeman. Luther loved his MSG.

By sunset she and the dogs will have reached the old line camp on the flanks of Gunflint

Mountain. The thought made Dani happy. She was anxious to see if any of the mares had foaled yet, and if the wildflowers were in bloom on the mountainsides. She wanted to once again hear the coyotes howl and admire a night sky so full of stars it made her heart ache with the beauty and mystery of it.

Before eight a.m. she was loading her Subaru with camping gear. The two dogs jumped into the backseat when she opened the side door, then she climbed behind the wheel and turned the key in the ignition.

"Okay, gang, let's hunt us up a herd of wild horses."

JOE WAS UP well before dawn. He was restless, and the time difference made it feel as if he should have been up far earlier. He dressed in jeans and a flannel shirt, the same clothes he'd worn the day before because he had no other clothes to wear. Just lucky that Rico had brought these clothes to the hospital yesterday morning. He wandered into the kitchen of the small house in Gallatin Gateway that Molly shared with her fiancé, Steven Young Bear. Joe had always been protective of his baby sister and had been skeptical that any man would be good enough for her, but the moment he met Steven, he knew instinctively that this man would take good care of her. Molly had told him that Steven was a Crow Indian and an attorney of great merit and integrity, *and* that she loved him very much. She spoke of him with such unrealistic praise that Joe hadn't been prepared to like the man, but from the first handshake he was sold. Young Bear was quiet and self-possessed, and Joe had no doubt that he could handle any situation life threw at him. Last night the three of them had shared a simple meal of stir-fried chicken in the cozy kitchen of the small post-and-beam home, after which Joe had retreated to the guest room, exhausted.

Yet in spite of his fatigue, he hadn't slept well. He couldn't blame it on being in a strange place. Nothing was stranger than a hospital. Maybe it was the absence of constant interruptions. No nurses, no doctors, no badges checking on him hourly. Maybe it was the silence. The sound of the wind pushing around the sides of the house was all he heard here no matter how hard he listened. No sirens, car horns or traffic noises. Maybe thirty-six years of city living had been what kept him awake his first night in the heart of the Wild West.

He wandered into the kitchen and saw that Molly had left the coffeepot ready to go. He pushed the start button. The coffee grinder whirred and the smell of fresh ground beans infused him with comfort. Water began to hiss and thump and drip through the filter and into the pot. He leaned his elbows on the kitchen counter and gazed out the window at a landscape that was both foreign and compelling. No snow remained on the ground and the grass was just greening up. The leaves of the aspen in the grove near the house were a pale, newly minted green, quivering in the early breeze. Majestic mountains in shades of blue and gray loomed on the horizon. He could easily get used to the big spaces, the tall mountains and the silence. For the first time he understood why Molly had never wanted to come back home. *This* was home for her, and she told him she'd felt it the moment she first stepped off the plane. *I just knew it in my heart, Joseph. I knew Montana was where I was meant to be.*

Montana was a far cry from the Boston Fergusons, and Molly loved her big Scots/Irish family, but she loved it here even more and appeared to be sublimely happy with her life. Joe wondered if he would ever find anything like what his sister had found. Last night he'd watched the pair at supper, watched the way Molly looked at Young Bear, the shine in her eyes, the way she so openly adored him. The feeling was obviously mutual. Mutual enough that when Molly opened the bottle of red wine and neglected to pour herself a glass, Young Bear had looked at her for a long, thoughtful moment before nodding and saying, "I thought that's what the doctor was going to tell you. I hope it's a girl, and I hope she has beautiful red hair, just like her mother."

Turns out his baby sister was going to be a mother, and watching the two embrace, Joe realized how empty his own life was. Oh, he wasn't sorry about the divorce. Nothing had made him more miserable than five years of being married to Alison Aniston, but their love-less marriage had ended a year ago and for the last few months his contact with women had been purely physical. Which had suited him just fine until meeting Dani Jardine yesterday. At first he thought maybe his lung had collapsed again, but the fact of the matter was, she'd taken his breath away. He hadn't realized a woman could be so naturally beautiful and vibrantly alive. Being Molly's best friend made her especially off-limits. Better for him if he kept far, far away from her.

He padded into the living room, dropped onto the sofa and cradled the hot mug of coffee. The picture window looked east, toward a big mountain range. Some of the taller peaks still cradled snow near their summits. The sun was rising behind the mountains, turning the snow crowning the peaks a pale shade of yellow. He took a swallow of coffee and watched the show. He thought about Molly's suggestion, of bringing Ferg out here. His son would love it, but would Alison allow it? She was fighting for sole custody, and she was a nasty fighter.

"Morning."

Molly's voice startled him. She'd come into the living room quiet as a wraith, red hair loose upon her shoulders and freckles plain in her pale face. She looked very much like a little girl, not a young woman soon to be married.

"Coffee's all made," he said.

She shook her head and made a face. "My stomach can't handle it lately. Sleep well?"

"Like a rock."

"Don't lie to me, Joseph. You didn't sleep at all and neither did I. All I could think about was Marconi and how he almost killed you. Once he's behind bars and after you've testified, you'll be safe, but I have a plan to keep you safe in the meantime."

"I can hardly wait to hear it."

"Don't tease me. I've already told Steven about it and he thinks it's a good idea. As a matter of fact, he called his sister, Pony, last night and she agreed that you should stay out at the Bow and Arrow. Nobody'd get within five miles of that place without being observed by everyone in Katy Junction. The ranch is extremely isolated and you have to drive through the middle of Katy Junction to get to it. There's only one road in or out."

"The Bow and Arrow." Joe wondered why it sounded so familiar, then he remembered the wedding invitation he'd gotten in the mail. "Isn't that where you and Steven are getting married?"

Molly dropped onto the sofa next to him, propped her feet on the coffee table and wrapped her robe about her. "It's such a magical place. You'll love it. Conveniently, we have to visit there today."

"Why's that?"

"Because today's Saturday, and they always have barbecue on Saturday. Besides, I really want you to meet Pony and Caleb and all the kids."

"I don't need to hide out there. I can take care of myself."

"Oh, yes, that's quite obvious," she said, giving him a skeptical up and down. "Don't worry, you'll earn your keep. Pony said they could always use another teacher."

"You told me it was a ranch."

"A huge ranch, with horses and buffalo. Steven's sister started a school there, too, for Crow kids who weren't making it in the reservation's school system."

"Troubled kids?"

"No. But special kids, for sure, especially Roon."

"I remember you mentioning him. The boy who talks to wild horses."

"And buffalo," Molly added. "Roon sometimes helps Jessie Weaver on her rounds, now that she's graduated vet school. Jessie used to own the Bow and Arrow until she sold it to Caleb, Pony's husband. Then Caleb deeded half the ranch back to Jessie as a wedding gift when she married Guthrie Sloane, so now they co-own it. Guthrie helps Caleb and Pony run the ranch, and Jessie doctors most of the horses in Gallatin and Park counties. You should see her truck—it's so cool. Anyhow, Roon's so good with the animals Jessie says whenever he comes along with her on farm calls having him there cuts the need for tranquilizers by half."

Joe took another swallow of coffee, dizzy from trying to keep up with Molly. "What's all this got to do with me teaching?"

"Roon was one of the toughest cases at the Bow and Arrow. He had a big chip on his shoulder to start with and then he lost his little brother in a car accident. Pony had her hands full with him, but being out there at the ranch turned him around. So they started a school for kids like Roon. I think Pony and Caleb have about five or six kids living there now. They've built an actual schoolhouse next to the ranch, with an upstairs bunk room big enough to house all the boys. The kids help with ranch chores and spend part of their days in class, but only a small portion. Most of their learning takes place out of doors."

"Sounds like my kind of school, but I'm no teacher."

"Of course you are, Joseph. We all are. They have guest teachers out there all the time. Some like it so much they come back more than once. All you have to do is talk about what you do. Tell them what it's like to be a big-city cop. Tell them what your work is like, what kind of education and experience you needed to land the job, tell them what you like and don't like about it."

"Kind of like show-and-tell?"

"Exactly."

"I'll show 'em all my bullet holes and tell them to avoid a career in law enforcement."

"Joseph, that's not the least bit funny." She gave his arm an affectionate squeeze. "Anyway, when you're done telling them all about your chosen career, you answer their questions and afterward you help with ranch chores. And then—" she paused for effect "—then you get to eat the most incredible meals west of our mother's kitchen. They have a cook named Ramalda and she's a real treasure."

"Good food?" Joe perked up at this.

"Great food, and lots of it."

"Sounds like you visit there frequently."

"As often as I can, and I've taught there, too, several times. I told them all about law school and different choices of careers within law and Steven's fight to save Madison Mountain from the mining industry. In exchange, the boys taught me how to throw a rope over a fence post... Well, they tried. I'm a terrible cowgirl. I rode horseback once up into their mountains to see the buffalo herd and it took me weeks to recover. But I love it out there. It's a perfect place to raise kids."

"And this place isn't?" Joe looked around the comfortable room and lifted his coffee mug to the view outside the picture window. "What more could you ask for?"

Molly just smiled. "Wait till you see the Bow and Arrow."

IT NEVER FAILED to amaze Dani how much food Luther Makes Elk could eat. She'd brought him enough to feed a family of six, and by the time she left, most of the Chinese take-out containers were half empty. He never said much when she arrived, didn't speak while she unloaded the bags of food and the small gifts she always brought. And she left him how she found him—sitting on his wooden bench in front of his shack, hat pulled low and blanket over his shoulders, gazing back through time and into the future. He shook her hand when she got ready to leave, the way he always did. Slowly, with a solemn expression. "Sometimes the best thing you can do is nothing," he said. Those were his only words the entire visit.

The lack of talk didn't bother her, though. She was a quiet person herself and always felt strangely revitalized by her silent visits with the holy man. Today was no exception.

Now she headed south for the Arrow Root Mountains, the sun slanting off her right shoulder, settling toward the Absaroka Range, the Crow reservation off to her left. Her dogs had abandoned all their manners and were jockeying for position in the passenger seat, craning their eyes out the windows with mounting excitement.

A convoluted series of dirt roads took her into the high country. This was a seldom traveled place, but she noticed fresh tire tracks today. She wasn't the only one with spring fever. Eventually, rotting snowdrifts closed off the road and she could drive no farther. She parked where someone else had parked very recently. Footprints in the mud indicated one person had continued up the unplowed road and returned, probably within the past day. A ranger from the forest service had no doubt walked up to check on the cabin, knowing she'd rented it for the weekend. The dogs bounded out of the Subaru, sprinting in tight circles of excitement as she shrugged into her pack and balanced the tripod over her shoulder. It was three p.m. and they had another hour or so of hiking ahead of them before reaching the forest service cabin. With any luck she'd have her camera gear set up by sunset and would get some good shots of the band stallion, his mares and hopefully some new foals.

She loved hiking in these mountains and photographing the mustangs that lived here. To Dani, they embodied the free spirit of the West, the part that would never be tamed. Her photographs had appeared in several major magazines, and she'd recently agreed to supply many more for a book that was being written about the wild mustangs of the West. The Bureau of Land Management, or BLM, had begun aggressive roundups in recent years to thin the population, but many felt their management goals were too low to maintain genetic diversity and long-term survival. The fight was on to preserve the purest strain of Spanish mustangs in North America, and Dani, through her love of horses, hiking and her photographic skills, had become a big part of it.

Her spirits were as high as those of her dogs as they hiked through mountain mahogany and juniper. The scenery was spectacular. Mountains framed every scene. The Bighorn, Beartooth, Wind River and Absarokee. Spring was in the air and the yeasty smell of the land, warmed by the afternoon sun, wafted in an earthy ferment around her. She knew in the higher elevations the wind would be thundering over the land like a herd of wild horses. When she was here she felt as if maybe there wasn't a city west of Saint Louis. As if, in the four-hour drive from Helena, she'd traveled back through two centuries. Sometimes she wondered if she just kept on hiking into the Arrow Roots, would she vanish into the past? She wondered if perhaps she hadn't already lived here in another life and maybe that was why, when she was with Luther Makes Elk, she felt no need for words. The silence between them was comfortable.

*Sometimes the best thing you can do is nothing.* His words came to her again as she took a breather. Luther didn't say much, so when he spoke, she listened. As did everyone. He was, after all, a legendary holy man. What had he meant? Had Luther been referring to Molly's brother Joe? Had he been telling her to leave the dark and dangerously handsome man well enough alone? Or had he been describing his own life, his days spent sitting on the old wooden bench in front of his shack, watching the occasional vehicle drive past?

She shifted the tripod to her other shoulder and continued on. Her breath came in short, hard gasps as the trail steepened. Her thigh muscles burned and her shoulders were already sore. She was pathetically out of shape. Cross-country skiing was good exercise and a fine way to enjoy a long Montana winter, but nothing beat climbing uphill while shouldering a heavy pack. She hadn't slept very well last night, but she had a feeling tonight would be different. Tonight she'd forget all about how Joe Ferguson had turned her insides to mush and instead focus on finding the bright golden stallion, Custer, and his little band of unbranded mares. With any luck he'd be grazing his mares in the high mountain park that surrounded the old camp.

She was going to get some great photos. She could feel it in her bones.

"THIS IS KATY JUNCTION," Molly narrated to Joe as Steven parked the Wagoneer in front of a small hole-in-the-wall diner called the Long-horn Café. The café comprised one of four buildings that made up a town that, except for the addition of telephone poles, didn't look like it had changed much in well over a century. There was even a hitch rail in front of the board-walk, which still looked well used, if piles of horse manure were any measure. "Guthrie's sis-ter, Bernie, runs this diner. She's wonderful— you have to meet her. She brews the best coffee in the West, so you must have a cup. Badger and Charlie are probably here, too. They help out at the Bow and Arrow and spend the rest of their lives hanging out at Bernie's counter and gossiping."

Joe climbed out of the passenger seat, trying to keep track of all the names his sister tossed his way. His chest ached. His gut ached. His head ached. He didn't want a cup of coffee and he didn't want to go to the Bow and Arrow. He was beginning to wish he'd never gotten out of bed that morning. He'd passed on his six a.m. painkillers and that had been a mistake. He felt punk enough that Molly had put off visiting Luther Makes Elk on the way to the Bow and Arrow, and it was a good thing, too. Just climb-ing the three steps to the diner really took it out of him. When he reached the top step, the wall of the diner began to move in a strange way, and he grabbed on to the hitch rail to catch his balance.

"Joseph?" Molly's face looked up at him, eyes full of concern. She'd been hovering ever since he'd arrived, as if he might drop dead at any moment. She had her hand on his arm and he felt another hand steady his elbow. Steven. Jesus. How embarrassing.

"I'm fine," he said. "Jet lag, that's all."

"Bernie makes good homemade soup. We'll stay for lunch," Steven said.

The cold sweat passed as they helped him through the door into a small room. The tables were empty, but two men, both on the far side of ancient and dressed like the cowboys of old, sat at the counter. The slender, pleasant-looking woman standing behind it took one look at them and came around, wiping her hands on a towel as she approached. Her smile was warm and genuine. She glanced at Joe questioningly, then at Molly. "Why, Molly Ferguson," she said, her smile broadening, "if this is your tall, dark and handsome older brother, you must introduce me."

"How'd you guess?" Molly said.

"Except for the lack of red hair, there's a strong family resemblance." She extended her hand. "I'm Bernie Portis. Welcome to Katy Junction and the Longhorn Café. Won't you have a seat?" Her hand gripped his arm firmly as she deftly guided him to the nearest table. He sat. Gave her a grateful look. She smiled and nodded imperceptibly in response. "Soup of the day is extra special because I'm using Bow and Arrow buffalo, not beef. Pony finally persuaded Caleb to take the plunge. They harvested a two-year-old bull, and I'm their first commercial account," Bernie said proudly. "Buffalo's wonderful meat—low-fat, low cholesterol and naturally raised on the prettiest wide-open range in the West."

"Sounds great. We'll take three bowls and three coffees, Bernie," Steven said.

"Make mine peppermint tea," Molly said.

Steven and Molly sat. Bernie looked between the two of them. "Are you feeling all right?" she asked Molly. "Is your stomach upset?"

Molly glanced questioningly at Steven, who gave her a calm nod. "We're going to have a baby," she announced, then to her visible mortification she burst into tears.

Bernie never missed a beat. She gave Molly's shoulder a reassuring squeeze. "Don't worry, Molly, babies aren't so awful. I've had two myself and I count them as two of the three best things that ever happened to me, my husband being the third. Joseph, how long are you planning to stay?"

"You can call me Joe, and I'll stay as long as Molly will put up with me." Given Molly's highly emotional state, Joe figured this was a tactful response.

Bernie nodded. "Good. It's tough facing such big events as a wedding and first baby when your family's all back east. Though I will say, Molly has plenty of family right here." She gave Molly's shoulder another affectionate squeeze before retreating to get their beverages. Meanwhile the two old codgers on the bar stools had slid off their perches and were turning in their direction.

"Did we hear correct?" the bowlegged bewhiskered one said as they approached the table. He removed his hat respectfully. "You're expecting a baby?" Then damn if he didn't pull a huge red bandanna out of his hip pocket and hand it to Molly, and damn if she didn't use it to blot her tears.

"I'm sorry, I don't know why I'm crying. Badger, Charlie, meet my big brother, Joseph," Molly introduced through her tears. "He's visiting us for a while. He lives in a big city back east and needs some vacation from all the smog. This is his first trip west. We're taking him out to the Bow and Arrow after lunch."

Joe shook hands with Badger and Charlie, feeling like he'd just stepped into a John Ford Western. "Good to meet you," he said. "And the name's Joe."

"Katy Junction might seem small to you, being a big city slicker and all," Badger said to Joe, "but some mighty big things happen around here. Just ask your sister—it ain't never dull."

"I've heard some of the stories," Joe said. "I'm looking forward to seeing how wild the West still is."

Badger rubbed his bewhiskered jaw. "Well, everyone knows the wildest critters live in the big city, and from the looks of you, some of 'em chewed you up good. But a few days out here'll get you back on your feet. And your sister's having a baby, that's real good news," Badger said. "It'll give that little one out at the Bow and Arrow something to play with."

"Little one?" Molly echoed.

"Ain't you heard? Pony just took in another'n, just knee-high to a grasshopper. I saw it this mornin' for the first time. Cute as a speckled pup. She don't like my whiskers, though."

"Who would?" Charlie said.

Molly wiped her eyes, blew her nose and cast an accusing look at Steven. "Why didn't you tell me about the new baby?"

Steven shook his head. "Pony is my sister but she doesn't tell me everything."

BY TWO P.M. Steven was driving his Jeep Wagoneer down the last stretch of ranch road leading to the Bow and Arrow. Joe was dozing off his lunch, but he roused in time to take in the sweeping views, the creek and the old log cabin on its bank, the ranch buildings beyond on the knoll and what looked like the Continental Divide rising up behind it. There appeared to be a lot of action down by the barns. Horses in corrals, boys riding horses, boys leaning over the top rail watching another boy on a horse in a separate smaller corral. Clouds of dust. Puddles of mud. Two Australian shepherd–type dogs chasing each other in play and yapping with excitement outside the corrals. Class was quite obviously in session at the Bow and Arrow.

They parked in front of the ranch house and a slender woman in blue jeans and a red flannel shirt with a long jet-black braid over her shoulder emerged almost immediately, balancing a toddler on her hip. "That's Pony," Molly said. "Isn't she beautiful? Oh, my, look at that baby girl." Molly was out of the Jeep and up the steps before Joe's feet hit the ground. "Steven!" she said, spinning around with the baby already in her arms and a wide smile on her face. "She's two years old and her name's Mary. Isn't she just the sweetest thing?"

While his sister showed Steven the baby, Pony came down the steps to meet him. Her handshake was firm, her eyes dark and intelligent, and Molly was right. She was beautiful in a soul-deep, earth-mother way. "I'm Pony, and I'm glad you came," she said. "I'll tell Ramalda there'll be three more for supper. She likes to set a big table. And, Joe? You're welcome to stay here as long as you like."

## CHAPTER THREE

DANI PAUSED AT the old line camp just long enough to shed her pack and sort out her camera gear. The boot tracks she'd been following hadn't stopped at the cabin, but had continued on toward the high park. Nobody had been at the cabin for several weeks. Now managed by the forest service, the camp was available by reservation year-round for twenty dollars a night, and Dani had reserved it for herself well in advance, though not many hiked up here in mud season. It was a simple setup: two bunks, a plank table with two chairs and a woodstove for heat. With the grizzlies out of hibernation and roaming the mountains, four solid log walls were a comfort. She stashed her pack at the cabin and hiked immediately toward the park. From there she would most certainly be able to spot wild horses. She called the dogs to heel and they fell in beside her. They knew not to chase after things or to leave her side when she spoke to them in that stern tone of voice. They knew work from play, and they knew this was her time to work. They also knew there would be plenty of time for play afterward.

She paused for a moment to take a deep breath of sweet, cool mountain air and drink it all in. It was so beautiful up here, so wild. One day she'd live on the edge of a wilderness just like this and be able to walk out in it every single day. And maybe, just maybe, there'd be a special guy in her life to share this with. Someone who wasn't gone all the time. Someone who'd worry if she didn't come home on time, and who would always be glad to see her when she did.

Dani laughed at herself. She'd sworn off guys after Jack left, and now she was spending way too much time thinking about Molly's big brother. Foolishness. Joe Ferguson was a city boy. He'd never take to this life. Besides, he was probably juggling a handful of women. Someone that good-looking couldn't be single. *Get to work*, she chided herself, and hiked onward.

She saw the vultures before she saw the horses, wheeling circles on mountain updrafts in their telltale, teetering flight. Something was dead or close to it. Rounding the crest of the broad sweep of high meadow, she spotted more vultures on the ground not a quarter mile distant. There were twenty or better scattered over the meadow in three undulating clumps, each clump feeding on something large and deceased. Vultures were big birds, and from a distance it was hard to make out what they were feeding on, but Dani's good mood instantly vanished, replaced by a growing feeling of dread.

Walking slowly, she descended the gentle slope. Ravens in nearby trees croaked an alarm and took to the air as she approached, and on cue all of the vultures flew away. Their take-off was heavy, loud and slow, and Dani stopped abruptly when she saw what the flight of the vultures revealed. She'd half expected this, but the shock ran through her like an electric jolt as she processed the scene. Three horses lay sprawled in the high park.

Three of the eight wild horses that made up Custer's band. Dead.

Shaken, Dani stood paralyzed. She couldn't believe what she was seeing. How could this have happened? How could three have been killed all at once? Lightning sometimes struck them in these higher elevations, but not in this number and not this early in the season. Was Custer one of the dead? Wild, beautiful Custer? The dogs looked up at her. They smelled death and sensed her distress. Their tails were still, their expressions solemn. This wasn't what she'd come to the Arrow Roots to photograph. Nonetheless, this was something that needed to be captured for others to see. Photographs needed to be taken. Whatever had happened to the wild horses of the Arrow Roots, people needed to know their fate. Dani blew out her breath and steeled herself for the task at hand. "Okay, boys, you stay right beside me," she said to the dogs. "Heel."

She shouldered her gear and started walking down the hill. The dogs walked close beside her to keep her safe.

CUSTER WAS AMONG the dead. Of course he would be. This was his little band of mares. This was his home range. He would have fought to protect all that was his. Dani was overwhelmed by the enormity of the tragedy. The three dead horses were widely scattered. From the hoofprints left behind in the soft spring earth it looked as though they had been running in a wild panic, changing directions, not knowing which way to turn when whatever happened, happened. And it had happened very recently. Late yesterday, perhaps? Though the spring sunshine was warm and flies had begun to gather, the carcasses had not yet begun to bloat or smell. Vultures, coyotes and ravens had begun their feast, and Dani saw the fresh imprint of a large bear in the churned-up earth near one of the carcasses. The dogs were uneasy and their hackles raised when they sniffed at the track. She knew from experience they didn't like the smell of bear. She snapped photos with her digital camera swiftly, but the hair on the back of her neck prickled. Where was the bear? Not far, she was sure, and it wouldn't like her being anywhere near the dead horses.

She took multiple photos of Custer, that wonderful wild stallion that she'd been photographing for the past few years, then bent and zoomed the lens in on the neck of a bay mare that was not as mutilated as the others. She focused on what could only be a bullet hole. Large caliber. Not fatal, but she had several other bullet holes in her chest area that were. These horses had been shot multiple times. Deliberately slaughtered. Both mares had been pregnant. Dani thought about the tire tracks back where she had parked. Big tires with aggressive tread. Truck tires. And the boot tracks that had walked here and returned to the parking area. Big footprints. A man had come up here with a rifle, spotted the herd grazing in this high meadow and shot them.

Who? And why?

Dani pulled her cell phone out of her jacket pocket and turned it on. No signal. But she dialed Molly's cell, anyway, just in case, and got nothing.

"Damn it." This was the downside of true wilderness. No cell phone towers.

Remmie and Win were looking toward the bushes at the edge of the meadow. Their ears were cocked. Dani took a few steps closer and saw the legs of a fourth horse protruding from the brush. This mare was lying well apart from the others near the edge of the tree line and mostly hidden by the brush. A dun-colored mare with a long black mane and tail. Dark stripe down her spine. Dark barred stripes on her legs. A beautiful Spanish mustang with classic markings, and except for the bullet holes in her neck and shoulder, she'd been untouched by the scavengers. She was the perfect subject to prove the horses had all been shot. Dani moved closer, raised the camera and took a burst of shots. The mare's eyes were open, which wasn't unusual in death, but at the sound of the camera's shutter, the mare's ears flickered ever so slightly, then she blinked and moaned, a deep gut-wrenching sound of agony. Dani lowered the camera, a different kind of shock paralyzing her.

This horse was still alive.

"Easy, girl," Dani soothed, but at the sound of her voice the mare thrashed her legs, struggled desperately to gain her feet, then lost strength, groaned again and collapsed flat on her side.

"Easy, girl, I won't hurt you." Dani's thoughts were as panicked as the horse. The mare was wild and didn't want her near, but she was badly injured and suffering. Dani cast around frantically, as if help might appear on the horizon, but all she saw were the three other dead horses, a sky full of circling vultures and two loyal dogs. She was on her own.

The dogs suddenly looked beyond her, ears cocked, and she heard the crashing of something in the thicker brush beyond the mare. She backed rapidly away, her heart in her throat. Bear? She saw a flash of pale color. Bears were dark. Was it another wounded horse? Please, God, no.

But it wasn't a bear or another wounded horse. A cream-colored foal stepped out of the scrub on long wobbly legs that could barely support it. When it spotted her it made a noise, the sound of a frightened young thing that needed its mother. The foal was a newborn. Tiny. Scared. Dani looked again at the mare. The blood from her gunshot wounds had masked the blood from the birthing. This mare had been shot twice and then, lying near death, had somehow birthed this foal, and very recently. The foal's coat was still damp. It staggered unsteadily toward its mother, who raised her head off the ground and made a noise in her throat that knifed into Dani's heart. The foal responded and came to her side, but the mare could do no more. Her life was nearly gone, bled out into the grass.

"I'll find out who did this and they'll be punished for it," Dani said in a choked voice to the dying mare. "I promise you."

Tears ran down her cheeks as Dani watched the mare draw her final shuddering breath. The foal nuzzled its mother, seeking comfort that would never come. Thin, watery milk leaked from the mare's teats, as if even in death she wanted to nurture her foal. The sun was setting and the night chill would kill the newborn quickly. It needed food and warmth. She couldn't just leave it here and run for help. Somehow she had to get the newborn foal down to her car and to the Bow and Arrow. They'd know what to do.

Would it let her approach? Was she strong enough to carry it down the mountain?

Dani laid her gear on the ground. She moved toward the dead mare and the foal watched with wide eyes but stood its ground. She reached a hand toward it. Her fingers gently brushed the damp, curly coat and combed through the short wisp of mane. She stroked its neck and could feel the taut skin trembling beneath her fingers. She removed her jacket slowly and used it to rub the wetness from the foal's coat. She rubbed gently at first, then with increasing vigor. The foal braced its legs, lowered its head and stood its ground. Then Dani dropped the jacket and tried to lift the animal. Heavy. Far too heavy for her to carry. She set it back down gently. "Easy now, easy," she soothed as she reached for her camera, took a few quick shots of the foal near its mother and slung the camera over her shoulder. She draped her jacket over the foal's back to keep it warm, tied the arms together under its neck, took hold of the make-shift collar and tugged gently. The foal took a step, then another. Wobbly steps, short steps, but it was walking.

Two steps later Dani had another thought. The foal hadn't eaten since birth and the mare's udder had been leaking milk. Would it be possible to retrieve some of the first milk from the dead mare? She had a stainless-steel water bottle in her day pack. Dani hesitated. She could try at least. The critically important first colostrum milk might save the foal's life. She wasn't sure how long a newborn foal could go without eating but surely mother's milk was best. She shrugged out of her pack, retrieved her water bottle, dumped the contents and returned to the mare's side, where she knelt and positioned the water bottle before trying to strip milk out of the mare's teat. *This is crazy*, she told herself. Even crazier with a grizzly bear lurking in the vicinity. But crazy as the idea was, and as clumsy as she was acting on it, milk finally squirted out of the teat and into the bottle she held on its side. Thanking her dairy farm upbringing, Dani stripped the milk as swiftly as she could, first from one teat and then the other, until no more came. It took less than two minutes but felt like hours while ravens called and vultures circled and she scanned the edge of the nearby woods for bears. She stood, capped the bottle, returned it to the day pack and shouldered it. The foal didn't try to escape when she reached for the dangling arms of her parka tied around its neck.

"You can do this," she said, wrapping one arm around the foal's neck to steady it. "You can do this. You have to, because I can't carry you. And if you stay here, you'll die." She looked over her shoulder. "Win, Rem, come on, boys. We're going down the mountain now."

SATURDAY BARBECUE AT the Bow and Arrow was a tradition that Ramalda presided over with the practiced efficiency of a seasoned military commander. Joe was seated on the porch beside Pony. She'd already given him a house tour, showed him where the bathroom was, where his bedroom would be if he chose to stay and poured him a tall glass of water from a pitcher with lemon slices and ice. "Just relax and watch the show," she told him with a smile. "I hope you are hungry, because if you don't eat a lot, Ramalda will think you are sick, and if she thinks you are sick, you are doomed."

Joe was content to sit and watch, and Pony was right—it was a show. Boys running every which way between the barn and corrals and ranch house. Stout, maternal Ramalda, blue bandanna tied over white hair, scolding them to no effect in nonstop heated Spanish while basting the ribs roasting over the coals with her special sauce, baking corn bread in cast-iron skillets in the reflector oven and stirring a huge pot of spiced chili beans. All of this was being cooked on a giant outside grill beneath a covered patio flanked by two picnic tables. Pony was in and out of the house constantly, setting the two picnic tables and helping Ramalda with the preparations. Joe sipped his water and enjoyed the aromas of mesquite smoke and barbecue. He marveled that in just one day he'd gone from lying in a Providence hospital room that smelled of rubbing alcohol and sickness to sitting on a Montana porch admiring a spectacular Rocky Mountain sunset and hearing the distant whinny of a real horse as the cool air sank into the river valley. His sister was smitten with the baby she still held in her arms as she interacted with the rest of the kids. She was clearly in her element here, among a pack of lively Crow children and some very good friends.

Steven Young Bear walked up from the corrals and dropped onto the bench beside Joe. "Do not let those young renegades talk you into any rodeo activities," he advised, brushing some dirt off his jeans. "You will pay for it."

"Don't worry," Joe said. "I've never ridden a horse and I'm not about to start now."

"That is what I said when I first came here."

Joe eased himself on the bench and took another swallow of water. "I can see why Molly likes this place."

"It grows on you," Steven agreed. "My sister has done a good job with the school. The boys were difficult at first, but two of them are about to graduate with their GEDs, and Roon is doing well enough that Pony thinks he might go on to college. She has made a big difference with these kids. Caleb has given her a good life here. She is happy but it is becoming too much. The buffalo herd is growing, the market for range-raised buffalo is getting bigger... Pony cannot do it all, especially with that little one to watch."

"Maybe Caleb should hire more help."

"When he gets here, you can tell him that. He's tried to hire outsiders, but Pony won't let him. She thinks the boys should be able to help keep the ranch running, but they are kids," Steven said, settling back on the bench. "Caleb will be back shortly. He took two of the boys to a livestock auction. He gives them each a certain amount of money to bid. He says it is the best way to teach them about math and critical thinking at warp speed."

"Huh," Joe said. "What happens if they win what they bid on?"

"If they win, he brings it home and they have to take care of it. This teaches them responsibility."

"And this is a livestock auction?"

Steven nodded. "Yes."

Joe thought about that for a moment. "We grew up in the city and couldn't even have a dog," he said. "I wonder if Caleb would be interested in adopting me. I'm good at math, but I'm not so sure about the critical thinking at warp speed."

Steven grinned. "You will have to ask him. He should be here soon. He just called Pony to warn her about the goats."

"Goats?"

"It would seem one of the boys bid successfully."

Sure enough, within minutes, a big Chevy Suburban towing a livestock trailer came into view, climbed the gentle grade from the creek and pulled up near the corrals. Doors opened and two boys climbed out. A tall, athletic, sandy-haired man with a mustache emerged from the driver's seat, raised an arm toward the house in a casual wave and turned to embrace Pony.

Steven pushed to his feet and brushed more dirt off his pants. "Do you like goats?" he said to Joe.

Joe stood. "Guess I'm about to find out," he said and followed Steven down the steps. When they reached the corrals he was introduced to Caleb McCutcheon, a retired baseball Hall-of-Famer, and the boys, Jimmy and Roon, who had pooled their auction money to buy the goats. "They're an Alpine/Saanen cross," Jimmy said as Caleb lowered the ramp on the back of the livestock trailer. "They make the best-tasting milk and cheese. It was a really good price for all five of them, and they're real pretty," he added.

"Pretty does not pay the rent," Pony said, opening the corral gate. "Let's have a look. We'll get them settled in, give them hay and water and then you boys better get washed up. It's time to eat."

"The owner said their milk makes the best soft cheese on the market, and it's really popular," Jimmy said as Roon began to lead the goats out of the trailer. They were smallish, brown-and-black colored with big udders, droopy ears and strange yellow eyes. They had collars around their necks with plastic numbered tags dangling from them. "He said we could make a lot of money selling the cheese."

"Is that right?" Pony said. "Do you know what Montana's rules and regulations are for making and selling cheese from a home dairy?"

Jimmy shook his head.

"Then you can probably guess what tomorrow's lessons are going to be about, right, boys?" she said. They all nodded. "Five goats, that's a lot of milking. Who is going to be in charge of that?"

"Only three are milking, the other two are dry but the owner thinks they could be pregnant," Jimmy said. He was stroking one of the goats, who seemed more interested in butting him than in being petted.

"How nice. An expanding goat dairy," Pony said. She caught Caleb's eye. "What's next? Llamas?"

"I think they're sweet," Molly said, still holding the little girl on her hip. "I'll buy some of your cheese, Jimmy. I love chèvre with herbs mixed in it."

"See, we have our first customer!" Jimmy crowed triumphantly.

At that moment Ramalda rang the dinner bell. She rang it long and loud, the sound peeling out across the valley. The boys didn't need much persuasion. They were hungry. They rushed to get the goats into the corral, lug water and bring hay. Then they sprinted for the house to wash up. The adults fell in behind, walking at a more sedate pace toward the barbecue pit and picnic tables. "Just so you know," Joe heard Pony say to Caleb, "I am *not* going to be the one milking those goats twice a day."

He heard Caleb laugh softly in reply. "They know the rules, and they know I'll enforce them. You won't become a milkmaid, I promise. I talked to the farmer who was selling them. He's in his late seventies, his wife's health is failing, so he's downsizing his herd. These five milk goats are gentle, they've been well cared for and they're all young and healthy. If it doesn't work out and we have to bring them back to the auction, the boys will make their money back. They really did get them for a steal, and it'll teach them all about the legal hoops a farmer has to jump through to sell home-raised and -produced product."

"And all about milking twice a day, rain or shine, winter or summer, which includes today right after supper because three of those goats need milking very soon, and then straining the milk and pasteurizing it and making the cheese. Don't forget making the cheese," Pony added. "Somehow I can't see the other boys helping out with this production."

"They don't have to. They didn't buy the goats. Roon and Jimmy did."

"Roon's going to be working with Jessie full-time this summer and they'll be on the road doing farm and ranch calls dawn to dusk. When is he going to have time to milk goats and make cheese?"

"Jimmy's thirteen and plenty big enough to tackle this project by himself," Caleb said. "Looks to me like he's about to find out what running a goat dairy's like." He pulled Pony close as they walked toward the ranch house together. "Don't worry. One way or the other, it'll all work out. It always does."

CHARLIE AND BADGER showed up just as Ramalda was ringing the dinner bell, and shortly after that another vehicle arrived and Joe got to meet Jessie Weaver and Guthrie Sloane, who were partners in the Bow and Arrow Ranch and lived a couple miles away in a cabin on Bear Creek. A good-sized crowd, but Ramalda and Pony handled the meal as if it were a common everyday occurrence. Joe supposed it probably was, if tonight's Saturday barbecue was any indication of the typical menu served. He'd never seen so much food, and every bit of it was delicious. Lively banter flew around the tables, blow-by-blow descriptions of all the animals sold at the auction, talk about Molly and Steven's wedding plans, the announcement of Molly's pregnancy, which caused a happy babble of commotion, talk about the buffalo herd and talk about making a fortune in goat cheese. And when the boys found out Joe was a big-city cop, there was a moment of guilty silence and darting eyes followed by a barrage of cops-and-robbers questions.

"Let the man eat," Pony said, putting another platter of ribs on the table. "Maybe if you're really nice to him, he'll come back and talk to you about what he does, but it's not polite to talk with your mouth full." She took the toddler from Molly's lap. "You need to eat, too. I'll feed Mary."

"I'm in love with her," Molly said, giving the little girl up reluctantly. "Is she staying?"

Pony shifted the toddler onto her hip and shook her head. "We don't know. Her mother was hurt in a car accident and is in the hospital. Her father can't take care of her. Mary is my nana's sister's great-granddaughter. I said I would watch her until her mother was well, but we don't know if she will get well. She was badly injured."

"Bring her over here, Pony," Caleb said. "I'll hold her while you sit and eat. You've been on your feet all day, which you wouldn't have to be if you let me hire another cook to help Ramalda. The boys have cleanup detail, and Ramalda will ride herd on 'em. You rest and eat."

Joe hadn't eaten this much food since last November's legendary Ferguson Thanksgiving. He was about to push his plate away when Ramalda marched over to the picnic table and added another scoop of spiced beans and a fresh hot buttered wedge of corn bread. "You're too thin," she said, scowling her disapproval. She picked up the platter of ribs and forked three more onto his plate. "You need much good food. Eat!"

"Don't even think about arguing," his sister cautioned. "You won't win."

MOLLY CLIMBED THE porch steps after supper, holding little Mary in her arms. She sat down beside Steven and Joe with a happy sigh and plopped the toddler in Steven's lap. "I just love this place. Those boys are great. I only wish I had a fraction of their energy."

"You have plenty of energy," Steven said.

"Any more and I wouldn't be able to keep up with you."

The sun had set, the twilight was thickening and cold air sank down from the high places. Steven had brought their coats from the car and Molly put hers on. "Did you get enough to eat, Joseph?" she teased, and Joe could only groan in response. Molly's cell phone rang and she fished it out of her jacket pocket and answered with her usual brusque, "Ferguson," listened for a few moments during which her expression changed from sublime to serious before she stood abruptly. "My God, Dani, are you all right?" A few more seconds passed. "And you have it in the *car* with you, and you're driving and talking on a cell phone?…Okay, listen to me. Hang up. You're almost to the ranch. I'll tell Pony you're coming. Roon and Jessie are here…Yes, yes, we're all here. I wanted Joseph to see the place. Just drive safe, okay? Hang up and drive!" She ended the call and looked at Steven. "That was Dani. She's pretty upset. She went hiking up Gunflint Mountain in the Arrow Roots earlier today and found the herd of wild horses she's been photographing, but four of them had been shot. She rescued an orphaned baby horse. She somehow got it all the way down to her car, loaded it in with the dogs and is on her way here. She just drove through Katy Junction, so she's about ten minutes out."

Steven pushed to his feet and handed the baby back to her. "I'll go tell Pony."

# CHAPTER FOUR

THE SUNSET WAS spectacular but Dani was too distraught to appreciate it. Twilight thickened into dusk. The Subaru's headlights illuminated the dirt road ahead. She glanced over her shoulder into the back of the vehicle, where the pale foal lay flat on her side as if dead. Maybe she was. Remmie lay beside her and Winchester was in the passenger seat. Both dogs were quiet and had been since she'd lifted the exhausted foal into the back of the station wagon. The walk down the mountain had seemed to take forever, one step at a time leading the wobbly foal, yet darkness was still only hovering on the far side of the mountains as she approached the Bow and Arrow. They'd made it to the ranch before full dark, something she hadn't thought possible. If the foal was still alive, Jessie could save her. Dani knew the Bow and Arrow was her best chance for survival.

Dani passed the old cabin by the creek and headed for the ranch house. There were old kerosene storm lanterns hung in the barbecue area, illuminating the picnic tables in their soft light. In the gathering darkness she saw kids clearing away the supper dishes, the glow of coals and the slow lick of flames in the fire pit. She parked the Subaru and saw Molly coming down the porch steps toward her. She climbed out of the driver's seat and the words rushed out of her, fueled by relief and adrenaline.

"Molly! I'm so glad you're here. The foal's in the back of the Subaru. I don't even know if she's still alive. She was just born when I found her and it was such a struggle getting her down the mountain. Where's Pony? Is Jessie around? The poor thing hasn't eaten and she had to walk all the way down to the car and she's so weak. I had the heater blasting to keep her warm but…"

"It's okay, you're here now, you're safe," Molly said, giving her friend a reassuring hug. She peered in the back, the interior light providing illumination. "Wow, she's so little. I think she just blinked—she can't be dead. Roon and Jessie are down at the barn. Steven went to get them. Come with me, Dani. Sit down before you fall down." Molly's arm slipped around her waist and she was guided up the porch steps. "Sit," she repeated. "We'll take it from here. I'll ask Ramalda to fix you a plate of food."

Dani sat. She'd begun to shake all over, not from the cold but from the relief of making it to the ranch and the release of her adrenaline. Molly vanished inside the kitchen and it was then that Dani saw the troops coming up from the barn. Steven was among them, and Roon and Pony and Jessie. Jessie was carrying her medical bag, and they all paused at the Subaru. Dani watched as the foal was lifted from the back of the car into Roon's arms. She was as limp as a rag doll. "Bring her in the kitchen— it's warm in there," she heard Pony say. If they were bringing the foal into the kitchen, then she was alive.

Dani felt her eyes flood with tears. "Thank God," she whispered.

"Don't worry, we'll take care of her," Jessie said as she climbed the steps, pausing to squeeze Dani's shoulder. "You did a great job bringing her here. Do you know if she nursed at all before the mare died?"

Dani shook her head and swallowed past the lump in her throat. "I don't think so," she said. "I think she was born just before I got there. Her coat was still wet. I got some of the mare's milk, though. It's in my water bottle on the front seat of the car."

"Excellent," Jessie said. "Colostrum could make all the difference. How did you know to do that?"

"I grew up on a dairy farm," Dani said. "All the newborn calves had to get colostrum."

Once they had all tramped inside the kitchen with the foal, Dani leaned forward and rested her head in her hands, overwhelmed with exhaustion and turbulent emotions. She drew a shuddering breath. The screen door banged and she heard Molly's voice. "Here. I brought you a mug of coffee with a shot of whiskey in it. I know you don't like whiskey but sip it. Slowly. Drink all of it. That's an order. I'll bring you a plate of food."

"I'm not hungry," Dani murmured into her hands, not lifting her head. "All those dead horses… Custer's dead, too. Who would have done this?"

"Joseph? Make sure she drinks this. She's in shock."

Dani lifted her head, and for the first time noticed the man sitting in the shadows, not four feet from her, sharing the same wall bench.

She sat up, startled. "I didn't see you."

"I'll take care of her, Molly. You go check on the patient," came Joe's deep voice.

Dani wiped her cheeks and drew a deep breath, letting it out slowly, struggling to get her emotions under control. Joe moved closer on the bench. She saw the reflection of lamplight on the mug he held out to her and took it from him.

"Thanks." She raised the coffee to her nose and the fumes made her eyes water. She took a tiny sip and felt the slow burn head south. "Awful," she gasped.

"Medicinal," Joe said. "You need it right now. What happened?"

"I went to photograph Custer's herd and he was dead, along with three of his mares. All shot, probably late yesterday or early this morning. There's good tracking snow in the higher spots, and on the road where I parked my car the boot tracks and tire tracks were clear in the mud."

"Who do you call around here to report something like that?"

Dani drew a steadying breath. "We'll notify Sheriff Conroy, and Ben Comstock's the warden in these parts. Jessie knows him well. He'll probably be the one to check it out." She took another tiny sip of the fiery coffee. "There's a big controversy over the wild horses on public lands. The ranchers who pay lease money to run their animals on the lands consider the horses an invasive species that steal the grass and water from their cattle."

"So, by their own measure, their cattle are also an invasive species?"

Dani's laugh was humorless. "Depends on your perspective. Anyhow, I doubt that little foal will live." She stretched out her legs and winced from the pain. "I stashed all my photographic equipment by the side of the trail and my camping gear's still up at the cabin. I'll go back and get it all tomorrow. I don't have the strength tonight and I seriously doubt anyone'll be up there. It's off-limits to motorized vehicles and not many people want to hike that far to camp."

"Any idea who might have shot the horses?"

Dani rubbed a cramp in her thigh and took another tiny sip of coffee. "Hard to say. A rancher, maybe. Legally, the horses are protected as long as they're on public lands, and Custer's band was in a part of the national forest, but sometimes they stray. It's tough to teach horses boundaries when they can't read. Drought years are hard—they gravitate toward water and that's usually a water source protected by a rancher. Even the water and graze on BLM lands is hotly contested. The situation can get really ugly. The government holds roundups yearly on public lands to keep the wild horse population in control, but a lot of ranchers don't think that's enough and want them all gone. Anyhow, my guess is, with the lack of snow this past winter, ranchers are already worried about the graze and water supplies. Any unbranded horse that strays off public lands is in danger, but this shooting was on public lands. Maybe a preemptive strike? They're legally protected by the *Wild Horse Act*, but that's in a perfect world, right?"

She heard a wry laugh in the darkness. "Right."

"Jessie Weaver's family owned these lands for generations, and let the wild horses run on them. She has some of the best bloodlines of pure Spanish mustangs, right here on this ranch. I met her through Molly but I actually heard about her before that through the Wild Horse Rescue. She's legendary." The whiskey made her stomach burn but Molly was right; she was feeling stronger. "She's not only legendary, she's really nice. She spoke at the Wild Horse Foundation meeting last fall, and she donates her time and experience to the Pryor herd during roundups. If anyone can save that little foal, Jessie can."

"If she lives, what's in her future?"

Dani took another sip. The whiskey didn't taste so bad now. "I don't have a clue. Do you want to adopt a wild horse?"

"I doubt she would be happy in a big city."

"Are *you*?"

"The city's all I've ever known, except for a four-year stint in the military before joining the police department. And I guess guns and violence are the sum of my life experience."

"So you get shot up back east and come to the Wild West for some rest only to discover we have guns and violence, too. But really, Montana's great. I love it here."

"So does Molly."

At that moment, Molly reappeared from the kitchen carrying a plate of food and a napkin rolled around silverware. "Ramalda won't let you leave without eating this first. *And* you're coming home with us tonight. You can leave your car here and we'll pick it up tomorrow."

"I can drive my car to your place, but I have Remington and Winchester, and your brother's staying at your house."

"We have three bedrooms, and your dogs are welcome, you know that. We even have a fenced yard. Besides, Joseph might be staying here. Now clean that plate before Ramalda comes out to check on you. That baby horse is alive because of you and Jessie's going to feed her through a tube into her stomach when it's warmed up enough. She's going to teach Roon to do it, too. But she says it's best to find her a foster mother, so she's going to make a bunch of phone calls once she's finished feeding her. Caleb's already reported the shooting to Ben Comstock and Sheriff Conroy, and Comstock said he'd go up there to check it out first thing in the morning."

"I'd like to go along," Joe said.

"That's too much climbing, Joseph," Molly said. "You're supposed to be recuperating."

"I've had enough bed rest to last me the rest of my life. I need the exercise and I'd like to scope out the crime scene. I'm not staying here tonight. There's no need of it."

Dani set the coffee down between them. She wondered why Molly thought Joe might be staying at the Bow and Arrow, but the food in her lap smelled good, and she suddenly realized she was starving. Ravenous. She unrolled her silverware from the napkin. "You can come with me tomorrow morning, if you want, Joe. I have to get my camera and camping equipment. It's not a tough hike if we take our time. We'll bring some bear spray."

"Bear spray?" Joe said.

Dani picked up a rib. "The Arrow Roots are grizzly country and they love fresh horse meat. I saw some mighty big bear tracks today."

# CHAPTER FIVE

DANI OPENED HER eyes to the predawn light, to the first birdsong of the morning, to the tantalizing aroma of fresh coffee brewing, and all was well until she remembered the wild horses. Things went downhill from there when she moved. Her tentative movement brought a moan of pain. She was lame, a combination of the struggle to get the foal down the mountain, the emotional stress of the rescue effort and the fact that yesterday had been her first climb of the season. How on earth was she going to walk back up there today?

Yet she had to go back. She had to stop by the Bow and Arrow and see how the foal was doing. Her very expensive camera equipment was stashed beside the trail, and her camping gear was in the forest service cabin up on the mountain. Those were all very big incentives to get out of bed. Plus she was curious to find out what Ben Comstock could discover about the shooter and what had happened to Custer's four surviving mares. Last but not least, the prospect of spending another day with Joe wasn't the least bit unpleasant.

"Remmie? Win?" At her softly spoken words, the heads of her two golden retrievers popped up beside her, all soft brown eyes and wagging tails. "Hey, boys. You were so gentle with that little filly yesterday—you're both such good dogs." Their tails flagged faster at her words. She moved again, moaned again, then swung her legs over the edge of the bed. "Give me five minutes and I'll take you outside. I need a hot shower first."

She limped into the little bathroom and emerged ten minutes later in a cloud of steam to face the two very impatient dogs. The hot shower had helped her sore muscles. She dressed quickly and they exited the guest room together, heading for the kitchen and the back door. As she let the dogs out into the fenced backyard, Dani was surprised to see Joe sitting on the back deck with a mug of coffee in his hands.

"Good morning," she said. "Sleep well?"

"Like a rock. You?"

"The same. The smell of coffee woke me up."

"Help yourself, there's plenty."

While the dogs wandered about the yard, Dani poured herself a mug of very strong black brew and rejoined Joe on the porch. He was dressed the same as yesterday, blue jeans, running shoes and a warm, fleece-lined jacket bor-rowed from Steven and zipped up to his chin against the chilly morning air. She dropped into the chair next to his and leaned back to admire the view. She took her first sip of coffee, prac-ticing her furtive sidelong glance. Joe had won-derfully thick wavy hair, a rugged masculine profile and the shadow on his unshaven jaw was very sexy.

"I've been sitting here trying to figure out what to get Molly and Steven for a wedding present," he said. "I'm not good at stuff like that."

"Your being here is the best present you could ever give her," Dani said. "She was right in the middle of her first solo courtroom appear-ance when she got the text from your younger brother that you'd been shot. She ran out of the courtroom and would've been on the next flight back east if Steven hadn't caught up with her."

"What happened with her court case?"

"The judge granted a recess of one day. That was long enough for you to go through surgery and get a 'two thumbs-up' prognosis from the surgeons. Next day she was back in court—she won hands down. She's very good. I don't think she realizes how good she is."

"Don't tell her. She has the Ferguson ego. Her head will swell."

"It's the swelling in her stomach that I'm worried about. I have to remake her wedding gown, but I think I've got it figured out. She's going to be beautiful."

"I didn't know you were a dressmaker. I thought you were an attorney."

"The dressmaking's a hobby. I enjoy it."

"You were limping when you came out here. You okay for today's hike?"

"I have a blister on one heel and I'm a little lame, but otherwise fit as a fiddle. You?"

"Never better. That meal at the Bow and Arrow yesterday rejuvenated me. If they served food like that in hospitals, survival rates would skyrocket, but the patients would never want to leave."

Dani laughed, took another swallow of coffee and wondered if she had any aspirin in her day pack, because she was going to need a handful. "Well, looks like you're going on your first mountain hike. We'll leave right after breakfast."

"If the warden's heading up there first thing, we should probably get on the road as soon as possible."

Dani canted her head to one side to study him. He did look better than he had yesterday. A lot better. In fact, if he looked any better, she'd be in big trouble. Who was she kidding? She was already in big trouble. She sighed. "At least let me finish my coffee. I don't function well without caffeine."

MOLLY SAW THEM off and told them to stop at the Longhorn Café to pick up an order to go that she'd phoned in for them. "You can't do that hike on an empty stomach, Joseph. You shouldn't be doing it at all," she scolded as they were getting into Dani's Subaru. He didn't argue. By the time Dani reached the Longhorn Café he was hungry. They ate the fried-egg sandwiches Bernie had cooked for them as they drove the final miles to the ranch. "Bernie said Ben Comstock was in bright and early for breakfast and he was headed up to check out the shooting when he left," Dani informed Joe en route. "He's probably already figured out who the shooter was, he's that good."

"He has some suspects in mind?"

"If he doesn't, he will. There aren't many ranchers in the area and he knows them all. Bernie fixed you a second egg sandwich, Joe. It's in the bag. Eat it. Could've been a hunter," Dani continued. "Some of them hate the mustangs as much as the ranchers. They don't like the wild horses because they think what they're eating is better left for elk and deer."

The fried-egg sandwiches were good and Joe ate his second with gusto. He was looking forward to the hike up Gunflint Mountain. He only hoped Dani didn't leave him too far in the dust. "Where'd this particular bunch of horses come from? Did they stray from the Bow and Arrow?"

"Doubtful," Dani replied. "Jessie's fence lines along that side are rugged enough to hold the buffalo, and her wild horse herd is semitame. She winters them in the valley near the ranch and provides them with hay, so they don't need to roam and forage for food. More than likely Custer and his mares originally strayed from the Pryor Mountains," Dani said. "The ranchers maintain fences, but there are lots of places where horses could get through, especially in winter. Like any wild animal, fences don't mean much to them. If they want to get around, they find a way. Custer's band has been in the Arrow Roots for several years now. The forest service is in charge of managing the herd but nobody really knows what to do with them."

WHEN THEY REACHED the Bow and Arrow, Dani was relieved to learn that the filly was still alive, still in the warm kitchen and being tended by Roon. Ramalda, a bright blue bandanna tied over her white hair, was cleaning up after breakfast, muttering in a mixture of Spanish and heavily accented English. "*Usted está girando mi cocina en un establo de caballos!* My kitchen now turned into horse barn!"

"I just fed her the last of the mare's milk," Roon told them as they gathered around. The foal was curled like a leggy dog in a big folded-up blanket.

Roon was a quiet young man, ruggedly built and still growing in height. Dani had met Roon several times and had always been impressed by his calm demeanor. "Jessie said that what you did was a good thing, getting the mare's first milk. Not many would know to do that, Dani."

"I was raised on a dairy farm. I know all about how important colostrum is." Dani knelt down next to Roon and the foal lifted her head and nuzzled her hand. "She's still very weak, isn't she?"

"She's tired. I took her outside and walked her around just before you got here," Roon said. "Jessie made phone calls this morning and she located a mare in a BLM holding facility who just lost a foal. Caleb has gone to pick her up. He should be back by noon." Roon was more talkative than usual today, despite having been up all night with the orphan.

"That's good," Dani said, gently stroking the foal's neck. "She has to make it."

"If anyone can save her, Jessie can." Roon placed a hand on the filly's withers. "But she has to want to live. Right now, she does not really want to."

Dani knelt closer to murmur into the flickering ear. "Sweet girl, I promised your mother I'd find who hurt her, so I have to go now, but you hang on. You fight. You live, you hear me? You're too beautiful to die."

She pushed to her feet. Joe was standing by the kitchen door, watching her. The jolt she felt when their eyes met was like an electric shock that left her whole body tingling. "We'd better get going," she said. "Comstock's probably already arrested the shooter."

The drive to the Arrow Root Mountains wasn't long, less than an hour, but it was midmorning before they reached the trailhead. Comstock's vehicle was still there, which surprised Dani. While she organized her day pack, Joe scouted tire tracks and boot prints at the parking area and snapped a few photos with his cell phone. He found a candy wrapper and a cigarette butt in the grass and brush beside the road and bagged both in an empty sandwich bag she'd had in her center console, stashing the bag inside his parka pocket.

"Your shooter drove a truck with oversize mud tires, wore size-twelve Red Wing boots, smoked Marlboros and liked Snickers. Time to climb Everest," he said, eyeballing the route ahead.

"It's not that steep," Dani said, adjusting her

pack on her shoulders. "We'll take it nice and slow. When you need a rest, just sing out."

Joe nodded and fell in behind her. Dani walked at half her normal pace, the dogs running up ahead, then racing back to give her questioning looks, wondering why she was traveling so slowly. She paused where she'd stashed her camera gear in the brush not a quarter mile up the trail. "I'll need this stuff to get more photos," she said, slinging the camera bag over her shoulder and picking up the tripod. "And I'll need to send the photos out so people know what's happened here."

"What kind of punishment is there for shooting wild horses?" Joe asked, lifting the camera bag off her shoulder and wresting the tripod out of her hand.

"On public lands, if they get caught, they pay a two-thousand-dollar fine and might get a year in jail, but I don't think anyone's ever been thrown in the slammer for shooting a wild horse," she replied, hiking slowly upward. "Not many are ever caught, even with the rewards that get offered. The West's a big enough place that if someone were to shoot a bunch of horses in a remote spot, like this, the scavengers would clean up all the evidence in short order. If I hadn't hiked up here yesterday, the bones of those four horses might've been scattered to the four winds in another couple weeks. The thing is, nobody would miss them. Nobody really cares."

"I wouldn't say you're nobody. Do you ride, too?"

"No. I just like horses." Dani paused to give him a breather. "I think wild is beautiful."

"Your photographs sure capture that sentiment."

The wind tousled his dark hair and made Dani want to run her fingers through it. He had wonderful shiny hair. And his mouth, and his jaw with the dark stubble, and those dark eyes of his with those thick, dark lashes, were to die for. She wanted to photograph him standing there, so she could remember this day always, this moment and this man. "I took a photography course in college, just for fun," she said, a little tongue-tied. "With the digital cameras available now, all that technical stuff is almost moot. Anyone can shoot a good picture."

"Not me. There's a lot more to it than just pointing and pushing a button. Did you go to school around here?"

She shook her head. "I'm a farm girl from Oregon. I went to law school at UCLA, then got a job in a Helena law firm as an estate planner. I feel like I'm helping people, and I like feeling useful, though it's not as exciting as what

Molly does. Molly and I used to live within a few miles of each other. I really miss her."

"There must be some law firms in Bozeman that could use a good attorney."

Joe's breathing was slowing down and his color was better. Dani felt her anxiety begin to ease. She nodded. "There are. I've already put in applications at two of them. I really want to be closer to Molly, and the timing just happened to work out, now that she's pregnant. I can't stand the thought of Molly having a baby and me not being there to help her with everything. She doesn't know I've applied for the jobs, so don't spill the beans. I don't want to get her hopes up. I've also listed my house in Helena with a real estate agent, so I'm ready to make my move, if the opportunity presents itself."

"Your secret's safe with me. I hope it all works out. I know Molly would like having you nearby. How much farther to the forest service cabin?"

Dani smiled. "Another mile or so. You ready to quit?"

"Never."

"Then we'd better get a move on, lawman."

By THE TIME they reached the forest service cabin, Joe was sure he was on the fast track to an early grave. Part of the problem was trying to keep his deteriorating physical condition from Dani, so he pushed himself to keep up when his sorely abused body was telling him to slow down. When the silvered old log cabin came into sight, his heart was beating like a war drum, with every beat generating a sharp pulse of pain. His lungs labored to breathe. There was a wall bench outside the cabin and he dropped onto it before he could fall.

"You okay?" Dani asked, pausing with a frown of concern.

"Just a little out of breath. Thought you said it was only a mile."

"Did I? It's probably closer to two and a half. This is part of the Gallatin National Forest. It's a wilderness study area, nonmotorized, which is what keeps it so wild and primitive. Snowmobilers can't come up here and neither can off-road vehicles. The forest service rents out this cabin for twenty bucks a night. Can you believe it? Incredible bargain, but hardly anyone uses it. Woodstove, spring water two hundred feet behind it in that little creek, bunk beds with decent mattresses. Best deal ever. Isn't this beautiful? It's like we're on our very own planet." Dani swept an arm out to encompass the rugged mountain scenery.

Joe raised his head from a bout of trying to cough up the pain in his wounded lung and looked around while blinking the sting of cold sweat out of his eyes. "Beautiful."

"We'll rest here a bit. Comstock must still be up where the horses are."

*"Up?"* Joe glanced up at her, alarmed. "You mean, we're going *higher* than this?"

"Not far. Just over that knoll there's a big meadow in a basin where Custer usually hung out when the grass was greening up. Obviously I'm not the only one who knows that, which is why he and half his mares are dead. I hope Comstock found something. He must have, or he wouldn't still be up here."

"Maybe he died of a heart attack."

Dani shook her head. "Comstock's as tough as they come. He has quite a reputation in these parts. I've never met him but I've always wanted to."

The admiring way she said it made Joe straighten up. He drew a cautious breath and pushed to his feet. "Then what are we sitting around here for? Let's go find out what he's dug up."

# CHAPTER SIX

DANI KNELT SLOWLY at the crest of the knoll and signaled to Joe, who was five steps behind her, to do the same. She called the dogs in a low voice, motioned to them to lie down beside her, which they did, then slowly shrugged out of her day pack and retrieved her camera from the bag Joe set next to her. "Bear," she whispered as Joe drew abreast. He lowered to a prone position on the other side of Remington and peered into the valley.

"*Big* bear," he agreed.

"Grizzly." Dani kept her voice down, though the bear was a hundred yards off and intent on a meal of horseflesh. "She has two cubs with her. See them?"

Joe was propped on his elbows beside her. "Yup. Looks like we aren't getting any closer than this."

"Nope," Dani said, zooming in on the trio of bruins and snapping a stream of shots. "We might see some wolves, too, if we're lucky."

"Where's Comstock?"

"Probably pinned down somewhere, waiting for that bear to leave. A mother grizzly is nothing to trifle with. She probably showed up while he was investigating the scene. Maybe that's why he's been up here for so long."

Joe bent his head to muffle a paroxysm of coughing, then lay silent, scanning the carnage in the meadow below. "It's definitely an all-you-can-eat wild horse buffet for whatever's hungry," he said.

"The wind's out of the west. As long as we stay where we are, she won't smell us. We just stay put until she's had her fill and leaves. Might as well eat our lunch while we're waiting." Dani nodded to her day pack. "Bernie packed us some sandwiches. There's a thermos of tea in there, as well, and some cookies. And two dog bones. She's the best."

"Which horse had the baby?"

Dani pointed to the dark mound lying at the edge of the tree line. "You can barely see her, just her legs sticking out of the brush. The foal was lying in the bushes next to her. When she got to her feet and made all that crashing noise, I thought she was a bear."

"You're lucky she wasn't."

Dani glanced sidelong at him. "I'll feel better once we've made contact with Ben."

"You think that bear might've gotten him?"

"No. He's too experienced, but he shouldn't have come up here alone. He's in his late sixties and it's quite a hike. The sheriff should've come with him, but according to Molly, Sheriff Conroy's gained too much weight in the past four years to make the climb. Rumor has it he won't run for reelection. So there you go, lawman. You could run for sheriff this fall and keep the county residents safe."

"Can't imagine a more exciting career than riding herd on a couple hundred widely scattered, self-reliant and independent-minded Westerners."

"Don't knock it. Too much big-city excitement can land you in a hospital bed."

"No argument there." Joe handed her a sandwich with her name written on the wax wrapper and poured two cups of tea. Dani unwrapped her sandwich, pleased to see it was turkey and Swiss on rye. She pulled a piece of the cheese out and broke it in half, giving a piece to each dog, who took the offering politely from her fingers.

Joe's designated sandwich was roast beef and Swiss on wheat with horseradish mayo. He lowered the top slice of bread after examining it. "How'd that woman at the café know what kind of sandwich I like?"

"I'm not a detective, but my guess is your sister told her." Dani took a bite of her sandwich. "How's that for brilliant amateur sleuthing?"

They ate their sandwiches lying prone, side by side, the strong spring sunshine warming them, watching the grizzly feed while her cubs wrestled with each other. If it weren't for the gruesome sprawl of dead horses in the meadow below and the circling and feeding vultures above, it would have been the most scenic lunch either had ever enjoyed. It would certainly be the most memorable. By the time they'd eaten their sandwiches and drunk half the thermos of tea, the mother bear had finished her meal. She sat and let her cubs nurse while Dani took more photos. When the cubs had their fill, all three bears slowly moved toward the lower end of the meadow and the forest's edge, and in half an hour's time, they were gone.

As mama bear moved off with her cubs, Joe inched forward on his elbows to carefully examine the ground just beyond them. "Someone else laid here, same as we did. Your shooter, I'm thinking," he said over his shoulder. "You can see where his boot toes dug in, and where his weight flattened the grass, see?" He searched some more and then uttered a triumphant, "Ha!" dug in his pocket for the sandwich bag with the cigarette butt and candy wrapper and used it to pick up something, then rolled over and sat up. "He left behind some critical evidence," he said, showing her the brass shell in the bag. "Must've driven it into the dirt when he stood up and couldn't find it. Lucky for us. Because this'll tell us a lot more than just the caliber of rifle. There could be fingerprints, and the imprint of the firing pin."

Dani packed up her camera gear and day pack and glanced at the disturbed ground. "I wonder if Comstock noticed any of this. I'm getting worried about him."

They both rose to their feet, but before they could move a man emerged from the woods and entered the meadow almost directly across from where they stood. He proceeded toward them without pausing by any of the horses, and they walked to meet him. Comstock was an experienced warden in his sixties who knew his way around the backcountry. He looked tough and capable, with the leathery skin of a lifelong outdoorsman, keen eyes and close-cropped salt-and-pepper hair beneath his warden service ball cap. He shook their hands when Dani introduced herself and Joe and explained why they were there, then bent to give the two dogs a friendly pat.

"I've been poking around here since early morning," he said. "There were a total of nine horses in this valley," Comstock told them.

"Four are lying down there, four ran up higher into the pass when the shooting started, but one of them was wounded and ran back down the valley. I followed the blood trail over a mile before I found her. She was dead, died sometime last night. A sorrel mare, shot once in the gut. Don't know how she made it that far, but she was one tough horse. Died hard. She wasn't one of the mustangs. She was wearing a brand I recognized right off. One of Hershel Bonner's quarter horses."

"How'd she get up here?"

Comstock shook his head. "Don't know. Hershel's place is at least five miles from here with some rough country in between. When I was tracking that wounded mare, I came on another set of tracks. Someone was up here on horseback around the same time as the shooting. They came in from the north end on a shod horse. I couldn't find any sign that whoever it was dismounted or came any closer than half a mile to this meadow, but the snow's spotty and the tracking's not that good, too many tracks overlapping. Horse, elk, mule deer, wolf, bear. Everything's moving around right now.

"Maybe the rider heard the shooting, or maybe they were up here before it happened, looking for that mare. I don't know, but whoever it was sat for a while in one spot, then went back the same way he came. Those tracks were no older'n a day, same as the shooter's. Right now I'm going to head back down to my truck and call my wife, then go talk to Hershel about his horse." He glanced up at the knoll where Dani and Joe had eaten lunch. "My guess is the shooter did his work from up there."

"He did," Joe said. "He shot from a prone position, and when he was done he picked up all his cartridges. But he missed one, and left some stuff behind down where he parked his truck, too." Joe pulled the sandwich bag holding the collected evidence from his pocket and handed it to Comstock, who pulled a pair of reading glasses out of his shirt pocket.

He examined the cartridge and other pieces of evidence through the plastic before putting it in his own pocket along with his glasses. "Smoked Marlboros, snacked on Snickers and used a rifle big enough to take a .300 Winchester Magnum. That explains the kill rate and the size of the two slugs I dug out of one of the horses. Thanks. This'll help with any forensic fingerprinting we might be able to do. I'll drop this off at Sheriff Conroy's office."

"I took some photos of the tire and boot tracks at the parking area," Joe added. "Just in case you need them."

"If you want, Joe and I can look for where

that rider might've come out on the lower road," Dani offered. "I have to drive back that way to get to Bozeman. We'll call if we find anything. Joe's a cop from back east. He's here on vacation, but I'm sure he wouldn't mind doing a little sleuthing."

"That right?" Comstock cast a brief, appraising glance at Joe, then dug a business card out of his jacket pocket and handed it to Dani. "I spoke to the sheriff early this morning. He was going to ask around. The forest service staff's been alerted, too. Will you two be in the area long?"

"I'm heading back to Helena tonight," Dani replied. "Joe's staying with his sister and Steven Young Bear in Bozeman."

"That your gear down at the line camp?"

Dani nodded. "I was planning to camp there last night, until I found the horses. Those four mares that you say went up into the pass. Did you see any signs of them?"

Comstock shook his head. "I only followed them until the snow got deep. Then I turned around. I don't think they can get through the pass yet, too much snow. They'll have to come back down eventually. I'm surprised they already haven't."

"Maybe they can't," Dani said. "Maybe they're bogged down up there."

Comstock's eyes narrowed as he looked up into the pass. "Maybe. But those wild horses are pretty tough and smart." He glanced at her. "You did good, getting a newborn foal down that trail. Jessie told me about that. That's not an easy hike, and the grizzly bears are out and about. How's it doing, by the by?"

"Still alive, but only barely. Jessie found a foster mother for her at a BLM holding area. They were trucking her in this morning."

"If anyone can save that orphan, Jessie can," Comstock said. "I'll do my best to find who did this, but no promises."

"I know," Dani said. "I really appreciate everything you're doing. I just can't imagine how anyone could have…" Her voice squeezed off. She shook her head, unable to finish her sentence. Comstock nodded again and gave her shoulder a squeeze.

"My Emma loves these wild horses the way you do," he said. "If we get lucky, whoever did it will have a few too many and say something in the wrong company. The Wild Horse Foundation will probably post a reward. That might help loosen up some tongues."

Dani nodded. She drew a shaky breath and shouldered her pack. They walked back to the line camp with Comstock, where they parted company. Comstock continued down the trail while Dani went inside the cabin to gather up her gear. She avoided looking at Joe, embarrassed that he'd seen her lose it twice. Once last night at the Bow and Arrow, and now in front of Comstock. Joe would think she was a crybaby, and she wasn't. She was finally getting her emotions in control when he said, "I'll do what I can to help you find who did this, Dani."

The sympathy in his voice destroyed her. She turned, raised her eyes to his and watched his face disappear in a blur of tears. She felt his arms go around her and she sobbed against his chest while he comforted her as if she were a heartbroken child. He held her until she pulled away, wiped her face on her shirtsleeve and continued gathering her things.

Packing up didn't take long, since the only thing she'd unpacked the day before was her sleeping bag and Primus stove. She looked around the cabin and made a promise that one day, in a happier time, she'd be back. But would she? Her reason for coming here had been destroyed. Senselessly slaughtered. When she turned away from the cabin she felt a terrible sense of loss. The wild, free spirit of the Arrow Roots had been broken and bloodied, and for her, this place would never be the same.

Joe thought the walk back down would be a whole lot easier, but he was wrong. One misstep could prove disastrous, and the going was slippery with patches of snow, loose gravel, mud and grass. Joe paid close attention to every step, but as it turned out, it was Comstock, hiking down ahead of them, who twisted his knee not a hundred yards from his Wagoneer.

"Got careless," he said when Dani and Joe caught up with him. He was sitting on a rock, contemplating the remaining distance to his vehicle. "I promised Emma I'd be home for lunch and I was hurrying to get to my vehicle to call her. I carry a satellite phone in there. She worries," he added.

"I can bring your phone up here," Dani offered.

"Oh, I can make it, all right. Nothing's broken." To prove his point, Comstock pushed off the rock, tried to stand but sat back down immediately, both hands wrapped around the offending knee and his face tight with pain.

Joe studied the rough trail. "Bet that Jeep of yours could make it up this far."

Comstock didn't have to think long before digging into his pocket and handing Joe the keys. "It's a standard," he said.

Joe nodded. "Sit tight. I'll be right back." On the way down the trail Joe rolled a few of the larger rocks out of the way. The going back up was rough and there was one ten-foot-wide drift of knee-deep snow, but a Jeep was a Jeep and they were made for terrain like this. Five minutes later he cut the ignition beside the rock Comstock was sitting on. He helped the man into the vehicle. Once he was seated, the warden placed a call to his wife.

"Emma, I'm going to be a little late. I have to go talk to Hershel Bonner about a mare of his that I found up there with the wild horses…Yep, she was dead and she was wearing his brand… Don't worry, I always am…Love you, too, Em." He ended the call and blew out a weary breath as he packed the phone back into the waterproof case. "Best woman on the face of the planet and all I've ever given her for the past thirty-odd years is a phone call telling her I'm going to be late. After all these years of me standing her up and making her wait, she just tells me to be careful."

Joe leaned on the passenger-side door frame. "I'll drive you over to Bonner's place. Dani can follow in her car. You can't drive this standard with a bum left knee."

"No, I can't." Comstock knocked back his ball cap and rubbed his forehead as if it hurt. He glanced up at Joe. "I hate to ask it of you."

"We're glad to help," Dani said, kneeling beside the open door. "You should get your knee looked at first. Talking to the rancher can wait."

Comstock shook his head. "Hershel lost a good mare yesterday and I'm interested to hear what he has to say about it."

Hershel Bonner's place was ten miles away, maybe five miles as the crow flies, but the ranch roads were twisty in the mountains. It was nearly forty minutes before they were rattling down the rutted road that led to a modest clapboard ranch house with a pole barn and a series of corrals out back. A battered blue Ford pickup was parked beside the pole barn and a late-model hybrid car was up near the house. Joe parked beside the hybrid, and a yellow dog came around the corner of the barn, announcing their arrival with gruff barks and raised hackles.

"That's Fang. She won't hurt you, she just sounds mean," a slender young woman in jeans and a plaid flannel shirt called out as she stepped onto the porch. The screen door slammed behind her. She peered through the windshield at Joe, sitting in the driver's seat of Comstock's vehicle, and frowned. "What happened, Ben?" she said as Comstock opened the passenger-side door and tried to disembark. He drew a sharp breath, gave up on the idea and remained in his seat.

"Twisted my knee hiking down from that forest service cabin up on the mountain. I'd like to talk to your father if I could, Josie."

Josie swept her dark hair back and secured it with a band. "Sure. I'll go get him." She glanced behind them as Dani drove up, then gave Comstock a lopsided smile. "This some kind of government raid?"

Ben laughed. "No. These folks were kind enough to help me out. They were up in the Arrow Roots when I hurt my knee."

"Well, we thank you both kindly, then. Ben's like family to us." Josie headed for the barn and Comstock leaned back in his seat, massaging his knee. They watched her walk into the barn with the gruff and bristling yellow dog at her heel. A few seconds later she reemerged with a man walking beside her, wiping his hands on a towel. Father and daughter were cut from the same cloth, both tall and rangy and not an ounce of fat on either of them. Hershel Bonner had silver hair, thinning and brushed back from his temples, and a mustache to match. His eyes were keen and clear and he walked like a cowboy.

"Come inside. I'll make coffee," Hershel said when he paused beside the passenger-side door and shook Comstock's hand.

"Can't," Comstock said. "I have a bum knee.

But thank you. Hershel, some wild horses were shot up in the Arrow Roots yesterday. A stallion and four mares."

"*Custer's* band?" Josie said in disbelief. "Custer was shot, too?"

Comstock nodded. "I think one of the mares belonged to you. Sorrel mare, wearing your brand. You missing a horse?"

Hershel rubbed his jaw and nodded. "Moxie. I kind of figured he'd run her off."

"Custer?"

Hershel nodded. "He ranges, that stallion does, especially this time of year. It's not far from here to there, once the snow melts in the pass, and Moxie liked to wander."

"Moxie's dead? *My* Moxie?" Josie said to her father, visibly stunned. "Why didn't you tell me she was missing? I've been here three whole days! I just assumed she was running with the rest of the bunch."

"She was," Hershel said. "I noticed she was missing about a week ago. I told Kurt about it when he stopped by last Friday, looking for you. I figured he'd tell you."

"Well, guess what? He didn't!" Josie snapped, glaring at her father. "You know we haven't been getting along, Dad. I've asked him for a divorce and that's why I'm staying with you, or have you forgotten?"

Hershel sighed and ran his fingers through thinning hair. "When I saw she wasn't with the rest of the bunch, I figured Custer'd stolen her, so yesterday I rode past Stony Gap and up toward the higher valley. Cut her tracks from time to time, so I knew she was headed that way. I meant to tell you," he said to Josie. "Thought we could ride up together and bring her back. Never figured anything like this would happen."

"Know anyone who might hike up past the old forest service cabin with the intent to shoot horses?" Comstock asked.

Hershel uttered a curt laugh. "I know a lot of people who'd like to shoot every last one of them," he said. "You've got your work cut out for you, Ben. Just about any rancher that runs cows or sheep on BLM lands, any hunter that hunts elk or deer, most of 'em want those horses gone. If you're trying to pin that shooting on somebody, good luck."

"That's national forest that Custer's band was on, not leased lands," Dani said, approaching the Jeep. "There'd be no reason for anyone to shoot those horses, and besides that, it's against the law."

"There're no fences holding them horses in. They're free to roam right onto BLM land and someone probably connected the dots and figured they were going to do just that," Hershel replied with a shrug.

"Whoever did the shooting shot your mare, too," Comstock pointed out. "They weren't all unbranded. You could bring charges against the shooter."

"You can bet we will!" Josie shot out heatedly. "Moxie was a great horse. I won a team penning championship with her just three years ago. She was the best cutting horse I ever rode. You have to find out who did this, Ben. They need to be punished." She spun to her father. "Whoever killed Moxie has to pay, Daddy. I know you like all your neighbors and don't want to stir up trouble, but if horse stealing used to be a hanging offense, horse shooting ought to be good for a few years in jail. I bet it was Don Chesley. He's a bigwig in the cattlemen's association. Hates wild horses. He's lobbying to get most of them rounded up and sold for slaughter in Mexico."

"Josie, Ches wouldn't be up there shooting horses," Hershel said. "He's a career politician and he plays by the rules."

"He could've hired someone. He's got the money. His family was involved in the Bell Creek deal. Oil," she explained in response to questioning looks from Joe and Dani.

"Josie," Hershel admonished wearily. "My

daughter has her opinions and likes to share them," he apologized to Ben Comstock. "I personally can't think of anyone who'd hike all that way just to shoot some wild horses. That's a steep trail. Most of the hunters around here don't stray far from the beaten path. Too lazy."

"Well, I'll have a chat with Don Chesley," Comstock said. "Thanks for your time, Hershel. Josie, I'm sorry about your mare."

"*I'm* more than sorry," Josie said. "I'm seriously pissed off. I'm going up there today to find her and say my goodbyes."

"There's a grizzly with two cubs in the valley," Comstock cautioned as Joe started the Jeep. "Be careful."

They left the Bonner place, and when the ranch road intersected with the main road, Joe paused the Jeep and made sure Dani caught up behind them. "You want to talk to Don Chesley now, Ben?" he asked.

Comstock shook his head. "He's probably not home. Spends most of his time lobbying at the state capitol. I'll touch base with him by phone."

"I got the impression Hershel Bonner knows more than he's telling."

Comstock gave him a sharp glance, then indicated Joe should turn right. "My place is about ten miles from here." After a few minutes of silence he blew out his breath. "I'm friends with most of them. That's the hell of it."

"Tough job."

"Everything from criminal investigations to ticketing litterbugs. I cover the entire district, and I also serve as a reserve deputy sheriff for the county. Emma keeps asking when I'm going to retire and I keep telling her, 'When they let me.' I love the job, though. Every day's different. I like being out in the field—never was cut out for a desk job."

"You might be sitting at a desk for a few weeks with that knee."

Comstock shook his head. "Hope not. Fishing season's in full swing and this is the time of year folks get lost hiking or get in over their head on the rafting rivers. Sheriff Conroy's son, Kurt, helps me out sometimes. He's a deputy sheriff himself. Married to Josie Bonner, matter of fact, though from the sound of things maybe not for much longer. I'll give Kurt a call, see if he can cover some bases for me, get this evidence to the lab. Then I'll take a chopper flight over the pass and look for the rest of Custer's mares, see if they're okay. If I don't do that, I'll be in big trouble with Jessie Weaver."

"If there's anything Dani and I can do, let us know."

"Will do. How long are you visiting for?"

"Until my sister's wedding."

"You like the city life?"

"It's all I've known, aside from four years in the military and some time in the Middle East," Joe said. "When I got out of the service, my uncle got me a job on the patrol beat and from there I worked my way up the ladder. But I can see why Molly likes it out here. It's beautiful country."

"That it is," Comstock agreed. "It's been said that if you stay long enough to wear out a pair of shoes, you'll never leave."

Joe glanced in the rearview mirror. Dani was right behind them. He wondered if she had to go back to her place in Helena tonight, and hoped she didn't. He also wondered how much tread was left on his shoes.

## CHAPTER SEVEN

WHEN THEY REACHED Comstock's house, he invited Joe and Dani inside for coffee. "Emma makes the best strudel, and her coffee's not too bad," he said. "Just don't mention Bernie's coffee at the Longhorn Café to her, and you'll be fine."

Emma herself met them on the porch. She looked just like Dani had pictured—a sturdy, capable woman with silvery hair pulled back into a twist, kind eyes and strong, beautiful features. She gave Dani and Joe a warm, grateful smile. "Thank you both so much for bringing Ben home safe," she said. "Come inside. I just took the apple strudel out of the oven and the coffee's fresh."

They drank coffee and ate warm apple and pecan strudel while Ben filled his wife in on the day's events. Emma put an ice pack on Ben's knee while he narrated and when he was finished talking she tried to convince him to let her take him to the hospital in Bozeman for X-rays.

"They'll do the same thing you just did, Em,"

he said. "They'll tell me to stay off my feet, elevate my leg, ice the knee, wrap it with an Ace bandage and take aspirin for the pain. Am I right?" he asked her.

"You're a stubborn man," she replied.

"You should know," he said. "Is there any more of that strudel left?"

Dani's cell phone rang. "It's Molly," she said. She rose to her feet and went out onto the porch to answer it. "Hi. We're just at Ben Comstock's place," she explained, filling Molly in as quickly as she could. "We'll be on the road soon. I have to get back to Helena tonight."

"Pony just called Steven and told him that Sheriff Conroy's out at the Bow and Arrow. He's hoping to get a statement from you—we thought you might be going back there to check on the foal. Is Joseph okay? I've been trying to reach you guys for hours."

"There was no cell reception where we were, but he's fine, really."

"His boss has been trying to reach him. Wants him to call, says it's important."

"I'll let him know. Joe did amazing on the hike up Gunflint Mountain. I'd say he's well on the road to recovery. Did Pony say how the foal was doing? Did the foster mare arrive?"

"Apparently the mare rejected the foal, but Roon's doing his best to keep her alive, and Jessie hasn't given up on the fostering idea. Pony says she has another plan."

"Good," Dani said, relieved to hear that the filly was still alive. "I'll drop Joe off at your house after meeting with the sheriff, but I really have to get back to Helena. I have a ten o'clock appointment with a client tomorrow morning."

"Can't you reschedule? Stay with us tonight, Dani. It's too far to drive after such an exhausting day."

Dani wavered. Molly had a point. She was tired and the drive to Helena was a long one. "Thanks, Molly. I'll call my client and see if I can work something out. We'll be there as soon as we can."

She went back inside the warm, fragrant kitchen and met Joe's eyes across the kitchen table. "Sheriff Conroy wants to meet us at the Bow and Arrow. He wants to get a statement about what we saw."

Ben Comstock pulled the plastic bag of gathered evidence out of his uniform pocket and handed it to Joe. "Give this to him, if you would. You have my card, so don't hesitate to call me if you want an update or have any information to pass along."

"Will do," Joe said, pushing to his feet and pocketing the plastic bag.

They said their farewells and moments later

were in the Subaru, headed back to the Bow and Arrow. Halfway down Comstock's driveway, Dani realized that Joe had climbed behind the wheel. She was glad to let him drive. She was more than just tired. She was discouraged, downhearted and downright exhausted. She gazed out the window at a landscape that was so beautiful it made her throat cramp up. She blinked hard. She was *not* going to cry again.

"Molly said your boss wants you to call him. It's important," she said when she could manage to speak.

"I'll call when we get to the Bow and Arrow. They've probably caught the bastard who shot me."

"I hope so."

"That strudel was great, huh?"

She heaved a sigh. "Yes, it was delicious. They're a nice couple. It's good to know true love exists and endures."

Two silent miles passed while she fought back the emotions that threatened to overwhelm her.

"It's going to be okay, Dani," Joe said, breaking the silence that was destroying her.

"What makes you so sure?" Dani turned her head to look at his profile, her eyes still stinging. "What's going to make it okay? They'll never find out who shot those horses. Hershel

Bonner's right. A lot of people around here want them gone."

"A lot of people care about those mustangs. You care. Ben Comstock cares. His wife cares. That young kid, Roon, at the Bow and Arrow, he cares. Pony and Caleb McCutcheon care. The veterinarian, Jessie Weaver, she cares. They all care. That's what makes a difference and that's what's going to make it okay."

"Is that how it works in the big city?" Dani said, sitting up straight. "Everybody cares, and everything's okay? Because out here, what happens is the BLM rounds the wild horses up using helicopters, and if they're not adopted out they're put in holding pens, or if they're considered too old and nonadoptable they get slaughtered. Right now there are over forty thousand wild horses being held in long-term facilities and the lobbyists for the cattlemen's association and hunting groups are pushing the BLM to have them all slaughtered. What's going to make that okay? Money talks, but we don't have any money. Big business has all the money. All I have is a bunch of photos, and maybe I can buy some support with those, but we need real money to make a difference. We need to have the legislators listen to us for a change. Wild horses deserve protection. They deserve the right to live on the land and eat the grass and drink the water. There are ways to reduce the population without slaughtering them, but viable numbers have to be maintained for genetic diversity."

"I'm not the enemy, Dani," Joe said. "I'm on your side."

Dani sank back in her seat. She drew a shaky breath and let it out slowly. "I'm sorry. It's been a long day."

"We'll meet with that sheriff and then head back to my sister's. I'll buy you supper at the Longhorn—they must have good burgers. And, oh, by the way, just to set the record straight, in the big city, your BLM dudes would get swallowed whole by the gangsters, the sex traffickers and the drug cartel. They wouldn't last a day in the concrete jungle."

ROON READ SOMETHING once when he was a young boy. It was written by Chief Dan George and it stayed with him because it resonated, and those simple words came to him now as he held the foal while she nursed from the bottle. He spoke the words softly to himself as the foal drank the mare's milk that Jessie had retrieved from the foster mare.

*One thing to remember is to talk to the animals. If you do, they will talk back to you. But*

*if you don't talk to the animals, they won't talk
back to you, then you won't understand, and
when you don't understand you will fear, and
when you fear you will destroy the animals,
and if you destroy the animals, you will destroy yourself.*

"So I am talking to you now and you are talking back to me. We are talking, and the spirit
between us is good, and you will know that you
have in you everything you need to live and we
will help each other to be strong."

RAMALDA HEARD ROON'S voice crooning to the
foal as she cleaned the kitchen after the evening
meal. She listened carefully to his words as she
scrubbed the countertops, wiped the dishes and
put them away. She shook her head, her expression grim. She turned the burner off under the
coffeepot and carried it, along with two mugs,
out onto the porch where the sheriff sat with
Caleb McCutcheon, awaiting the arrival of the
girl who found the orphaned foal. She set both
mugs on the side table and filled them with
fresh coffee. "The boy talks, the little one eats.
He will not let her die."

Caleb nodded and picked up one of the mugs,
handing it to Sheriff Conroy. He took the other

and gazed down toward the creek. "That sounds about right."

"But the boy, Roon, he will get sick if he does not eat and does not sleep! This is no good! *No good!* Is his life worth less than that of a horse?" She turned on her heel and stomped back into the kitchen. The screen door banged shut behind her.

SHERIFF CONROY TOOK a cautious sip of the scalding coffee. "I see Ramalda hasn't changed."

"Nope. I hope she never does."

They heard the crunch of tires on gravel and the two young cow dogs snoozing on the porch jumped up and barked in response. Dani's Subaru wagon climbed up the road from the creek crossing and headed toward the ranch house.

"Does Dani Jardine know anything about this business going on back east with Joe Ferguson?" Sheriff Conroy asked.

"Not to my knowledge."

The screen door squeaked open and banged shut. Pony came out onto the porch and stood beside her husband. "Both guest rooms are ready," she said, and Caleb felt her hand rest on his shoulder. "The filly just finished an entire bottle of milk."

"That's good news," he said, covering her

hand with his own, giving it a gentle squeeze. "Maybe she's turned the corner."

"Ramalda's fixing supper for Roon and our guests."

"It's been a while since I've eaten Ramalda's cooking. It'll be a real treat," the sheriff said.

Dani and Joe climbed out of the Subaru, along with her two dogs, who were greeted happily by the cow dogs. The boys, per Caleb's instruction, stayed down by the barn and corrals and left Sheriff Conroy to question Dani and Joe. Caleb didn't want them to hear everything the sheriff had to say because not all of it was about the shooting of the wild horses. Besides, they had a herd of dairy goats to milk. And Charlie and Badger were down there with the boys, coaching them on something they knew nothing about, but that had never stopped those two old geezers from dispensing advice.

"Come inside," Pony greeted. "We've eaten but Ramalda's fixing you a plate."

They all gathered in the kitchen. Dani knelt beside Roon and the foal and ran her fingertips through the short soft wisps of curly mane. "She looks much brighter," she said to Roon, and Roon nodded.

"Her spirit is strong now. I think maybe she wants to live."

Ramalda set a big kettle of beef and beans in

the center of the table with a resounding thump. "You eat!" she said to Roon. "Or your spirit will get weak and you will starve, and who will take care of her then?" She scowled at the sheriff and Joe. "Sit! Biscuits are coming. Eat while it is hot!"

Nobody argued. They all pulled out chairs and sat. Caleb and Pony had coffee while the others filled their bowls with stew and plucked fresh hot biscuits from the basket Ramalda put on the table. The food was so good nobody spoke until most of it was gone. Then the sheriff scraped back his chair, picked up his coffee and heaved a contented sigh. "Ramalda, you're the best cook west of the Mississippi and that includes my wife, who's darn good, which is why I'm so fat. And by the way, what's said at this table stays at this table."

Caleb grinned. "Amen."

"Okay. So you have some photos on your camera," Conroy said to Dani. "I'd like copies of them, if you could email a file to me." He fished a card out of his shirt pocket and slid it across the table to her. "Tomorrow I'll be talking with the forest rangers who patrol that district. I've already spoken with Ben Comstock. He filled me in on how many dead horses there were. He also said you had some evidence for me."

Joe fished the plastic bag out of his pocket

and handed it to Conroy. "Most of this was re-trieved where the shooter parked, all except for the shell casing, which we found up on the mountain. He picked up all his shells except this one. I took photos of the tire and boot tracks with my cell phone."

The sheriff eyeballed the contents of the bag for a moment, stone-faced, then tucked it into his pocket. "You flew out here two days ago?" he said to Joe.

Joe nodded. "That's right. Came out for my sister's wedding."

"And some R and R, from what I understand," Conroy prompted. "I've spoken to your sister. She tells me you were shot multiple times in an undercover drug bust gone bad with a high-profile organized crime cartel." Joe and the sheriff locked eyes. "Molly also informed me that you'll be staying here at the ranch until you head back for the trial."

"That's not necessary. Once the big cheese is rounded up, this will all die down."

"Roon," Pony said quietly. "Why don't you go help Jimmy with the goats and I'll keep an eye on the foal."

"He doesn't need my help. He knows every-thing about everything," Roon said.

"Go help him, anyway," Caleb said, and Roon pushed away from the table and left the room with a scowl. The screen door squeaked open and banged shut behind him. Caleb leaned forward, resting his elbows on the table, and looked at Joe. "Turns out the big cheese, Marconi, flew the coop. He's not in Providence—the feds have tracked him to Mexico. You need to touch base with your boss. Apparently a death threat's been made against you. We all agree that it's best if you stayed here for a while. This is a tough place to sneak up on. Not that anything's going to happen, but just in case."

"I'll post a deputy in the area to keep an eye out for any strangers in town," the sheriff said. "I'll also contact the Bozeman police and fill them in on the situation, have them stake out your sister's house until we know what Marconi's up to."

"With Badger and Charlie on the lookout, nobody can get into or out of Katy Junction without being seen," Caleb added. "This really is the safest place for all of you, until this matter is resolved."

"You are welcome to stay here as long as you like," Pony said. "You, too," she added, looking at Dani.

"Thank you, but I really have to get back to Helena," Dani responded.

Joe panned the faces at the table like a cornered wolf. "If the feds say Marconi's holed up in Mexico, there's no need to hold me in protective custody. Marconi's death threat is just a lot of hot air."

"Was this death threat made against Joe specifically?" Dani asked.

"According to Molly, Joe's testimony will crucify Marconi," Caleb said. "Marconi's had lots of people killed during his career, and more than a few were police officers."

Dani looked at Joe, who shrugged. "It's just their way of making sure nobody messes with the Mob."

"So they make you a pair of cement overshoes and two years from now your body's found at the bottom of the harbor," Dani speculated.

"I'm not worried. The feds are hot on his heels—they'll nab him soon. And after a while he'll forget about me," Joe said.

"I doubt he'll forgive and forget so easily," Caleb said. "Seems you got some lead into him."

"Really?" Joe brightened. "I did my damnedest."

"That's how the feds tracked him," the sheriff said. "There's an excellent west coast surgeon who has a villa in Puerto Vallarta. This surgeon was on vacation and apparently taken against his will to keep Marconi alive after the shooting. Soon as he was able, he notified the authorities. He was also the one who passed along Marconi's death threat. The surgeon said that Marconi holds a personal grudge against you now, since you almost killed him."

"Great," Dani said. "So what happens next? You get put into a witness protection program? New name, new identity, new life?"

Joe rolled his coffee mug back and forth between his palms. "This'll blow over."

"Or blow up," Dani said. "They use bombs, too, don't they?"

"Would anyone like a slice of apple pie with their coffee?" Pony said.

Her comment was so out of context that they all stared at her blankly for a few moments. "I'd love some pie," Joe said.

The sheriff patted his ample stomach. "I don't need it, that's for sure, but I'd be crazy to pass that offer up."

Pony cut slices of pie and distributed them. She poured more coffee and sat back down, her dark eyes on Joe. "Molly's right, Joe. You should stay with us until this blows over."

"This is a school, not a safe house," Joe said, picking up his fork. "You have a pack of kids here, along with a two-year-old toddler, as I recall."

"Little Mary was picked up by her grandmother today. Her mother's being released from the hospital tomorrow," Pony corrected.

"Molly's right," Caleb repeated. "Nobody can get within ten miles of this place without being seen. There's only one road in. If anyone comes snooping around, they'll stand out like sore thumbs. Don't worry, we'll put you to work—no free passes here. We're always bringing in people to talk to the boys. You can lecture them about careers in law enforcement."

"Yes, you can show them all your bullet holes and then explain why you can't ever go back home again," Dani added. When Joe looked at her she flushed and dropped her eyes to her untouched pie. She pushed back her chair and stood. "Thank you so much for supper, Ramalda. It was delicious. Right now I have to feed my dogs. They must think I've abandoned them. Excuse me, please."

DANI FLED THE kitchen and stood on the porch for a moment, breathing the cool evening air. The mountains were aglow with sunset and the faint murmur of voices and the rush of the creek reached her ears from down near the barn. Winchester and Remington were sitting on the porch waiting patiently for her. They rose to their feet like the true friends they were, flanking her one on each side as she descended the porch steps and crossed to the car.

Her thoughts were jumbled. First it was the shock of the wild horses being shot, and now Joe Ferguson's life was in danger from a vengeful Mob boss. It was a lot to process on the tail end of a challenging day, but she had no idea why she'd just sniped at Joe. His life and how he lived it was none of her business. She'd have to apologize, but first she'd feed her dogs.

She rummaged in her pack for the sealed bag of dog kibble and the two soft-sided dog dishes she carried on her camping trips. The dogs jumped willingly into the back when she opened the hatch and waited patiently while she fixed their supper and then filled a third bowl with water from the jug she always carried in the car. "You're such good boys," she murmured, watching them eat. They were perfect traveling companions. They never chased after anything or ran off. They were cheerful in all weather and loyal no matter what. They would have waited all night on that porch for her.

Her eyes stung with self-pity as she thought about Jack's infidelity, his matter-of-fact announcement that he'd fallen in love with someone else and would be moving his things out of the house they'd shared for years. Then she thought about Ben Comstock and his wife, Emma, and how clearly devoted they were to each other. Why did relationships work out for some couples and not for others? What had she done wrong? Had it been her fault, or had she just been a victim of Jack's restless heart and his flying career?

Dani pulled her cell phone out of her pocket and rescheduled all her clients for the following week. She felt guilty doing so, but it was in her clients' best interest. She was in no shape to advise anyone about anything at the present time.

She sat on the tailgate while the dogs finished their supper and checked her voice mails. One was from the law firm of Hacker, Whetstone and Swindleman in Bozeman, where she'd recently sent a résumé. A man who identified himself as Harold Swindleman left a well-modulated message requesting that she schedule an appointment for an interview and stating that he was impressed with her credentials and experience.

She played the message a second time before listening to a message from her real estate agent. She'd shown Dani's house to a couple on Saturday. Apparently they loved the place and were going to make an offer. Dani stuffed her cell phone back into her pocket. Her spirits improved considerably as she contemplated the first stars of evening. At least one law firm thought she was worth an interview. *And* someone might be buying her house in Helena. She glanced over toward the ranch house. They were still talking inside, finishing up their apple pie and probably thinking she was quite a rude individual. They were right. But Dani couldn't go back in there, not after how she'd behaved. Her eyes narrowed as she thought about her alternatives. She needed more than anything to talk to Molly, and Molly was only an hour and a half away. Molly and Steven lived very close to Bozeman, which was where the law firm of Hacker, Whetstone and Swindleman was located. If she climbed into the Subaru and drove off right this very moment, Joe would be stranded here, in a very safe place, which is exactly what Molly wanted. It would be rude of her to leave without saying goodbye, but she'd be doing it to keep Joe safe.

Plus, if she just sneaked off, she wouldn't have to face him again this evening. She'd just call the ranch when she reached Molly and Steven's place, and make her explanations, beg forgiveness, do whatever necessary to stay in Pony's and Caleb's good graces. It was a cowardly strategy but, at the moment, one that held a strong appeal. Dani slid off the tailgate.

"Okay, boys, how about we go for a little ride," she said, quietly closing the hatch.

Sixty seconds later, she was stealthily driving the Subaru across the bridge over the creek, heading west into the sunset.

# CHAPTER EIGHT

JOE ACCOMPANIED SHERIFF CONROY outside when the sheriff announced his departure. He was reasonably sure he could talk Dani into going back to Molly and Steven's place for the evening, especially if he offered to drive. That would give them plenty of time to talk. Dani was peeved with him for some reason, and he wanted to smooth things over with her. He stepped out onto the porch and came to an abrupt stop, staring at the empty place on the other side of the sheriff's vehicle, where Dani's Subaru had been parked.

"Looks like she's flown the coop," Conroy said.

Joe rubbed his jaw and lifted his gaze to where the road threaded through the valley. He saw the rooster tail of dust trailing behind Dani's Subaru as she headed toward town. "Looks to me like she's driving over the speed limit," he commented. Conroy grunted in agreement. They stood side by side, staring. "She's really stressed out from everything that's happened, probably shouldn't be behind the wheel. Think you could catch her in your rig?" Joe asked, nodding to the sheriff's battered white-and-gold SUV with the blue light bar on top. "If you could pull her over before she reaches the main road, I'll drive her to Molly's place. I'm sure that's where she's headed."

Conroy nodded and started down the steps. "Climb aboard and buckle up."

DANI DIDN'T MAKE it as far as the ranch gate before she noticed the flashing blue lights through the cloud of dust behind her and slowed to a stop. Joe walked up alongside her door. She rolled down the window but kept her eyes fixed straight ahead, hands gripping the wheel.

"License and registration please, ma'am," he said.

"I don't believe you have any jurisdiction in this state, Officer," she replied, lifting her chin slightly and keeping her eyes straight ahead.

Joe leaned his forearms on the window ledge to bring himself down to her level. "Well, you see, Counselor, the thing is, I've been deputized by Sheriff Conroy. He thought you were driving at an excessive speed on a private road and wanted me to have a word with you about that."

She turned to look at him, her expression stony. "I didn't want to stay there," she said, but her voice had a waver despite her attempt at bravado. "I need to talk to Molly about all this."

"So you just drove off and abandoned me?" Joe shook his head. "That's rude behavior. I might have to write you another ticket for that."

"This isn't a laughing matter. This is dead serious stuff. You were safe there, Joe. You heard what they said and I believe them."

"But the thing is, if I'm a target, I don't want to be a target surrounded by kids, and for that matter, I don't want to be a target at my sister's home. So, if you'll be so kind as to give me a ride back to Bozeman, I'll hop a flight back east in the morning. That's where I belong, in that concrete jungle where dogs eat dogs."

Dani glared at him. "Dogs don't eat dogs."

"Maybe not, but they can get into some nasty fights and tear each other apart. So what do you say? It beats getting two tickets."

Dani blew out her breath. "Fine. And, by the way, I'm sorry I said what I did at the table. It was way out of line. Your life is none of my business."

Joe straightened up from her window. "I'm sorry to hear that," he said. "I was beginning to think things were going well between us," he said. "Look, you've had a rough couple of days. At least let me drive you to Molly's place, then if you want to go all the way back to Helena

I'll drive you there and you can drop me off at a hotel near the airport. I'll go cut the sheriff loose if you promise not to speed away."

She hesitated for a moment, then unlatched her seat belt, opened her door and walked around the front of the Subaru and climbed into the passenger seat. Joe waited until she'd buckled herself in before walking back to the sheriff's window. "Thanks," he said.

Sheriff Conroy nodded. "That's a dangerous outfit you're dealing with. I'll tell my deputies to watch for anything suspicious, but you be careful." He put the SUV in gear and pulled around them, continuing down the ranch road. Joe watched him drive away. This wasn't how he'd envisioned his trip to Montana. He did a slow three-sixty, standing beside Dani's Subaru, memorizing the mountains, the sky, the push of the wind, the smell of the wild places, the colors of the sunset. He wanted to remember it all, because after tomorrow, he might never be in a place this beautiful again.

THE DRIVE TO Molly and Steven's began in stony silence. Dani sat with her hands folded in her lap, watching the scenery flow past. After a brief pause at the ranch gate, they were driving on the main road toward Katy Junction. The Longhorn Café was closed for the evening and the four buildings that made up the town looked as if they were from another century, standing side by side, bathed in the golden light of sunset.

"So, this Marconi," Dani began in an attempt at conversation. "Just how powerful is he?"

"I'd rather talk about mustangs," Joe said, glancing briefly at her.

"Was he involved in a drug ring?"

"He was into it all. Sex trafficking, drug running, insurance fraud, stock market fraud, you name it. He had his fingers in all the pies. Federal prison didn't slow him down one bit, just gave him time to hone his techniques and build his clientele."

"I'm from a little dairy farming community in Oregon. You'll have to forgive me for being ignorant about organized crime in big cities."

"I think it's great you don't know anything about it," Joe said. "I wish I could've grown up on a farm."

"That dairy farm had been in my family for generations. It was a big farm, too, nearly seven hundred acres. My great-great-grandfather built the house the 1800s. We all loved that farm, especially my father. The land gets in your blood. It's a powerful bond that's hard to describe. My dad died of a massive heart attack when he was forty-five. It was very sudden. I was away at school, in my first year of college. I didn't even get to say goodbye." Dani's voice caught. She was amazed at how painful the memory still was. She turned her head away and felt her heart twist when Joe's hand reached out and closed around hers.

"I'm sorry," he said, giving her hand a comforting squeeze.

Dani nodded and struggled to compose herself. "After years of us nagging him, Dad had finally bought all new equipment and upgraded the dairy barn, just a few months before he died. New automated milking parlor and the whole nine yards. He'd had to mortgage the property to upgrade the business. The stress of that mortgage is probably what brought on his heart attack. We all felt guilty, like we'd killed him. When he died, the federal and state death taxes were so high my mother couldn't pay them *and* make the mortgage payments. She was forced to sell. She kept the house and twenty acres at least. But developers snapped up the rest of the land and turned it into big housing developments. A developer built a strip mall where the best hay fields once were. When I saw what losing my father and the farm he loved did to my mother, I wanted to keep the same thing from ever happening to anyone else's family farm. That's why I went into real estate law and estate planning."

"Any brothers or sisters?"

"Two sisters, both married with kids, living so-called normal lives. I'm the oddball."

Joe gave her hand one more squeeze before returning his to the steering wheel. "I think your father would be really proud of you," he said. He let a respectful amount of time pass before asking, "So how do we find the guy who shot the wild horses?"

Dani twisted sideways in her seat to study his profile. In spite of herself, she was getting mighty attached to Joe Ferguson's profile. "Until Marconi's caught, I really think you should stay out at the Bow and Arrow. It's safer than going back east."

Completely ignoring her statement, Joe said, "Comstock mentioned commandeering a chopper and flying up into the pass to look for those four mares. Is that sort of aerial search for wild animals in a warden's budget?"

Dani faced front with a frustrated sigh. "You know why I went to law school. What made you get into police work?"

"I went into law enforcement because I wanted to single-handedly abolish organized crime."

"A noble cause," Dani said with a note of skepticism in her voice.

"Okay, truth of the matter, an ex-soldier only has so many skills to market in the job place.

And who knows, maybe it's a genetic thing with the Irish."

"You're half-Scottish," Dani reminded him.

"Yeah, I figure that's why Molly moved out West. My mother's side of the family were the explorers, the fur trappers, the mountain men. The fiery redheaded environmental lawyers."

Dani smiled. "Molly's one of a kind."

"She's an icon in our family. Smart, college educated, beautiful, successful and somewhat famous after the successful fight to save Madison Mountain. Makes me kind of ashamed of teasing her when she was little about her red hair and freckles."

"Molly adores you. If you stayed out here, she'd be the happiest gal on the planet and you'd get to watch your niece or nephew grow up."

"So, getting back to the wild horses. If Comstock finds them, what then?"

"Then we tell Jessie Weaver, and Caleb and Pony, and figure out some kind of game plan. Odds are most of those mares are ready to foal. They need to be down in the valley, in a protected place."

"A place the shooter could access, to finish off the job?"

"Hopefully we'll find out who did it before it comes to that."

"So these four surviving mares, the last of Custer's band, what happens to them?"

Dani shook her head. "That's just it. Right now their future is up in the air. If the BLM decides to slaughter all the wild horses being held in long-term holding areas, which they're being pressured to do, they'll probably end up in dog food cans or being shipped to Europe for people food."

"Do you think that's really going to happen?"

She shook her head again. "I don't know. The cattlemen's association is a powerful lobby. But people truly connect to the mustangs and the image of the Wild West. It's an emotional subject and it's hard for people to be objective. But these wild horses have a very successful breeding rate. Without some way of controlling that, how do you control the population? Managing the wild horse herds is complicated."

"Isn't there some way to fix them?"

"Vaccines have been developed that will inhibit pregnancy in mares for up to three years. The problem is administering them to mares in a wild herd. And then there's the problem of how these vaccines might effect other animals who eat horse carcasses, and that includes the horses that get sold for human consumption. Castrating the colts and stallions is ineffective because just one animal that's missed can impregnate a whole lot of mares. There are no easy answers. Wild horses can't be managed the way you'd manage a deer or elk population, by hunting them, and as far as natural predators, there aren't many that can take down a horse. Roundups are ineffective, too. There just aren't enough people who want to adopt these horses, so they end up being held in pens and fed at the taxpayers' expense.

"Jessie Weaver has probably the most genetically pure Spanish mustangs, and her program works because the Bow and Arrow is a huge ranch with plenty of land and water, and her mares are only half wild and she can easily manage her herd. She's able to administer the three-year vaccine to specific mares. She chooses when to breed and which mares to keep open, so when the foals are born, they're wanted. They're waited for. That's what the kids at the Bow and Arrow help with. They're great at working with the young horses. Once the foals are weaned off their mothers and the colts are gelded, the kids take over, and by fall time the horses are ready for new homes. Any remaining yearlings are handled regularly and they're trained to be ridden when they're two-year-olds. Unfortunately, Jessie Weaver's wild horse management is the exception to the rule."

Joe drove in silence for a while, digesting

Dani's words. "So, what's the answer?" he finally said.

"I don't know," Dani admitted. "But I do know shooting them isn't the way to solve the problem." She brooded for a few moments. "Sometimes I wish I'd never discovered that little band of mustangs up in the Arrow Roots, but I did, and I've gotten attached to them over the years. If I had a place with some land, I'd take those four mares myself. My house in Helena's on the market. It's a beautiful old house in the historic district and should sell fast. The real estate agent showed it on Saturday to a couple who loved it. She thinks they'll make an offer. I'm shopping for something that might have enough space for a few horses but haven't found anything yet."

Joe hit the brakes and Dani braced one hand against the dash as he swerved to avoid a Hereford cow and calf that burst out of the brush and trotted across the road in front of Dani's vehicle. "Damn!" he said after the close call. "Don't they fence in their cattle around here?"

"BLM lands are leased to cattle ranchers, and there are fences but not all of them are in good shape," Dani explained. "Driving can be hazardous after dark."

"Then I better slow down," Joe said. "I prefer my steak on a plate, not on the hood of a car."

"THEY SHOULD HAVE been here by now," Molly said for the umpteenth time, pacing to the window.

Steven looked up from the newspaper. "Pony said they only left the Bow and Arrow two hours ago. They probably stopped somewhere along the way."

"Where? There's no place to stop. The Longhorn isn't open at night. Something bad's happened, I know it. Joseph should have stayed at the Bow and Arrow—it's the safest place for him! Marconi's hit men are probably here already, waiting to pick him off. You almost got killed the same way, or have you forgotten?"

"That was different."

"No, it wasn't. A crazy man with a gun almost killed you. Someone shot at Joe and almost killed him. There's so much violence in the world. I hate guns! They should all be banned."

Steven folded the paper and set it on the coffee table. "They're here."

*"What?"* Molly ran to the window. "How do you know? I didn't hear anything!"

"That's because you're too busy pacing and talking."

Molly crossed to the door and opened it just as Dani's Subaru swung into the drive and headlights swept across the front of the house.

"Oh, thank God!" she said, and rushed toward the station wagon. "Joseph!" She plastered herself against her brother as soon as he got out of the car, then did the same to Dani when she emerged. "I was so worried. Why didn't you stay at the Bow and Arrow? You weren't supposed to come back here—it's too dangerous. Come inside, Dani. You can let the dogs out in the yard. It's not safe out here—anybody could be hiding in those bushes." She rushed them into the house and made sure the curtains were drawn tight. "What took you so long? I tried and tried to call you but you weren't answering. Have you called your boss yet, Joseph? Have you talked to Rico?"

Steven folded his newspaper, pushed out of his chair, added another chunk of firewood to the fireplace and went into the kitchen. "I'll fix the drinks," he said. "What is everyone having?"

MOLLY LOOKED AT Steven as he stood behind the kitchen counter taking drink orders, and wondered how he could be so calm.

"How about a glass of milk for Molly?" Dani said, leading her to the couch and sitting her down. "I'm sorry we scared you. It's been a long day for everyone." Dani sank down beside Molly. "I'll have whatever you fix, Steven, and thank you. I'm sorry we're so late getting here. It's a slower drive at night."

"Joe?" Steven said.

Joe had moved over by the fire and was nudging the log with a brass poker. "Whiskey, straight up, if you have any."

Steven brought a glass of milk for her, a shot of whiskey for Joe and a glass of cabernet for Dani. "Red okay?" he asked her.

"Red's perfect," she said. "Thank you, Steven."

Steven sat on the other side of Molly and opened a bottle of cold beer for himself. "So, what's next?"

Molly set her untasted glass of milk on the coffee table. "First thing in the morning, Joseph goes back to the Bow and Arrow. I'm sure Marconi knows I'm living in Montana and his goons have probably already tracked you here."

"You've watched too many cop shows," Joe said. "Anyway, you won't have to worry about Mob goons after tomorrow because I'm catching a flight out of Bozeman in the morning and heading back east."

"You'll do no such thing!" Molly said.

"Let's drop this subject," Joe said. "I'm sick of it."

"Agreed," Steven seconded.

A gust of wind rattled a loose shutter. Molly jumped up nervously and paced to the window, fiddling with the curtains, making sure they were tightly shut. Nausea made her stomach roil and her fingers trembled as she adjusted the curtains. "Rico told me about the death threat," she said.

"Rico talks too much."

"Joseph, this is serious. Until they're all rotting in prison, you won't be safe. Are you forgetting how our very own grandfather died?"

Joe met her gaze with an expression that made her feel like a naughty child, then drank his shot of whiskey in one swallow. He walked into the kitchen and set his glass in the sink. "I'm hitting the sack," he said. "Thanks for the drink, Steven. I'll see you all in the morning."

He paused by Dani, reached in his pocket and handed her a business card. "Sheriff Conroy's contact information. You'll want to make sure he follows up on that bag of evidence we gave him." Then he left the room, and the silence that filled it after he'd gone made Molly want to cry. She sat back down beside Dani and hugged a throw pillow to her stomach.

"He's so stubborn," she said.

"How did your grandfather die?" Steven asked.

"He was an honest Irish cop, and honest cops who made big waves with the Mob didn't last long. He was found in Boston Harbor. Authorities said he likely slipped and fell off the pier one foggy night and drowned. They called it a tragic accident and said it was just a coincidence that it happened two days before he was to testify against a member of the Mob."

Molly jumped to her feet and flung the throw pillow onto the couch. "So you see, I won't let history repeat itself. Joseph's not going anywhere except back to the Bow and Arrow. That's the safest place in the world for him right now."

"He won't go willingly," Dani said.

Molly paced to the fireplace and back, then stopped. Her frown vanished and her expression brightened. "Unless we make him think that staying was his own idea," she said. "And I think I have the perfect plan."

WHEN THE PHONE rang at ten p.m., Ben Comstock groaned aloud. He and his wife had just gone to bed and turned the lights out. The aspirin and ice pack had taken the edge off the pain and he was tired enough that he was almost asleep.

"I'll get it," he said. He reached for the phone before Emma could lean over him, but she beat him to it. "You're not going anywhere tonight, no matter who's poaching what," she informed him before picking it up. She listened to the caller for a few moments, then covered the mouthpiece. "It's Molly Ferguson, the attorney who has the law practice in Bozeman with Steven Young Bear. Not an emergency—she just wanted to ask you something."

Comstock took the phone from his wife. "Hello, Molly. What's up?"

Molly's voice was taut. "It's about my brother Joseph. You met him today. He was with Dani when she went up the mountain where the wild horses were shot," she began, and Comstock settled back on his pillow to listen.

# CHAPTER NINE

DANI ROSE BEFORE dawn to let the dogs out into the fenced yard. She was grateful for the neat stack of clothing Molly had provided the evening before, knowing that Dani had packed very little for her hiking trip. She was a few inches taller than Molly but about the same size, which was helpful. Their tastes in clothing, however, were vastly different. Molly, being a redhead, preferred understated and conservative styles. Getting dressed meant choosing between dull and boring, as far as Dani was concerned, but the clothing was clean and that's all that counted.

The sun was an hour shy of rising over the mountain range to the east and the world was still quiet and peaceful. Steven and Molly's house was way off the beaten path. No neighbors, no traffic noises. Just the wind blowing across the distance, the first clear notes of birdsong, the last of the stars fading from the sky. She smelled coffee in the kitchen. Joe must already be up. He was an early bird, and the time difference was probably still influencing his routine. She poured herself a mug and carried it out onto the porch. Sure enough, he was sitting in the same chair he'd been in the morning before. Had it been just a day that they last sat side by side, drinking coffee? So much had happened since then.

She sat down in the chair beside him with a quiet greeting, which he returned. "Did you sleep, Joe?"

"Like a log. You?"

"I don't have anyone trying to kill me."

"Don't start," he said. "Molly gets carried away sometimes, and yesterday was definitely one of those times."

"Are you still dead set on going back east?"

"It's the best way to nail Marconi, especially if he's gunning for me. Lure him back into the city where the local cops and the feds know his every move."

"Maybe I'm way out of line here, but I sense this thing with Marconi is some sort of personal vendetta with you."

Joe balanced his mug of coffee on his knee and gazed out across the distance. "It is, I guess," he said slowly. "My ex-wife, Alison, was a model featured in a lot of glossy magazines doing perfume and makeup campaigns. Her photo was also often found on the society pages and in tabloid rags. And several times over the five years we were married she was photographed with Marconi. She shrugged it off when I asked her about it when we started dating, said they just happened to be at the same party. But the way they were looking at each other in some of the photos..." Joe's voice trailed off. He raised his coffee mug, took a swallow and set it back on his knee. "Doesn't matter, I guess. She played around with a lot of men after we were married and made no secret of it. It's just the thought of her and Marconi being together, especially when she knew I was working so hard to put him away for life... It really bothered me."

Dani took a sip of coffee, momentarily tongue-tied by this revelation. "That's pretty heavy stuff," was all she could think to say.

"She was in love with him. She admitted it after our divorce was finalized." Joe's voice was flat, devoid of emotion, but she could almost feel the tension radiating from him. In spite of the terrible way his ex-wife had treated him during their marriage, Joe had loved Alison, and her infidelity had hurt him deeply.

They sat in silence, each caught up in their own thoughts as they drank their coffee. Finally Dani sat up a little straighter and looked right at him. "I understand how you feel about Marconi, Joe—at least I think I do—but I wish you wouldn't go. I could use your help finding the person who shot those horses. The sheriff's not going to put any real time into it, and Ben Comstock's out of commission. I've been thinking of taking a few days off from work to talk to the forest rangers who patrol the Arrow Roots and maybe go see Josie again, without her father around. She had some pretty strong opinions, and she might have seen something on her ride up into the pass yesterday. Besides, if you go back east, what'll you do? I mean, other than be used as bait to lure Marconi and his men."

"I have a friend with a boat who likes to striper fish. You ever fished for striped bass?" Dani shook her head. "They're a great fighting fish. Fun to catch. Been years since I've been deep-sea fishing. I'd bring Ferg with me, take him out of that stuffy private boarding school and teach him how to fish. Six years old is the perfect age to get 'em hooked."

"But what about Molly's wedding? Don't you want to be here for that? Couldn't you fly your son out here and get in some father-son time before the wedding?"

"Bad plan. Think about it. Marconi wants me dead for a number of reasons, so he sets his dogs on me. They find out Molly's engaged, not hard to do since the engagement's been published. They easily figure out the wedding date and place. What better place to nail me than at my sister's wedding? Ever see that movie *The Godfather*? That's the sort of bloody drama the Mob likes. You want me to do that to Molly? If I go back east, I can at least keep the fight on the East Coast."

"If you bring the fight out here, you'll have the advantage," Dani argued. "Those goons are city dogs. They'd be like fish out of water in Montana. Everybody in this neck of woods has a gun and knows how to use it. Those kids at the Bow and Arrow? You're worried about them? They could probably tie you up in knots. If you leave now, before the wedding, you'll wreck Molly. You have to know that's true."

Joe took a swallow of his coffee and was quiet for a moment. "For someone who doesn't care about my personal life, you're getting awfully personal," he commented.

"Molly's my best friend and I care about anything that affects her," Dani said. "If that offends you, I apologize."

"You can get as personal with me as you like. I'm all for it," Joe said.

Dani felt the heat climb into her cheeks and declined to respond. She took another sip of coffee instead as they shared a few minutes of uneasy silence. Then she said, "I just think you should stay, that's all. That's my opinion, for what it's worth. Molly needs you right now." Without waiting for a reply, she pushed out of her chair, called the two dogs and went back inside.

JOE WAS POURING his second cup of coffee and looking up the number for the airlines on his cell phone when Molly came into the kitchen. Her magnificent red hair framed her sleepy face. "Good morning, Joseph." She picked up the coffeepot, started to pour herself a cup, then set it back on the warming plate with a grimace. "I can't drink this stuff anymore," she said as she drew a glass of water instead. "I don't know why they call it morning sickness when it lasts all day." The house phone rang. Molly carried her water with her and picked up the call. She spoke briefly, then held the phone out to Joe. "Ben Comstock. He'd like a word with you."

Comstock didn't beat around the bush. "Morning, Joe. Last night I made arrangements with Yellowstone Helotours to fly up into the pass today to look for those four mares, but Emma's taking me to the clinic this morning. My knee's hurting pretty bad, figure I better get it checked out. I know it's asking a lot, but could you meet the chopper pilot at ten a.m. this morning, at the airfield just south of Gallatin

Gateway, and have a look for me? I'd appreciate
it. The sheriff can't go—he gets airsick—and I
promised Jessie Weaver and Caleb McCutcheon
I'd make sure those mares weren't bogged down
up in the snowpack. Some of those horses are
probably pregnant, making them more vulnerable to predation. I also need someone to talk
to the forest service employees. I was hoping
you'd be able to do that, too. I know that's asking a lot, son, but you said you'd be in the area
for a few weeks. And this gives you a good opportunity to see the lay of the land."

Joe glanced suspiciously at Molly, who stared
back with wide-eyed innocence. "Actually, sir,
my plans have changed. I'm flying back east
today."

"Oh? I'm sorry to hear that. I could have used
your expertise on this case. Guess I'll have to
find someone else. I want you to know I appreciated your help yesterday, though, and so
does Emma."

"Does the warden service usually use choppers to look for wild horses?"

"They do when the chopper's being paid for
by the Wild Horse Foundation, and the wild
horses were shot and harassed illegally. Caleb
and Jessie are helping with the air search costs,
as well. They have a vested interest in Custer's

herd, being as they're nursing the foal that Dani rescued."

Joe ran his fingers through his hair. "I suppose I could delay my departure for one day."

"I'd really appreciate it. The pilot's name is Nash. I told him where to look for the mares. He just needs a second pair of eyes to help search when he's flying in the mountains. The downdrafts and turbulence can be tricky but Nash is experienced. If Dani wants to go along, her photos would be appreciated. There're a couple good pairs of binoculars on board, too. They provide them for the tourists."

"I'll be sure to let her know, though somehow I think she already does."

"The forest ranger's main office isn't far from the airstrip. You'll pass it on the way there. You could stop in and get the name of the ranger who was patrolling that area of the Arrow Roots when the shooting occurred. Anything you could find out would be a help. I told Jessie Weaver she might get a firsthand report from you around suppertime out at the Bow and Arrow."

"That right?" Joe said. "She's expecting us around suppertime?"

"That's when I usually show up. A man would be foolish to pass up a meal like that."

Joe hung up a few moments later and gave his sister a calculating stare. "I suppose Pony's also expecting me to give the boys a lecture after supper?"

"I think that would be nice," Molly said.

Dani chose that moment to enter the kitchen. She was still carrying her mug of coffee and looked as beautiful as the morning. She gave him a smile that took his breath away. Joe looked between the two of them and admitted defeat.

"I've been ambushed," he said. "I'll stay one more day, but that's it."

NASH HAD BEEN flying for Yellowstone Helotours long enough for the job to have become mundane, but every time he got a call from Ben Comstock he felt the old adventurous spirit kick-start his heart. Comstock's requests were usually search and rescue, and that sure beat flying a bunch of picture-snapping tourists over Old Faithful. He and the warden had a long and colorful history, but any differences of opinion over hunting ethics were laid to rest during times of human travail and tragedy. When Comstock had called him the previous evening, he'd been sitting at the bar contemplating putting the moves on a woman he'd taken sightseeing two days earlier. She was with two girlfriends and had just given him what could only be described as a seductive smile when she entered the bar and spotted him.

At that very moment his cell phone rang. He fished it out of his pocket.

"Comstock here," came the warden's gruff voice. "Need you to fly over South Pass area in the Arrow Roots tomorrow, first thing, the area north of Hershel Bonner's place in the national forest. Know that high valley where the old ranger cabin is?"

"I know that whole area like the back of my hand, but I can't do it first thing. I have a geyser tour. Can it be second thing? Say, ten a.m.?"

"That'll have to do."

"Search and rescue?"

"Search, for sure. Not sure about the rescue part."

"I'll be waiting."

Nash figured it could be a challenging day, so he gave up on the idea of seducing the sexy tourist, left the bar early and got a good night's sleep. He flew the geyser tour, a one-hour narrated flight, and was waiting at ten a.m. when a tough-looking, rangy dude with a knockout girlfriend approached the office and asked for him by name. "I'm Nash," he said. "But if you're looking for a flight, I'm booked this morning."

"Joe Ferguson, and this is Dani Jardine. Ben Comstock sent us. He can't make it—he hurt his knee and is having it looked at this morning. Said he told you where to fly us in the Arrow Roots to search for the horses."

"Horses?"

"That's right," Dani Jardine said. Her dark hair was pulled back in a ponytail and she wasn't wearing a stitch of makeup. Didn't need any. She was a natural beauty. She had some expensive digital camera equipment slung over her shoulder and was wearing a pair of sexy mirrored sunglasses. "Wild horses. Four were shot in that high valley by the forest service camp, along with a domestic quarter horse mare. You probably heard about it, I'm sure it's been in the news."

Nash shook his head. "Nope, haven't heard a thing."

"Four other horses managed to escape by running up into the pass. The snow's still deep in the higher elevations and Jessie Weaver's afraid they might have gotten bogged down. They're pregnant mares."

"Do they belong to Jessie?" Nash asked. Jessie Weaver was somewhat legendary in Park County.

"No. We think they're a small band that may have strayed from the Pryor Mountains. We're hoping you can locate them for us."

"Don't worry. If they're up there, I'll find

them," Nash said. He fed a stick of gum into his mouth and nodded to the chopper on the tarmac behind him. "It's kind of bumpy today. Hope you two don't get airsick. I'm all out of barf bags. Passengers used 'em up on the last ride."

DANI HAD NEVER ridden in a helicopter before, and Nash's words and the borderline malicious grin that had accompanied them had done nothing to ease her anxieties. She strapped herself into a window seat in the back, adjusting the belt tightly. Joe sat up front with the pilot, who had pulled on his aviator glasses as he did his preflight check. He wore a headset over his ball cap and was talking into the mic. She checked her camera gear while the chopper's engine warmed up and tried not to think about her irrational fear of flying, and how her airline pilot boyfriend, Jack, used to tease her about it. "I don't like not being in control," she'd repeatedly told him.

"What's that?" Joe said, turning in his seat.

Dani flushed. "Nothing. Just talking to myself."

"Relax," Joe said with a grin. "This is going to be fun."

Dani realized she must be wearing her anxiety like a flashing neon sign and forced a smile. "I'm just worried about the horses, that's all. I hope they're okay. I don't want to see any more dead mustangs."

Within minutes they were airborne, and within several more minutes it was obvious to Dani that Nash knew what he was doing, which helped settle her nerves. The scenery helped, as well. It was hard to think about crashing and burning while she scanned the landscape beneath them. The Gallatin National Forest and the Absaroka-Beartooth Wilderness were a spectacular backdrop to the snowcapped mountain ranges that soared into a deep blue sky. Dani had hiked many of these mountains, but she'd never flown over them like this, up close and personal. Nash narrated as he flew; it was part of his job giving the tours, and he seemed to enjoy sharing his knowledge and history of the area.

"We're flying over the boundary of the Absaroka-Beartooth Wilderness Area, where it abuts the Gallatin National Forest," he narrated. "To your left you'll see the river that runs through the Bow and Arrow, which is just beyond the park boundaries and not all that far from Hershel Bonner's place. It's not impossible that these wild horses you're looking for have been hidden in these valleys for generations and could be related to Jessie Weaver's herd. It's a wild area with lots of canyons and valleys that are hard

to access. The Arrow Roots are part of the Absaroka, which are dead ahead, just south of the
Livingston Road. The Absaroka Range isn't as
harsh as the Beartooth so there's more vegetation, more wildlife. This was Crow country—
they called themselves the Absaroka—and I
doubt a prettier piece of America exists than
what we're looking at right now."

The chopper rode on the turbulent air cur-
rents as they climbed over the mountains. Dani
braced one hand against the roof as the chopper dropped into a bottomless pit, then clamped
her camera between her knees to remove the
lens cap. High winds, updrafts and downdrafts
buffeted the chopper and made it difficult for
her to steady the camera for a few shots of the
highest peak as Nash narrated the geography
unfolding beneath them. "South Pass coming
up," she heard him say. "Those tiny buildings
to the north are Hershel Bonner's place. We're
climbing into the valley where you saw the dead
horses…" Dani lowered the camera and tried
to identify the valley. "There's the old ranger's
cabin," Nash said. Dani recognized the place
where she'd camped so often and snapped a few
aerial shots. "There's your dead horses—what's
left of 'em." The laconic narration continued as
the chopper descended for a better look.

The dark carcasses were sprawled against

the greening grass of the high meadow and the brightening spangle of wildflowers blooming in shades of yellow, blue and white, creating a startlingly beautiful backdrop to the gruesome scene of the slaughter. They soon left the meadow behind and the chopper ascended into the pass, circling as it gained altitude so that the buffeting up and down and the circling motion began to affect Dani's equilibrium. She tried to concentrate on taking photos, on searching for the missing mares, but it became increasingly difficult. "Lotta snow up here still," she heard Nash say as she struggled with increasing nausea. "I can see where the horses came up through the pass. See those dark smudges? Those are deep shadows made by their tracks."

"I see them," Joe said. "Dani?"

"I see them," she said, blinking the sting of cold sweat from her eyes and swallowing a mouthful of saliva.

They climbed higher and then she heard Nash say, "I'll be damned, somehow they made it through. Look at that, the snow must be chest-deep through there. They could've turned around and come back into the valley, but didn't. We'll see if they made it down the other side, but it's damned rough country through there. Wilder'n hell and lots of creeks to cross."

The chopper was being tossed around like a

toy in the mountain updrafts. Dani figured it was only a matter of time before they crashed. She drew deep breaths, determined not to throw up, and braced herself, camera in her lap. There was no hope of getting a photo that wasn't blurred in turbulence this severe. She watched the dizzying mountain landscape blur past her window. Snow, rocks, granite ledges, snow. Then she saw the tops of trees and a few minutes later she heard Nash say, "Well, their tracks go into the tree line down there, so I have to guess they're okay. Tough horses, those mustangs. Let's see if we can find them in one of these valleys."

The turbulence lessened as they descended onto the forested flanks and flew over high valleys lush with grass and sprinkled with spring wildflowers. Creeks were ribbons of dark laced with the frothy white of rapids. "Hey, would you look at that!" she heard Nash say. "Three o'clock. Four horses in that meadow, running for cover. I'll get you a good photo angle."

Nash maneuvered the chopper and Dani barely had time to snap a photo before the horses vanished into the trees. Joe turned to catch her eye. He looked excited. "Did you see them?"

A nod was all she could manage.

"Well, they're safe for now. Nobody's going

to be climbing up here to shoot at 'em," Nash said with an abrupt laugh. "They don't like the sound of choppers much. That's what the BLM uses to round 'em up every year."

The rest of the flight was less turbulent. Nash took them back to the airfield by skirting the high passes and flying them over the Bow and Arrow at a high enough elevation not to disturb the buffalo. He showed them the lay of the land on the northern and western edge of the Absarokas, the high places where the buffalo calved, the broad, low plateaus along the river where the graze was good. "This is all part of the Bow and Arrow," he said. The size and beauty of the historic ranch was impressive.

Dani saw the four tiny buildings of Katy Junction, the dirt road that headed west toward Bozeman and Gardiner. She sat back in her seat and wiped the cold sweat from her face. Her heart was still beating fast and her stomach was still roiling, but she was relieved that Custer's four mares, the survivors of his little band, were still alive.

Back at the airfield, Joe had to help her out of the chopper. Her knees were weak and she was pretty sure she didn't resemble the dashingly beautiful Amelia Earhart. Nash pushed his aviator shades onto his head and shook her hand with a grin that was genuinely friendly.

"You did all right," he told her as he handed her his card. "That was a rough flight. Any time you want another bird's-eye view of the Rockies, you let me know."

When they reached the car, Joe opened the passenger door for her and she climbed in on shaky legs, stashed her camera gear in the back and fastened her seat belt, taking deep, slow breaths to settle her stomach. Joe was wearing a broad, satisfied grin as he climbed behind the wheel. "What a ride," he said. "That was kick-ass. I'd do that again in a heartbeat." Dani moaned in response as he pulled out of the parking area and headed north. He gave her a sidelong glance. "You're looking a little off-color. I remember passing a saloon on the way to the airfield. I'll stand you to a stiff drink."

"I'm fine," Dani said as cold sweat beaded on her forehead.

"We should stop at the district office and see what they have to say about this whole messy situation, then I'll buy you lunch. I could use a greasy hamburger."

With an abrupt forward lurch, Dani reached for the door handle with one hand and covered her mouth with the other. "Pull over!" she blurted.

Joe didn't waste any time. She ripped open the door as soon as he put the car in Park and lunged out into the roadside grass and brush, heaving up her breakfast and wishing she were dead rather than have Joe see her like this. She felt a hand between her shoulders as she bent over; another hand brushed her hair away from her face and cupped her forehead. Joe, steadying her while she threw up. She'd never felt more miserable and humiliated. Mortified, she straightened and accepted the wad of Kleenex Joe retrieved from the box in the car.

"Feel any better?" he asked.

She nodded, avoiding his concerned stare and wishing a bolt of lightning would strike her dead.

"C'mon, we'll sit over here for a few minutes," he said, guiding her to a grassy knoll. They sat in the strong wind and bright sunshine. An occasional vehicle whisked by. The wind made a sound like thunder, pushing across the land. Dani took deep breaths of the cool fresh air and slowly became aware of Joe's arm around her shoulders. She leaned against him gratefully.

"Sorry about that," she said.

"Don't be," Joe said, giving her a reassuring squeeze. "Gives us a chance to get to know each other better and do some serious cuddling."

Dani laughed in spite of her misery. "Right now I don't care if I ever eat again or take a ride in another chopper," Dani said, "but I'm glad we found the mares and they're okay. Now we just have to figure out how to save them." '

"Maybe they don't need saving," Joe said. "Maybe they're fine where they are. They're wild horses living in a wild place. Isn't that how it's supposed to be?"

Dani had no answer for that, but she was remembering what Luther Makes Elk had said to her when she visited him last. *Sometimes the best thing you can do is nothing.*

After dwelling on this conundrum for a few moments she said to Joe, "Maybe you're right. Maybe we shouldn't tell the forest service where those four mares are."

THE STAFF AT the forest service office was polite but not very helpful. Yes, they had been informed of the shooting and one of the rangers would be dispatched to the scene as soon as they could be spared. It was a busy time for them right now, getting ready for the hikers and campers. All the sites had to be cleaned and stocked. And no, they hadn't a clue who might have shot the horses.

"What's the forest service policy on wild horses running in national forests?" Joe asked.

"The forest service administers a total of thirty-seven wild horse or burro territories located in Arizona, California, Nevada, New Mexico, Oregon and Utah," the uniformed ranger responded. "There are no territories listed in Montana that are currently being managed by forest service personnel, so we don't have a policy on wild horses in the Arrow Roots. The Pryor Mountain herd is managed by the BLM. We coordinate with the BLM in the management of adjacent territories as well as the removal of wild horses and burros in excess of the territory capacity, or horses that stray onto forest service lands that don't belong in the wild horse territories or on land that isn't designated as such."

This delivery sounded carefully rehearsed. The ranger must have been expecting a visit from the media or wild horse groups. Joe could almost feel Dani spooling up to say something heated, and he headed her off with another question of his own. "In other words, the wild horses that were running in the Arrow Roots weren't under your active management?"

The ranger shook his head. "We don't recognize those horses as part of any designated wild mustang unit, so they aren't a part of any management plan. For all we knew they strayed from some ranch."

"They're unbranded mustangs, not strays," Dani corrected. "I've been photographing them for the past four years. You had to have known they were up there."

"We were aware," the ranger said. He was being put on the spot and was clearly uncomfortable. "There's been some discussion, but the supervisor hasn't decided on what to do about them. The solution would be to move them onto BLM lands and let them handle their removal."

"So, you were planning to remove them from the Arrow Roots?" Dani challenged.

"I think you'd need to speak to my supervisor," the ranger said. "I'm not authorized to answer your questions."

"Is he here?" Joe asked.

The ranger shook his head. "He's at a national conference in DC and won't be back until next week."

"Does a ranger usually check out the forest service rental cabins when the snow melts, to make sure everything's in order?"

"A lot of those cabins are used year-round, including the one in the Arrow Roots. Skiers and snowshoers will go up there occasionally."

"So, nobody checks periodically? Who's the ranger in charge of that cabin? Did he check on it recently?"

"That would be Chad Marquis, and no. His wife had a baby on Friday, so he didn't go up there."

"Do you have any ideas who might have shot those four horses?" Dani asked.

The ranger shook his head. "None."

"Well, you don't have to worry about what to do with the ones that survived. They're gone. The shooter ran them off," Dani said before turning to leave.

Joe escorted her out of the building and opened the passenger-side door for her. She hesitated before getting in. "How can they pretend Custer and his mares aren't wild horses?"

"They're probably getting pressured by hunters and ranchers who want them gone, and then by folks like you who like having them there. They're caught in the middle and don't know what to do."

"Well, I do. We need to get them recognized as a wild horse herd. If they're a designated band, they'll have to be recognized as mustangs and managed according to the *Wild and Free-Roaming Horses and Burros Act*."

"Would that be such a good thing?" Joe said. "Right now, as far as the forest service knows, they've vanished into the wild. Maybe those mares won't come back into that valley and they'll live out their lives in the wilderness."

Dani shook her head. "Maybe. I don't know. I can't think straight."

"Let's stop by that saloon we passed and grab

a sandwich," Joe suggested. Dani didn't look overly enthusiastic about the idea but he was reasonably sure a little food would make her feel better, and he was starving.

THE SALOON NEAR the forest service office was called the Hairy Dog, and their luncheon special of the day was Salt Horse in a Sinker with Whistleberries. "Real cowboy grub," Dani explained after the bartender interpreted the menu item as a Reuben on a house-made biscuit with a side of beans. Dani said she wasn't hungry but Joe ordered two of them. "Six Shooter Skink is cowboy coffee," she added, still perusing the menu and hoping the luncheon plates were small.

"What if I wanted a beer?"

"You'd ask for a John Barleycorn." Dani grinned at him. "Molly says the grub's good here, even if you aren't a cowboy."

"Good. 'Cause I don't ride horses."

"Most don't anymore. They use ATVs to get out on the land and check the herds."

The bartender set a mug of coffee in front of Joe, tea in front of Dani and returned a few moments later with two large plates heaped with cowboy fare. Joe lit into his while Dani picked carefully around the edges. She was definitely still feeling the effects of the helicopter ride.

No point in courting a repeat performance. She pushed the plate away and focused her thoughts on the four mares stranded up in the high valley. "I sent photos to the Wild Horse Foundation last night," she said. "We should call Comstock after lunch and fill him in on our helicopter flight. He'll want to know those mares are okay and he can pass the information on to the sheriff."

"Not hungry?" Joe asked.

"Not really," Dani admitted. "I don't particularly like flying."

"I have to admit, after that wild chopper ride, I was thinking what a kick it would be to do that every day."

Dani regarded him skeptically. Jack used to talk like that. He was always flying off somewhere; kissing her goodbye and trying to look sad that he was leaving, only deep down inside she knew he wasn't. He was glad to be getting back in the air. Eventually, of course, he flew right out of her life. "Maybe you should take lessons, if you like flying so much."

Joe raised an eyebrow at the edge in her voice. "Did I hit a nerve?"

"Something wrong with your food?" The bartender appeared to check on them before Dani could respond to Joe's comment.

She shook her head. "No, it's fine. I'm just not that hungry."

"She's a little queasy—went for a helicopter ride this morning and it was really rough," Joe said.

The bartender raised his hand. "Say no more. We get a lot of that in here on windy days. Must've been Nash you flew with. He's a real professional, best pilot around, but sometimes he flies when he shouldn't. Nothing keeps him out of the air. What you need, little lady, is a bowl of salty beef broth and some dry crackers. That'll settle your stomach." He disappeared into the kitchen.

Dani frowned at Joe. "I'm not queasy. I'm just not hungry."

"You still look kind of green around the gills to me."

The bartender reappeared with a steaming bowl of beef broth. "Here. Try to get some of this down—it should help."

"Thank you," Dani said, picking up the spoon. "Eat my sandwich, Joe."

"You sure?"

"You could stand to gain at least ten pounds." She tasted the broth. It was salty and good, and the bartender was right. It settled her stomach. By the time she'd finished the bowl of broth, Joe had polished off everything on her plate.

She gazed unabashedly at him while he finished his coffee. He was the handsomest man she'd ever laid eyes on, and every single time she looked at him she felt that curious jolt in the pit of her stomach that had nothing to do with being airsick, and a flutter in her heart that had everything to do with being lovesick. Which was ridiculous. She'd heard stories about Joe ever since she'd known Molly, but on a personal level she barely knew him…although she had thrown up in front of him, an intimate act if ever there was one.

Joe set down his mug and turned his head to meet her gaze. They were sitting so close together on the bar stools their shoulders were almost touching. For a moment they studied each other in a pretty intense silence. Dani had the distinct impression he was about to lower his head and kiss her. Her heart trip-hammered. She felt a little light-headed and breathless in anticipation, and was hoping her kiss measured up, but the bartender chose that moment to deliver the check, and the moment was ruined. Dani flushed, and she retrieved the check before Joe could. "We'd better get on the road. It's a long drive to the Bow and Arrow, and I'd like to stop by Molly's place first to pick up my dogs and get some Chinese food for Luther Makes Elk. He doesn't live that far from the Bow and Arrow. I think you'll like him."

## CHAPTER TEN

DANI'S DOGS WERE happily sprawled in the back of the Subaru while Joe drove. Dani chatted about her childhood growing up on a dairy farm, and Joe talked a bit about his years in the military and the different perspective that being deployed in a war-torn country gave him upon his return. It was quiet conversation. Reflective. And when they were talked out, they drove in a comfortable silence, until Dani dozed. She seemed startled when she woke to find that she'd fallen asleep and that they were near their destination. "It's just another mile or so," she said.

"Your miles out here are a lot longer than our miles back east," Joe said. "But the scenery's a whole lot better, so I'm not complaining."

Dani sat up and fixed her hair, taking out the ponytail, smoothing it with her fingers and then replacing the hair band. "Luther's always been home when I call on him—always seems to know I'm coming, too."

"Maybe that's because this road's so flat you can see clear to Billings?"

"He's a holy man, and he saved Steven's life. So I expect you to be on your best behavior—Molly's told me about all the awful tricks you used to play on your parish priest."

"I was a lot younger then, and a little wild," Joe told her. "I'm older and wiser now. If this holy man saved Steven's life, that's good enough for me."

"He doesn't say much and I don't usually stay long. I never really know how long I *should* stay."

"I'm sure he's glad to have a visit from you, long or short. I would be."

"He's officiating at Molly's wedding."

"No priest? I hope she's kept quiet about that. Our mother's as Catholic as they come."

"Luther Makes Elk was at Caleb and Pony's wedding, too. I'm sure Molly's will be just as beautiful. It's going to be at the Bow and Arrow. I can't think of a more romantic setting for a wedding." Dani sighed and gazed out the window.

"My ex-wife wanted a big wedding," Joe said. "I never saw anything as pretentious as the extravaganza she put on. We could've bought a mansion in Newport for what she spent. She wanted the perfect wedding that all her friends would envy her for and talk about for the rest of their lives. I guess all brides want that one big day because they know it's downhill from there."

"Oh?" Dani said in a prickly voice.

"Maybe not all," Joe conceded, "but mine was. The courtship, the proposal, the huge fancy wedding, the romantic honeymoon in the Greek islands, all followed by a five-year-long nightmare until the divorce papers were signed." Joe shook his head. "When I saw those photos you took of the wild horses, I realized why I connected with them. It's what I saw in their eyes. The wildness. They were free. Unbranded. And finally, so am I, and I plan to stay that way."

"Unbranded."

"That's right. I'm not letting myself be roped and tied again. Marriage is a fine institution for some, but I was never meant to be institutionalized."

"It's the next shack on your left," Dani said tartly. "The one with the warped asbestos siding, the rusted tin roof and the two old Crow sitting on a bench in front of it. And for the record, Joe Ferguson? What Molly and Steven have is really and truly special. I'm sorry that you never found a love like that. I've been burned, too, but I'm not giving up. Love is a risky business, but truly loving someone is the one thing that makes life worth living."

DANI'S LEGS WERE stiff when she climbed out of the Subaru at Luther Makes Elk's shack. Her back was stiff. Her neck was stiff. She was stiff all over and seriously pissed off at what Joe Ferguson had just said. She didn't quite know how to transition from his abrupt declaration of war against serious commitment, to being in a holy man's spiritual presence. The two old men watched with dark eyes as she and Joe approached the bench. Dani held the bag of Chinese takeout in her arms like a peace offering. She handed the warm, greasy paper bag with the savory smells to Luther and nodded to Joe.

"This is Molly's brother Joe Ferguson," she said. "He's visiting from back east. We're on our way to the Bow and Arrow and thought you'd like some Chinese food."

Luther took the bag and nodded. "I hoped you would bring some," he said. "Did you get the egg rolls?"

Dani nodded. "And the hot mustard and sweet-and-sour sauce."

"Good." Luther nodded again. "I like that hot mustard. It clears my thoughts." He looked at the old man sitting next to him. "This is Johnny Old Coyote. He visits me sometimes when he wants to save me from my own company." Then he studied Joe for a long quiet moment, eyes narrowing in his deeply wrinkled face. "Dani, tell Redhead her brother needs a sweat lodge before her ceremony. His blood is not strong, and his strength will be needed."

Dani had never heard Luther speak more than a few words at a time in the four years she'd been visiting him. "I'm pleased to meet you," she said to Johnny Old Coyote, who was dressed, like Luther, in a faded flannel shirt, old blue jeans and scuffed boots and was holding a pipe in one gnarled hand. Johnny Old Coyote nodded gravely in response. She stood for a few moments more, hoping Luther might speak further about Joe, give some hidden words of meaning about Marconi and the Mob, but he remained silent, intent on studying the take-out bag's contents. She didn't want to stay any longer and keep him from enjoying his meal. "I'll be sure to give Molly your message," Dani said to Luther. She waited a few more moments to give him a chance to respond, then said her goodbyes, turned and walked back to the Subaru. She heard Joe's polite farewells and his footsteps behind her.

She claimed the driver's seat as Joe took the passenger one and headed out the short drive to the main road, turning back toward Katy Junction. Miles passed. The silence grew as big as the mountains in the distance and as cold as the snows that still crowned their summits. Dani's hands were wrapped around the steering wheel so tightly that her fingers were beginning to cramp up.

Suddenly Joe broke the icy silence. "I met my ex-wife, Alison Aniston, when I pulled her over for running a red light and arrested her for drug possession. But as I'm booking her at the station house she starts telling me about all the rough knocks she's had in life and how a drug conviction would ruin her modeling career. So I book her for running a red light, conveniently forgetting about the bag of heroin I found on her. Then she asks me what time I get off my shift so she can buy me a drink. Our relationship was toxic from the start. She was working for one of the biggest and best modeling agencies in the city. Her photo was in all the magazines. She had me so turned around I couldn't think straight. I couldn't believe how lucky I was to have a woman like her in my life. She asked me to marry her after we'd been seeing each other only a few weeks. I bought her the biggest diamond I could afford, which on a cop's pay wasn't very impressive.

"The wedding happened two weeks after she proposed. I thought it was incredible she could pull that kind of wedding together practically overnight. I found out later that it had actually taken her twelve months to plan—apparently she'd made all the arrangements and done all the planning only to break up with her fiancé one month before she met me. Seems I came along just in the nick of time. I found all this out on our honeymoon, of course. She told me that running that red light was the best thing that could ever have happened to her because she'd landed herself a dumb cop who'd played right into her hand. Then the icing on the wedding cake? She told me she was two months pregnant. And that was the beginning of my five-year nightmare."

Dani struggled to process what Joe was telling her. "You're Catholic—wouldn't that confession from her grant you the right to an annulment?"

"I loved her. I thought once she got to know me better, she'd feel the same way. So I stuck with her, proving her theory that I was a dumb cop."

"The child she was pregnant with...was that Fergie? Molly never told me you weren't his real father."

"I never told anyone until now, and I'm listed as the father on the birth certificate. It was the right thing to do," Joe said. "I'm his real father, as far as I'm concerned. James Frederick Ferguson is my son. He's a good kid, a great kid, almost six years old now. Alison just enrolled him in a private boarding school so he wouldn't be underfoot and cramping her style. I stuck it out for five years just to stay in Ferg's life. The only good thing about our marriage was that kid. I love him and miss him like crazy. We share joint custody, but I don't think I'd stand a chance of getting Ferg away from her. I'm telling you this so you'll understand that when I say I'm a little gun-shy when it comes to romantic involvement, there's a reason."

"I'm sorry," Dani said. She took her hands off the wheel one at a time and flexed her fingers to relieve the cramping. "Your story makes my relationship with Jack sound like a fairy tale. All he did was fall in love with one of his young, sexy flight attendants. No kids and no messy marriage."

"I just wanted you to understand where I'm coming from."

"Thanks for telling me." Dani shot him a sidelong glance. "I'm sorry all that awful stuff happened to you, but I still believe two people can be happy together and share a good life."

"Did you have any clue Jack was going to leave you?"

Dani sighed. "Hindsight being perfect, I should have wondered about his recurring changes in scheduling, his increasingly shorter visits and the decrease in phone calls and text messages that had once been so frequent. I guess I was just so busy at work and assumed he was, too. His announcement that he was leaving me came out of the blue, but I should have expected it."

"So, having been through that, how can you ever trust anyone again?"

As Dani concentrated on the dirt road in front of her, she recalled how stunned she'd been when Jack had walked out on her. How, for days, she lived in a world filled with self-doubt and the feeling that she was a failure because she hadn't seen it coming, hadn't prevented it from happening. "I want someone to share my life with," she said. "I want my life to be about more than just me, so I'm willing to take a chance on loving again, and maybe being hurt again. I have to believe there's someone out there for me, someone to grow old with. I don't want to go through life alone."

Joe was quiet for so long that she wondered what he might say when he finally spoke again. Would he admit that the past few days spent in her company had made him feel like maybe, in spite of everything, he could take a chance on love again, too? She wondered if he enjoyed being with her, if he wondered what sharing that first kiss might be like? Back at the bar, had the sexual tension sizzling between them been just a figment of her feverish imagination?

Finally she prodded him with, "You're being awfully quiet."

He gazed out the windshield. "I was thinking about Luther Makes Elk and Johnny Old Coyote, two old friends sitting side by side on that bench all day long, sharing a pipe, and how ancient their faces were and how looking at them was like looking back through time. And I was thinking about what Luther Makes Elk said to me, about my blood not being strong and my strength being needed." He looked at her, his expression pensive. "What's a sweat lodge?"

Dani shot him an incredulous stare and shook her head with frustration. "For the life of me, I don't know how anyone as nice as Molly could have a brother who is such an insensitive jerk."

IT WAS CLOSE to suppertime when they reached the Bow and Arrow. Dani had gone all silent on him again, even though he'd tried his best to be open and honest with her when she'd brought up the subject of marriage. For all his efforts, all she'd done was call him an insensitive jerk. He wasn't sure what to say that would make things right, so he just kept his mouth shut. She was definitely a romantic and expected a whole lot more out of a relationship than he could ever give, so it was best to leave the subject alone. Besides, he'd be heading back east tomorrow. The most that could ever come out of any relationship they shared was a one-night stand. Dani was a class act and deserved a whole lot more than that from a guy.

She parked the Subaru next to a battered old pickup below the main house, unfastened her seat belt and gave Joe a dangerously neutral stare. "I'm going to let my dogs out, take them for a short walk, feed them and then check on the filly. I guess I'll see you around. It's a big ranch but we all share the same supper table. And by the way? I promised Molly I'd make sure you stayed put here tonight. It's all been prearranged, and I'm staying, too, just to make sure you don't run off. You can consider this a house arrest. She put an overnight bag together for you. It's in the back, with the dogs."

She got out and popped open the back hatch and let the dogs out. Joe watched her walk off toward the barn, hands shoved in her jacket pockets and the two golden retrievers gamboling in big happy circles around her. He sat listening to the tick of the hot engine and the sound of the wind pushing against the car.

He was content to sit and watch and listen. He could hear voices from down near the barns, the bark of an excited dog, a horse whinnying, a boy laughing. Domestic sounds came from the kitchen—the rattle of cutlery, the clank of a pot being set on the stove, the squeak and thump of an oven door being opened and closed. He wondered what it would have been like, to have grown up in a place like this. He heard the hinges on the screen door and glanced up to see Pony come onto the porch. She spotted him sitting in the car and came down the steps and up to his open window.

"Should I have the boys tie you up, or are you going to stay put this time?" she said with a smile that took the sting out of her words.

"We're staying put," Joe said. "I appreciate your hospitality."

"We are glad to have you. The boys are looking forward to your talk. Molly said you could tell them about the time you spent in the military, and how you got into law enforcement."

"I can talk to them about searching for wild horses by helicopter, too," Joe said. "We found the four mares. Dani can show you on a map where they are."

"Safe?"

"Yep. Made it all the way over the pass through some really deep snow."

Pony nodded. "They are tough, those mustangs. Jessie Weaver will be glad to hear that they're all right. The filly is doing well and is strong enough to stand and walk on her own. Roon has been with Jessie down in the barn, and they have had success getting her to nurse from the mare. They had to restrain the mare the first few times. It was difficult because the mare came from the BLM holding corrals and had not been handled much, but today's been a good day."

"That's good news. Dani's been worried about that little orphan all day long."

"It does not take much for an animal to get under your skin, if you have a soft heart," Pony said. "Dani loves horses. Not many could have gotten that newborn foal down the mountain. That was a brave thing she did. Has she gone down to the barn?"

"She took her dogs for a walk in that direction." Joe glanced down toward the corrals, then back at Pony. "We stopped to see Luther Makes Elk on the way here. Dani said he's officiating at Molly's wedding and I should meet him."

"Luther Makes Elk married Caleb and me," Pony said. "He is a Crow holy man and Steven's adopted grandfather. It was a great honor to have him at our wedding. Did he speak to you?"

"Not much. Just said my blood wasn't strong and I needed a sweat lodge."

Pony nodded thoughtfully. "A sweat lodge is a special ceremony among my people. We have a sweat lodge here, up near Piney Creek. I will speak to the boys. They will prepare it for you."

"No need. I just thought it was a strange thing for him to say since we just met."

"If Luther Makes Elk says your blood is not strong and you need a sweat lodge, then you must have one," Pony said. "It would be foolish of you not to. My brother, Steven, would not be alive today if it were not for Luther Makes Elk. He has strong powers, and you must heed them."

DANI WAS AMAZED at the way the little foal had rallied in one day's time. She was standing on her own and nursing from a roan mare who'd lost her own foal two days prior. Roon held the mare by a halter rope on the other side of the stall partition, but it was only a precaution. The mare had clearly accepted the foal. Her initial hostility had been replaced by a rapidly strengthening maternal bond. Jessie Weaver leaned over the partition, watching the foal nurse with an expression Dani could only describe as pure contentment. She caught Dani watching her and smiled.

"I love this part of my job," Jessie said. "Just this morning I had to tranquilize this mare. She was so ornery with the filly, tried to kick and bite her and wanted nothing to do with her. But now look at them. If we took that foal away, she'd tear the barn apart trying to get to her. We've turned the corner, Dani. This little filly is going to make it, thanks to you."

"Thanks to you and Roon," Dani corrected. "All I did was find her. It was a group effort that saved her."

"Did you find Custer's mares?"

"We spotted all four over on the other side of South Pass. They seemed fine. It was rough weather for flying. I got a little airsick."

Jessie smiled. "Nothing stops Nash from flying. He'd fly in a hurricane. He's a rogue and a rascal, but he's the best pilot around. He can spot a flea on a dog's back at one thousand feet. He always comes through in a pinch for us."

"I sent a bunch of digital photos to the wild horse rescue sites last night," Dani told her. "One of the groups was setting up a GoFundMe page to raise reward monies for finding the shooter, but what we really need is a workable solution for these horses, so they can stay on the range, so the bands don't get broken up." Dani watched the filly nursing and was filled with despair. "I wish I didn't care so much," she said softly, her eyes stinging. "I don't know how to help them."

Jessie had lived in this land her entire life, but she had no easy answers, either. They looked at each other, then looked away. There were

no words, just the hurt of it, the wrong of it—
Custer lying dead up in the Arrow Roots, half
of his mares shot dead, the other half struggling
to survive without him. There were the cattlemen who wanted the grass and water for their
beef cows so they could make a decent living.
There were the hunters who wanted the grass
and water for the game animals they liked to
shoot. There were the wildlife biologists trying
to find that elusive and imaginary sweet spot
where everything could coexist and thrive in a
world driven by the all-powerful bottom line.

But all Dani could think about were the
horses lying dead on that high alpine meadow
in the Arrow Roots. And Joe Ferguson, whose
own life was in danger. Oh, yes, she couldn't
stop thinking about him, either, even if he was
an insensitive jerk. "I wish I didn't care so
much," she repeated so softly that nobody else
heard.

RAMALDA WAS OLD enough now that she sometimes had trouble remembering where she put
her grocery list or what she'd made for supper two nights ago, but she remembered her
early days at the Bow and Arrow before it was
the Bow and Arrow. She remembered when it
was called the Weaver ranch, and her husband,
Drew, rode for John Weaver, and Charlie and

Badger had made up the rest of the full-time crew. She remembered those days very clearly, so when Charlie and Badger showed up at suppertime most every night, it was like those old times wrapped themselves around her. Memories of being young and strong and how they'd laugh together and how good the land was to them in those days. When Charlie and Badger walked through the door in the evening, she'd forget how many years had passed, and how those years had slowly robbed her of everything. She'd feel that glad kick inside of herself that she used to feel every time Drew walked in with the two of them. Seeing Badger and Charlie made her feel as if they were all young again, and life was still full of promise.

But today when they walked in, they looked old and twisted and arthritic—did she look the same to them? "Wash up. *Lávate las manos!*" she commanded with a scowl. "You have been with goats and you stink."

"Goats don't stink," Charlie said, shuffling obediently to the sink and reaching for a bar of soap. "Girl goats don't, anyway."

"And that's all we got is girls," Badger added, shouldering up beside his friend and lathering his hands. "A whole bunch of milk goats that don't give milk. That Jimmy bought himself a pig in a poke this time."

"What do two old cowboys know about goats?" Ramalda scoffed, laying a hand towel on the sideboard before taking a roasting pan full of chicken out of the oven.

"I may not know much about goats, but I know a pig in a poke when I see one," Badger said, wiping his hands on the towel. "They should take those goats back to auction and pawn them off on some other fool."

Pony came into the kitchen in time to hear this declaration. "The goats are fine—there's nothing wrong with them. They just need to be milked properly. Jimmy needs a lesson from someone who knows how to milk cows, not from two old cowboys."

Badger squared off to Pony, smoothed his wiry gray mustache and puffed out his chest. "I'll have you know I've milked a cow or two in my day. Wild ones, too. Why, when Jessie Weaver was just knee-high to a grasshopper me'n Charlie had to get milk for her when her mother got sick. You remember, Charlie? We had to find one of them longhorn critters that had a calf and rope it and hog-tie it, then milk it while it was all trussed up, lying on the ground."

"And I got kicked pretty bad," Charlie said. "Limped the better part of a year after."

"We got the milk, though, and John Weaver

was mighty glad to get it," Badger reminisced. "I'm not stretching the blanket to say that that milk probably saved Jessie Weaver's life."

Jessie herself entered the kitchen in time to hear the last exchange, with Dani right behind her. "I've heard that story more times than I can count," Jessie said. "I guess I owe my life to a wild longhorn cow and two old cowboys."

"It was I who fed you that milk," Ramalda said, hurt to have been excluded.

Jessie gave Ramalda a hug and kissed her cheek. "You've always been like a mother to me, Ramalda. I was a very lucky girl to have had you then and I'm just as lucky to have you now. We all are. Why're we talking about milking wild cows?"

"Somebody needs to teach Jimmy how to milk his goats," Pony said. "I refuse to milk his goats for him. Because if I do it once, I will be stuck doing it every day, twice a day."

"I grew up on a dairy farm," Dani said. "I'd be glad to show Jimmy how to milk his goats. Where is he?"

"Behind the barn is a small shed," Pony said. "The goats are there, and so are most of the boys. They like to tease him when he is trying to milk. If you go down there, could you please tell them supper will be on the table in half an hour and they must wash up first."

Ramalda sighed and shook her head after Dani had left the kitchen on her way to the barn. "*Este es un rancho, no una granja lechera*," she said.

"The times, they are a'changing, old gal," Badger said, giving her a fond pat in passing. "You might find yourself making goat cheese when she comes back with all that milk."

## CHAPTER ELEVEN

DANI DESCENDED THE porch stairs and marched right past Joe, heading for the barn again with her dogs by her side. She hadn't looked at him when she went into the house, either, and he was sitting right here on the porch bench. He pushed to his feet and started after her. She ignored him when he caught up.

"Mind if I tag along?" he said.

"Suit yourself." She kept walking. She had her hands shoved in her jacket pockets and her shoulders were rounded over as she walked.

"Look, I'm sorry if I offended you by something I said or did."

"You didn't offend me, Joe," Dani said. "Whatever makes you happy, do it. That's what most men usually do, isn't it? You want to go back east tomorrow? Go. I don't care what you do and it clearly wouldn't matter if I did." She came to an abrupt stop. "Strike that from the record," she said when he swung to look at her. "I care very much if you hurt Molly. She's my best friend, she's pregnant and her wedding's coming up, so if you can find it within your-self to think about what might be best for *her*, I'd be very grateful."

She resumed her determined walk toward the barn. Joe hesitated a moment before following her. He sensed he was treading in dangerous territory. So he silently followed her out behind the barn to a corral with pole-and-wire fencing that surrounded a weather-beaten shed with a rusted tin roof.

"No, stupid!" he heard a boy's voice say as they opened the corral gate and walked toward the shed. "That's not how Badger showed us to do it."

"She keeps kicking the bucket over," another voice said. "She won't hold still!"

"Anyways, Badger doesn't know nothin' about goats," a third voice said.

"Neither does Charlie," a fourth voice added. "They think they know everything."

"Yeah, and I don't believe that story about him and Badger milkin' that wild longhorn cow," a fifth voice pitched in.

Joe was right behind Dani when she pushed open the shed door. All five boys looked up from the goat that was tethered to the wall. The rest of the milk goats milled restlessly in the en-closed space. Joe saw a tipped-over stainless-steel pail under the tethered goat and a bale of hay and a couple buckets of water against the other wall. Dani closed the door behind them and addressed the situation with brisk efficiency.

"Hey, Jimmy. Pony said you might need help milking your herd before supper. I grew up on a dairy farm so I can give you a hand, if you like. Many hands make light work."

"Cows aren't the same as goats," Jimmy said, picking up the small pail and looking defensive. "They only have two tits, not four."

"That's *teats*, Jimmy," Dani corrected as the other boys snickered. "Goats have two teats, and it doesn't matter how many teats an animal has, they all function in basically the same way. I've never milked a wild longhorn but I milked a wild mustang a few days back, and my technique worked on her, too." The boys paid a little more attention after she said that, and Jimmy reluctantly handed her the pail.

"When I bought them at the auction the owner said they were all trained," he explained. "But they won't hold still and they keep kicking the bucket over."

Dani took the pail from Jimmy and looked around the shed. "Do you have any sweet grain up in the barn?" When Jimmy nodded, she smiled. "Good. Go get a couple quarts in another pail. We're also going to need a platform about knee-high for the goat to stand on while she's being milked—that will make it easier to reach her udder. And you'll need a stool or an overturned bucket to sit on while you milk. We can look up plans later for how to build a goat stand for milking—that's an easy project you can do tomorrow. But right now we have to get all these goats milked before supper, so a bucket of sweet feed and a bench will have to work. Can you fetch those things?"

The boys nodded and dashed out of the shed, leaving Dani and Joe alone with the goat herd. Joe thought these goats were mighty strange-looking animals but they seemed gentle enough, and Dani seemed comfortable around them, patting them and talking to them while he tried to think of something intelligent to say to her. He searched for the right words and was beginning to feel desperate when his cell phone rang. It was Molly.

"Joseph? I'm just making sure you're still at the Bow and Arrow," she said.

"We are. We're about to milk a herd of goats. Dani's right here, if you want to talk to her."

"Did you see Luther Makes Elk?"

"We did."

"Did he say anything about my wedding?"

"No. Was he supposed to?"

Joe heard Molly heave a frustrated sigh. "I just wondered, that's all. How's Dani?" she said.

"Dani's fine. She's in complete control of the current situation. I have a feeling these goats will all be milked in record-breaking time. Here, you can ask her yourself." He handed the phone to Dani and it was his turn to hear a one-sided conversation.

"Your brother's fine," Dani said in a carefully neutral voice. "We're both fine, just tired. It's been another long day…Yes, we found Custer's four surviving mares. They're okay and in a safe place for now. Everything's good here. How are you feeling, still sick to your stomach?… Well, that'll pass. You just have to suffer it out. I think Steven's right, you should take a couple weeks off and work from home…I'm not sure what Joe's plans are. I think he's giving a talk to the kids after supper…Don't worry, I won't let him out of my sight." Dani frowned with concentration as she listened to Molly's long reply. "I'm sure everything's going to be okay. Joe's safe and sound, and he's not going anywhere, so stop worrying. Take care of yourself."

Dani handed his phone back with a cool glance in his direction. "I didn't tell her you were still planning to go back east. You can do that yourself, but you better let her know before she drives all the way out here. She told me she wants to visit tomorrow. She's going stir-crazy."

Joe shoved the phone back into his pocket as the boys entered the shed, two of them carrying a mounting block, one carrying a pail of grain and an empty bucket and a fourth carrying a bale of hay.

"That's great, boys," Dani said. "Put the mounting block right up against the wall, we're going to make the goat stand on it. The bucket's going to be a seat. Okay, that's good. Now let's get the first goat up there, and when she's in place, one of you stand in front of her holding the grain so she can eat it while I show Jimmy how to milk. Ready?"

The first goat was soon in position and enthusiastically munching on sweet feed. "See how she likes that grain?" Dani said. "You want them to associate the milking with pleasurable things." She sat on the upended bucket and put the stainless-steel pail beneath the goat's udder. "Now watch, Jimmy, it's easy. Be gentle when you grip the teat, then squeeze your fingers firmly, starting from the top finger, right next to her udder and going to the bottom pinky finger. See how I'm doing this? You're forcing the milk that's in the teat out of the nipple, like so." A stream of white frothy milk entered the pail, with the boys all watching intently. "You keep doing the same thing, over and over, until no more milk comes out of that teat, and then you milk the other teat. Sometimes it helps to bump her udder with your hand, just like a baby goat would. This bumping gets the milk to let down easier. Wow, this is a good doe—look at all that nice creamy milk!" Dani said. "What a good girl she is. You must praise her, speak softly to her, let her know what a special girl she is for giving you this milk. Be kind to your milk goats and treat them well and they'll produce gallons of milk for you. Do you want to try?"

Jimmy nodded. They switched positions and Dani helped him perfect his technique. An impressive amount of milk was produced by the first doe and was poured into a clean pail. The second goat was brought to the bench and given a treat of grain while Jimmy milked her. All the boys took turns milking the three goats who were producing. Dani praised their efforts, offered her tutoring and answered their questions. When the last goat had been milked there was almost two gallons of milk.

"Who's going to make the goat cheese?" Joe asked.

The boys looked at each other. Jimmy picked up the pail. "Ramalda," he announced.

THE LONG TRESTLE table in the ranch house kitchen held twelve people when every chair was filled, and tonight three extra chairs had been added. It was a full house, and as the serving dishes were passed around, the room filled with the noisy chatter of five boisterous boys, two garrulous old cowboys, Pony and Caleb, Jessie and her husband, Guthrie, and Joe and Dani. Ramalda's chair always remained empty because she refused to share the table at supper or any other meal. She was in complete charge of the kitchen and it was a full-time job to run the food to and the empty dishes from the table. When Pony tried to help her, Ramalda took it as a personal affront, so in the end Ramalda presided over the kitchen while the rest of them ate.

Dani lit into her food. She was ravenous, completely recovered from her airsickness. As she ate, she tried to answer Jessie's questions across the table about the helicopter flight and the whereabouts and condition of the four mares, while to her right Joe was listening to Badger talk about buffalo cows and how dangerous they could be during calving season. And to her left Pony was coaching the boys about proper table manners and suggesting that they go up to Piney Creek and start heating the stones for a sweat lodge directly after supper because tonight's evening lecture by Joe Ferguson was going to be followed by the sweat lodge ceremony.

With all the different conversations flying around the table it was somewhat astonishing that the food vanished as quickly as it did. Ramalda refilled empty serving dishes until the eating frenzy gradually abated. Dani could only wonder what the food bill was at the Bow and Arrow. These growing boys appeared to eat their weight in fried chicken, biscuits and mashed potatoes with gravy, and they were fed three square meals a day.

Caleb had joined the conversation with Jessie, and Dani and was mentioning Sheriff Conroy and the fact that he wasn't running for sheriff in the fall. "He says he's been wanting to retire for a few years now. His son Kurt's a deputy sheriff, and the rumor is he's going to be running in his father's place. Kurt's married to Hershel Bonner's daughter, Josie, and I heard you mention you wanted to talk to her again. You might want to talk to Kurt, too, while you're at it."

Dani sighed. "Right now I'm more worried about what will happen to Custer's surviving mares without a band stallion to protect them."

"But with the shooter still out there, those mares could still be in danger," Joe said, startling Dani, who looked at him with eyebrows raised. "I think it would be a good idea to talk to both Josie and Kurt. Where do they live?"

"They have a place south of Billings," Caleb said. "I'll look up the address and phone number for you. Another thing, Hershel Bonner's on the cattlemen's association board, so he's caught between a rock and a hard place when it comes to the mustangs. It's a tangled web, for sure. There's a meeting coming up tomorrow night. I get the invites because I joined to keep abreast of what's going on. You could attend the meeting yourself and ask some questions of the local cattlemen."

"That's a good idea, too," Joe said. "Where and when do they meet?"

"I'll get you that information, too," Caleb said. "Matter of fact, I might go myself. I'd like to hear what they have to say about the shooting and let them know about the reward that's been posted for any information leading to the conviction of the shooter. We run some fine Spanish mustangs on the Bow and Arrow and if they should stray off our lands or our BLM leases I want the locals to know they'd better not be used for target practice."

"How do they work, those grazing leases?" Dani asked, confounded as to why Joe had jumped into the conversation like he did. Had he changed his mind about heading back east?

"Supposing I was thinking of buying a small ranch and I wanted to lease some BLM land to run wild mares on."

Caleb reached for another piece of fried chicken and nudged the platter toward her. "That's a question Jessie'll have to field. The rules and regulations of the permits and leases spin my head around. Jess?"

Jessie pushed her plate away. "Basically, anyone can lease grazing rights on BLM lands if the allotments are available and if the lessee has a privately owned home or ranch or some type of livestock operation. The leases usually last for ten years and are renewable, as long as the terms of the lease are being met.

"When Caleb bought this ranch from me, the BLM leases were transferred with it because he wanted to keep the grazing rights. If you're seriously shopping for something that already has BLM leases, there's a run-down place for sale about twenty miles from here, belonged to Shep Deakins. He ran beef critters on his land. When he died it took a lot of digging to find any family. He has a cousin in Illinois, but she doesn't want the place. Anyhow, Shep had a bunch of BLM leases and they're scheduled to expire at the end of the year. Nobody's bought the property yet, so those leases might come up for bid."

"And if someone buys the property, the leases would be transferred?"

"Yes, unless the new owner specifies that they aren't interested in renewing them. Shep's property isn't in great shape, but he had three good leases with the BLM, all fenced and totaling about nine hundred acres. Caleb and I went over and looked at the place as a potential satellite property for the wild horses and buffalo we run here. In the end we figured it was too far away from the Bow and Arrow, but it has a lot of potential because the graze is good, the fences are in good repair and it has reliable water. With close to three hundred acres of privately owned land, including a barn and some corrals, and the three BLM leases, the right buyer could make a go of that property with a small ranching operation." Jessie paused and gave Dani a long calculating stare. "Are you really thinking of buying a ranch just so Custer's mares can be safe?"

"I'm selling my house in Helena and shopping for a place with some land. Could you give me directions to Shep's ranch?"

"Sure." Jessie grinned. "Sounds like you have a busy few days planned. I'll show you on a map where it's at. You can probably look it up on the Realtor's website, too. It's been on the market for about eight or nine months now. Shep died last fall, just before the first big snow."

"Shep was one of the last of the old rounders," Badger volunteered, reaching for another biscuit. "Quite a character. You gonna take up mustang ranching and give up lawyering?"

Dani shook her head. "Maybe I'm just dreaming, but my real estate agent thinks I'm about to get a good offer on my house."

"Don't let so much reality into your life that there's no place for dreams," Badger said. "Shep's place would make a mighty fine homestead. Needs a little elbow grease, that's all."

Charlie let out a guffaw. "Needs a gallon of gasoline and a match. Shep never threw nothin' away, including his trash."

"Charlie, you never miss a good chance to shut up," Badger said. "Shep did all right out there. He lived good and he died good."

"If you can call dropping dead at the mailbox holding a fistful of unpaid bills good."

"Sure beats a nursing home," Badger said around a mouthful of biscuit.

"If you're interested in that property, maybe the thing to do is attend the cattlemen's meeting from a potential rancher's perspective rather than someone from a radical mustang preservation group," Joe contributed. "The people at that meeting wouldn't know who you were. Well,

Hershel Bonner would, but if we talked to him first he might keep quiet."

"Mustang groups aren't made up of radicals," Dani said testily. "We're trying to protect a wild horse's right to survive and remain wild."

"Joe has a point," Caleb moderated. "Why don't you two attend the meeting tomorrow, see if you can learn something. Be a couple of perspective ranchers thinking of buying Shep Deakins's place. Ask about the leases, what happens if other animals stray onto them—can you shoot them? Ask how you protect your grazing lands and water. See what they have to say. They might be more forthcoming if they think you're just going to be running a bunch of cattle."

"I could do that, I guess," Dani said. "Gives me another reason to look at Shep's place, too. What about Custer's mares? Should we leave them where they are? Will they come back into the high valley and be in danger again?"

"By the end of the week the pass will probably be rideable," Jessie said. "We could trailer some horses to the forest service camp and ride up there, check things out."

"I'd like to go along," Dani said. "I don't ride, but I could learn."

"We have a few gentle horses," Jessie said. "I'm sure Badger could rustle one up for you."

"You bet I could," Badger said. "Matter of fact, I'd like to go myself. Been a while since I've ridden through that high country." He smoothed biscuit crumbs from his whiskers and gave Dani a nod. "Don't worry about not knowing how to ride," he told her. "The trail's a real gully whumper, but you can just about always handle more than you think you can, and I'm sure you'll do just fine. I'll pick you out a nice steady horse."

Dani helped clear the table and then poured coffee and distributed slices of pie. She helped Ramalda at the sink while dessert was being eaten. "I had so much of your delicious chicken and mashed potatoes I'll explode if I eat another bite. I might have a piece of your pie later, if that's all right."

Mollified, Ramalda allowed her to help with the dishes. Dani avoided looking in Joe's direction and concentrated on drying and stacking the plates while Pony gave the boys instructions to light the fire at the sweat lodge and start heating the rocks before Joe's after-supper lecture began. Three of them jumped up from the table to do it. Jimmy had intentions of joining them, but as he made for the door Ramalda said in a brusque voice, *"Jimmy."*

Jimmy stopped in his tracks. Ramalda carefully wiped the soapy water from her hands with a dish towel. She walked to the pantry wearing a stern expression, disappeared for a moment and then reappeared holding his bucket of goat's milk. "You have your own chores to do," she said, handing him the bucket. "*Este no es mi trabajo.* This is not my job."

Jimmy's shoulders slumped. Clearly, he would rather go up to Piney Creek with the other boys and start the fire for the sweat lodge. He looked at the milk in the pail, then raised pleading eyes to Dani. "Can you show me how to make goat cheese?"

WHEN THE BOYS made their exit to light the lodge fire at Piney Creek, Joe pushed out of his chair and carried his dishes to the sink. Ramalda was talking to Jimmy in a stern tone of voice, a scramble of English and Spanish, something about making his own goat cheese. To his credit, Jimmy seemed to be accepting his responsibility.

Joe brushed up against Dani's shoulder as he slid his plate into the hot soapy water and washed it. "You coming to my lecture tonight?" he asked, leaning closer and drawing the sweet scent of her hair, the warmth of her skin, the strength of her spirit into his soul. She was smart and beautiful and sexy, and being near her made him forget all about his five torturous years with Alison. But for some reason Dani always seemed peeved at him.

"You inviting me?" she said, concentrating on the plate she was drying.

"I think you might find it educational."

"Really," she commented with complete indifference, adding the dried plate to the stack on the counter and taking the washed and rinsed plate he handed her. "You must think very highly of yourself, Detective."

"I do," he said. Her scent was like the elixir of life. "And I also think very highly of you, Counselor."

"Really," she repeated in that same disinterested voice. She added another dried dessert plate to the stack.

"I do."

"Enough to stick around for a while?"

"Maybe."

She glanced up at him, eyebrows raised. "Really?"

"I'd also like to see Shep's place and go to that cattlemen's meeting with you."

"Well, if that's the case, maybe I'll think about coming to your lecture, Detective."

"Good. And by the way? I'm not a detective."

"Really? What are you, then?"

"Maybe you'll find out at my lecture," he

said. "Pony said to head to the school around seven. See you there?"

"Maybe," Dani said, but he saw her lips curve in a smile before she turned away.

DANI BARELY HAD time to help Jimmy with the chèvre making before it was time to attend Joe's lecture. "Making soft goat cheese is easy, Jimmy," she said as they waited for the goat's milk to heat up in the stainless-steel pot. "We get it to a temperature where bubbles form around the edges, and after it cools to about eighty-five degrees, we'll add the curdling agent. In our case, it's going to be lemon juice since we don't have any rennet. That's something we'll need to order. But Ramalda's lemon juice will work. After we heat the milk and add the lemon juice, we'll let the mixture curdle, then strain it through a cheesecloth to separate the whey from the curds. Then we'll salt the curds and refrigerate them. The chèvre can be seasoned to taste with herbs and will keep for about ten days in the refrigerator. Easy, huh?"

"Will it be ready tonight?"

"Nope. Making chèvre is a multistage process. We'll let it cool and add the lemon juice, then leave it at room temperature overnight to curdle. We'll strain it in the morning and refrigerate it in the afternoon. Tomorrow night you can serve it up with supper and I bet everyone will love it. See the bubbles forming around the edges of the pot? It's hot enough now." Dani turned off the gas burner and shifted the pot onto the countertop. She glanced at the clock. "It's six thirty. At seven, add the lemon juice and then head over to the lecture. Think you can manage that?"

Jimmy nodded. "Good," Dani said. "I have to feed my dogs and get cleaned up."

Dani fed Remington and Winchester in the back of the Subaru, then left the hatch open so they could come and go as they pleased while she went inside to wash up. The room Pony had showed her was over the kitchen and had a dormer window that looked east, toward the mountains. There was a quilt-covered double bed tucked under the eaves, a small bureau with a mirror atop it and a desk and chair. A braided rug covered the pine plank floor. Cabbage rose wallpaper adorned the walls and plain muslin curtains hung at the open window and blew gently in the breeze. It was small, simple and very homey. Next door was a bathroom, and she carried her kit in to wash up.

It felt like ages since she'd looked in a mirror. She studied her reflection for a few moments, then pulled out her ponytail, shook her hair loose and sighed. It was hopeless. She was a mess. She needed a long hot shower but there was no time. No time to fancy herself up and no fancy clothes in her pack. She'd packed for a weekend camping trip, not a hot date, and Molly's clothes just didn't cut the mustard. Too bad her house in Helena was so far away. She wished she had some basic makeup in her kit instead of just a toothbrush and toothpaste, hairbrush and sunblock. She wanted to make herself look pretty for Joe.

He'd said he might be staying, and she was hoping he did. Even if he was an insensitive jerk.

## CHAPTER TWELVE

BY THE TIME she entered the schoolhouse, it was ten past seven and Joe's lecture was already in progress. The school building had an open classroom and bathroom on the first floor and upstairs there were three bedrooms, with two bunks in each, and a bathroom. The open-concept school had different sections. The classroom section had ten desks and chairs arranged toward a blackboard and looked quite conventional, with a desk for the teacher up front and a podium in one corner. There was a lab section, with microscopes and high worktables. There was another section with woven blankets on the floor and pillows, where the kids could lounge and talk, an area with computers set up like a small office and finally a small kitchen with a propane stove and refrigerator. Joe was in the standard classroom area, standing behind the podium, wearing his five o'clock shadow, flannel shirt and blue jeans like a genuine cowboy. He was handsome as hell and just looking at him caused her heart to dance that fluttering jig.

He stopped talking when she entered and waited until she sat at a desk in the very back and folded her hands. The boys sat in front of her, along with Pony and Caleb.

Joe grinned. "I'm glad to see Counselor Jardine has decided to join us."

"I wouldn't have missed it," Dani said.

"The boys were telling me they enjoyed the lecture about your legal career very much. They said you volunteer your time helping out at the school, as well as the Wild Horse Foundation."

"Molly and Steven got me involved in this school, and I fund-raise and write legal briefs for the Wild Horse Foundation," Dani said. "I also help make goat cheese, which is why I'm late."

There was a ripple of laughter and Jimmy caught her eye and grinned.

"I was just telling the boys how growing up in a big low-income family influenced my career choices. There wasn't any money for college," Joe continued. "If we kids wanted to continue our education, our parents encouraged us, but we were on our own as far as paying for it. My sister Molly's the smart one—she got a full scholarship and did us all proud. She was the first Ferguson to graduate from college. My grades weren't that great, so I opted to go to college via the armed forces, and here's how that works. First you have to enlist in a branch of the armed forces. In my case it was the army. The post-9/11 GI Bill is fairly generous. You put in your time and you get your four-year degree paid for by the military, including living expenses and books. Sounds great, right?

"Let me state right here and now, this is a tough way to get your education. You're signing away eight years of your life to the military, to being a soldier who takes orders and has little freedom. But for me, it worked. I was a street kid growing up in Roxbury, on the outskirts of Boston, and I was in trouble a lot. I was a fighter, and I hated school. My father told me once that he was sure I was on the path to a full-time prison career. My dad's a cop, like his father was. So's my uncle, his brother. Law enforcement runs in the family. Anyhow, I enlisted to avoid a life in prison and I served my time, including multiple deployments in the Middle East. If this is the route you choose, be prepared for a tough road. And never forget, you can be killed in active duty. There's a chance you might come back home in a body bag. Something to think about.

"After the army, I got my bachelor's degree in criminal justice, did a short stint with the Boston Police Department, then transferred to the Drug Enforcement Agency. The DEA's a federal agency and my background growing up in a big, bad part of the city and my years in the military worked out well for me. I graduated from their program as a Narcotics Bureau special agent, and I've worked on the Providence Division's organized crime drug enforcement task force for five years now. We like to think we're making a difference, keeping drugs off the street, but sometimes it seems like nothing ever changes. And sometimes things can go wrong. You have a question, Jimmy?" he said when Jimmy's hand shot up.

"Were you in a shootout with the Mafia?"

Joe hesitated. "I walked right into a bad situation without waiting for backup. By the way? Never do that. It's a stupid thing to do. Always play it safe."

"Did you kill any of them?"

Joe leaned his forearms on the podium and thought for a moment. "The court hearing's coming right up and I'm not allowed to discuss the case, so I can't answer specific questions. All I can tell you is, if I had it to do over again, I would have waited for backup, even if it meant letting the big cheese get away."

"Did you catch the big cheese?" one of the other boys asked.

"Nope. He escaped, and the only good thing that came of that whole fiasco is that I got to take some vacation time, which is why I'm here."

"What's the biggest arrest you ever made?"

He pondered the question for a moment. "Last year there was a collaborative dragnet utilizing the state police, Providence police, the DEA and the FBI. We arrested thirty-five drug dealers and confiscated fifteen weapons. That was a good bust, but I was only one small part of the team. Every day isn't all excitement and drama, but the job has its moments of glory. It's never finished, though. Drugs are a huge problem and probably always will be."

"Do you like being a special agent?" Roon asked this question.

"I was a regular cop for a while, wore the uniform and badge and drove a cruiser around. Arrested people for all sorts of things and broke up domestic arguments and street gang fights. That's what a cop's life is. A lot of the time we're dealing with the worst side of humanity and tragedies like traffic fatalities and house fires. Cops get burned out. So, as far as careers go? If I had a kid, I don't know if I'd suggest a career in law enforcement. I can't stand up here and tell you, yeah, law enforcement is the way to go, or even that the military is a good choice. It might not be for you. You're good with animals, Roon. I think you already know your path. Do any of you know what you might like to study in college?"

"Making goat cheese." One of the boys snickered, and Jimmy leaned over and cuffed him.

"Basket weaving," another said, and all the boys laughed.

"Do you have tribal police on the Crow reservation?" Joe asked.

"The Bureau of Indian Affairs oversees the police force on the reservation," Pony responded. "There are about twelve officers employed, about half of them native Crow. The police chief is a white man. He is doing a good job, and he has brought in more officers to increase patrol areas as well as school resource officers for Lodge Grass High School. Things are getting better."

"Have any of you boys had any experience with the tribal police?"

The boys shifted in their seats, so Pony spoke up. "They have all been in trouble, and were all kicked out of school, which is why they are here. People called them the Rez Dogs."

Joe nodded. "Well, you Rez Dogs got real lucky. You've been given a second chance to get your high school diploma, and I can't think of a better place to be doing that than on this ranch."

"What's it like, working undercover?"

"Lonely. You can't live in your hometown because everybody knows you. It would be a really bad thing if you were in the middle of a big drug transaction under the fake name of Eddie Bender and your old girlfriend walks up to the bar and says, 'Hi, Joe! Good to see you. It's been quite a few years since high school, hasn't it?' So the DEA assigns you to a city where it's unlikely anyone will recognize you. In my case I moved from Boston to Providence. Not a real long ways, but far enough to make me reasonably anonymous. You almost have to give up your old identity and start over, and that makes it tough, especially if you happen to be married. But that's life. You make decisions, you live with them."

"Are you going back?" Jimmy asked.

"I have to go back for the hearing at the end of the month, so yes, I'll be heading back to Providence. I can't stay on vacation forever, much as I like it here."

"What about the wild horses?" Roon asked. "Are you going to help find out who shot them before you go?"

"I'll do my best," Joe said.

"Badger and Charlie said some mobsters might come looking for you here," Jimmy said. "What do you want us to do if we see anybody suspicious?"

Dani met Joe's eyes while Caleb flinched under Pony's gaze. "My fault," he said, contrite.

"I told Badger and Charlie to keep their eyes open because someone had made a death threat against you," he said to Joe. "I guess probably the entire county knows about it by now."

"This is not a bad thing," Pony said. "We are a close-knit community. Outsiders cannot hide. That is why you are safer here than anywhere. The boys have eyes like the eagles, very sharp—they see all things. And they will not talk about this to their friends, will they?" Pony turned to look pointedly at the boys. They all shook their heads.

"Badger and Charlie already told us not to," Jimmy said. "They made us swear."

"You don't have anything to worry about. Nobody's going to come after me here," Joe said. "I'm not worth the effort."

"But in case they do," Caleb said, "if you boys see or hear anything out of the ordinary, let one of us know right away, and don't take any chances with folks you don't know."

"Yeah, don't take rides with strangers and don't eat the candy," Jimmy jeered. "Don't worry, nobody's gonna take us by surprise."

"Good," Pony said. "Now you boys go up to Piney Creek and put more wood on the fire. Make sure those stones are good and hot. Roon, you are doing the ceremony?"

Roon nodded. "Steven taught me, and Luther

Makes Elk taught Steven. Jimmy and Martin said they would join us, so there'll be four in the sweat lodge."

"Good," Pony repeated. "I will bring Joe up after I explain the ceremony to him. And, Roon? This will not be a ceremony like Luther Makes Elk does. This will be a healing sweat."

Roon nodded. The boys rose and filed out of the schoolhouse as Joe sat down in the desk next to Dani. "How'd I do?" he said.

"You did very well, Special Agent Ferguson," Dani replied. "Thank you for not showing them your bullet holes."

"That's what they really wanted to see," Joe said with a grin. "Blood and guts."

"Typical boys," Caleb said. "Blood and guts were huge with me at that age."

"Thank you for sharing your world with them," Pony said. "The more they hear of other lives, the more they will think about their own. There is not much of a future for reservation kids. They have lost their culture, their connection to the past. Many drop out of school and end up living off government money, spending it on alcohol and drugs. They must discover other paths, and one of the best ways is to learn a skill or to go to college and get a degree. But that is expensive. Your words will give them something to think about."

"I have a feeling the talk is just beginning," Caleb said. "That's what part of the sweat lodge ceremony is, as I recall. Sweating is only a part of it. Talking is the other."

"Is this sweat lodge ceremony something that women can do?" Dani asked.

"Yes, although traditionally, women and men have separate sweat lodges," Pony said. "It would be all right if you wanted to attend tonight. This is a medicinal sweat to strengthen Joe's blood."

"I have to admit, a sauna would feel pretty good right now," Joe said.

"A sweat lodge is nothing like a sauna," Caleb cautioned. "I didn't have a vision like some people do, but when I was in that lodge I was worried about permanent brain damage. It gets really hot."

"Caleb. It does no good to say such things," Pony admonished.

"How about it, Dani?" Joe asked. "You in?"

"Well, it's like Badger said tonight," Dani replied, "'You can just about always stand more'n you think you can.' So yes, count me in. I could use a good vision right about now. Maybe I'll find out who shot those horses."

MOLLY POKED AT her untouched supper until Steven pushed out of his chair, picked up her plate and carried it into the kitchen. He returned with a banana and laid it in front of her, along with a knife and a cereal bowl. "You must eat something," he said. "You like bananas in milk."

"I'm not hungry. I know you cooked that nice meal for me and I'm sorry I didn't touch it, but this pregnancy thing isn't much fun. I feel sick all the time, and I'm worried about Joe. I know he's safe but I keep feeling like the house is being watched."

"That's just your imagination. I've already checked a dozen times. There's nobody out there, unless it's one of the sheriff's deputies doing a drive-by. I don't think you should go anywhere tomorrow. Stay home and work on the Madison Mountain papers."

"I'm done sitting around the house," she complained. "It's driving me crazy. If I do something I'll feel better, even if it's just driving to the Bow and Arrow to hang out with Dani and Joseph. I'll be home by supper. Nothing strenuous. No mountain climbing or anything like that. I might stop and see Luther Makes Elk, though."

"Every time you stop to see Luther, you read too much into what he says and it makes you worry even more."

"Steven, he's your grandfather and he's a holy man and he saved your life. He might have something to say about Joseph, something that could help my brother stay safe. How can I not visit him? And besides, he's going to be marrying us in a few weeks."

Steven brought her a glass of milk and set it beside the banana. "So this means you will bring him more Chinese food, and I suppose that Pendleton blanket that arrived yesterday is for Luther, too?"

"I thought he might like it," Molly said, picking up the glass of milk. "It's a very handsome wool blanket, three points, red-and-black stripes, his favorite colors."

"A wool blanket and some Chinese food will not change the future," Steven said.

"I like your grandfather," Molly said, setting down her glass of milk. "You should be glad I want to go see him and that he likes me, or he might not have agreed to perform our ceremony."

"I am glad that you like each other, but I think you should stay home until this sickness passes. You should not be driving out to the Bow and Arrow, or visiting Luther. It's a long ways."

"Take tomorrow off and come with me," Molly urged.

Steven shook his head. "I have three appointments and I can't cancel them. We are barely making it as it is."

"Young Bear and Ferguson." Molly sighed. "It's been quite a struggle, hasn't it?"

"Are you sorry you left your law firm in Helena?"

Molly shook her head. "No regrets, not a single one. I'd rather eat macaroni and cheese for the rest of my life than go back to that law firm. I've never been happier, Steven." She reached across the table and gripped his hand. "I love you. It might seem like hard times now, but our baby's going to be the luckiest baby in the whole wide world to have a father like you and grow up in a place like this. I wouldn't change a thing."

"Good. Neither would I, but I do not like macaroni and cheese," Steven said, "and I am hoping it does not come to that. Go and see Luther Makes Elk, and spend the day with Dani and your brother, but be home by dark. You are not the only one who worries."

PONY TOLD THEM a little bit about the history of the Crow sweat lodge ceremony while she walked with Dani and Joe to Piney Creek. The trail ran up behind the old cabin and paralleled the creek as it climbed. Joe was quickly out of breath. The pain in his side grew worse with every step. Dani seemed unaffected by the steepness of the trail. Her leather hiking boots hadn't gotten worn like that from sitting in a closet. She climbed like a mountain goat.

"The sweat lodge ceremony was an important part of Crow culture, but the sweats were banned by the US government until 1978. Now it is part of our culture again, but a real sweat lodge ceremony must be performed by someone who has been taught the old ways, like Luther Makes Elk taught my brother, Steven, who then taught Roon.

"There are many spiritual connections in the actual ceremony. Four is an important number in Native American culture, as it represents the four directions and four seasons. You must be quiet when the first four rocks are brought in, but as more rocks are added, you can start to talk. There are four rounds in the sweat, but there are breaks in between each. In the first round, water is poured on the rocks four times. Water is poured seven times in the second round. The seven pours symbolize the Big Dipper and the seven buffalo that once helped the Crow tribe. During the third round, there are ten pours, which represents the number of moons between conception and birth. On the final round, there is no limit to the number of pours, which symbolizes that our spiritual life goes on forever. Herbs and medicines are also used during sweat ceremonies, but in

Crow tradition, the most commonly used herb is bear root. When the door is closed and the ceremony starts, the bear root is thrown on the rocks, which lights up like stars. It also emits a peppery and soothing smell.

"The spirit and body are two different things," Pony said. "The body is temporary, as it grows old, weak and tired. But the spirit is infinite—it never ends—and like water, it is always the same. The sweat lodge ceremony is about celebrating life and living it to the fullest. It is about self-discovery. It is a form of prayer."

JOE WASN'T SURE what to expect when he walked with Dani and Pony up the trail to the place where the sweat lodge had been constructed. He'd pictured a towering teepee with smoke curling out the top. What he saw, there on the edge of the creek, tucked into the woods, was a low dark mound. The lodge was maybe eight or ten feet in diameter, no more than four feet high and covered with what looked like blankets and buffalo skins. A flap lifted and served as the entrance, and inside strips of red cloth hung from the frame and fluttered when Pony opened the flap. She told him they were tied to the willow framing poles as reminders of the prayers said when each was fastened. The rich herbal odor of bear root hung in the air inside the sweat lodge, and a pit to hold the fire-hot rocks was dug in the far corner.

A fire burned in a pit close by and stones had been arranged in and around it. The creek tumbled into a deep pool in this spot, which, according to Roon, was why the sweat lodge had been constructed there. "We can just stand on the edge of the pool and dump buckets of water over our heads," Roon explained as he added more firewood to the pit that heated the rocks. "It's deep enough to swim but sometimes the shock of so much cold water after being in the heat of the sweat lodge can make a person pass out, so it's best just to use the buckets of water. It's good, having the creek close by like this. Your skin will get so hot it will feel like it's on fire. You can come out whenever you get too hot and dump water over yourself."

"Do people have visions during a sweat lodge ceremony?"

Roon nodded. "You might see things."

"So, what do we do now?"

"Strip," Roon said. "You don't want to be wearing any clothes when you go in the sweat lodge. It gets too hot."

The boys snickered. Pony frowned. They stopped. "You can go into the sweat lodge with your underclothes on," she said.

Dani scanned the trio of leering boys, then

said, "You're on your own, Special Agent Ferguson. I'll settle for a long, hot shower."

TWO HOURS LATER, Joe stood beneath the bright spangle of stars and poured one final bucket of ice-cold creek water over his head. He was light-headed and dizzy.

The boys had chanted. Roon had beaten on a skin drum and thrown handfuls of bear root on the hot rocks, filling the scorching air inside the lodge with a pungent herbal scent and whirls of colorful sparks. Just when he thought he couldn't stand any more heat, Roon would announce a break, and they'd come outside and pour water over themselves. This was the end of the fourth and final round. The sweat lodge ceremony was done.

The boys were quiet. They passed around a towel as they stood dripping in the cool night air. Nobody spoke. They pulled on their clothing, then sat on rocks beside the creek to put on their shoes. An owl hooted in the darkness. A gust of wind tugged through the trees. The creek rushed past, carrying the water that was life itself, the spirit that never ends. The owl hooted again and Joe stared into the starlit night for a long moment, then rose and began the downhill walk back to the ranch, where the boys filed into their building and Joe continued toward the ranch house. He climbed the porch steps slowly and sank down onto the wall bench. He wasn't as dizzy now, but he still felt strange, as if adrift, untethered. His muscles were like water but his lung felt better. The pain was gone.

A few minutes passed as he sat listening to the night sounds. A horse blowing down in the corrals. A whip-poor-will calling in the meadow beyond the creek. The murmur of voices in the kitchen. Then a patch of light spilled out onto the porch as the door opened. Dani emerged, carrying a pitcher of water and two glasses. She sat beside him and filled both glasses, handing one to him. "Water with lemon slices," she said. "Pony said you'd need to drink a lot of water after the sweat."

Joe took the glass and drank the cool, tart liquid. She refilled his glass and he drank that one down, too. The third glass he drank more slowly. "Thank you," he said, and his voice sounded strange to his ears.

"You're welcome. Did you have a vision?"

Joe leaned his shoulders against the weather-bleached boards of the house. He thought about seeing Molly walking away from him, looking back over her shoulder, and the incredibly sad feeling that came over him as she moved farther away. But he kept the vision to himself and shook his head. "No profound visions, but I felt like I was floating outside of myself. Still do."

"Maybe you're dead and having an out-of-body experience."

Joe laughed. "If a sweat lodge is supposed to strengthen your blood, I should be good for another hundred years."

Dani sat quietly beside him while he finished his third glass of water. Then she said, "I'm sorry I called you a jerk."

"You called me an *insensitive* jerk."

"I'm sorry," she repeated.

Joe gazed at her in the darkness. "Don't be. What you said was absolutely true. I am an insensitive jerk. Any other red-blooded man would have kissed you back at the Hairy Dog."

"What makes you think I'd have let you?"

"Because you were hoping I did."

"I can think of more romantic places to share a first kiss than the Hairy Dog."

Joe thought he sensed a smile in her response. "Is this place romantic enough for you?"

"I think this is the perfect place," Dani murmured, but just as Joe had resolved to make his move, she added, "But now's not the time. You were right about something you said to me."

Joe froze. "What was that?"

"You asked me how I could be sure if what I felt in a relationship was real, or if it was even reciprocated, and I've been thinking a lot about that. Maybe the strong attraction I feel toward you is just a rebound reaction from Jack walking out on me, and me wanting you—someone— to be attracted to me. I had no business talking about commitment. You're right about wanting to stay unbranded. The last thing either of us needs right now is another relationship."

Joe sat back, baffled. "Did I say all that?"

"You're a lot wiser than me, Joe. I apologize for being such a fool."

At that moment the kitchen door opened and Jimmy's voice called out into the night. "Dani? Can you come look at the cheese? I think something *bad's* happening."

She rose to her feet. "I'll be right there, Jimmy." Then to Joe, who was struggling to rise, she said, "You still want to come with me tomorrow?"

"If you don't mind my tagging along."

"I'd like it if you came."

They stood facing each other. Even though Joe couldn't see her clearly in the darkness, the nearness of her drove him wild. The sexual tension flowed between them like an electrical current. He was sure if they touched, sparks would fly. "Well, good night, Joe," she said softly, and turned to go into the kitchen. Joe stood for a few seconds more. He should have thrown all caution to the wind, pulled Dani into his arms and kissed her. Instead, as the kitchen door closed behind her, he dropped back onto the wall bench with a defeated groan.

He needed another sweat lodge to get Dani out of his blood.

## CHAPTER THIRTEEN

THE FOLLOWING DAY, after tossing and turning through mutually sleepless nights, Dani and Joe were on the road directly after breakfast. They left Jimmy in the kitchen straining his curdled goat cheese through the cheesecloth with Ramalda keeping a watchful eye. "Be sure to refrigerate it when it's finished draining, and don't rush it. Making good chèvre takes time," Dani instructed him.

Before they left the ranch, they stopped at the barn to check on the filly and Roon solemnly presented Joe with a cowboy hat. The hat was a genuine felt Stetson, tan colored, with a leather hatband. "It's too big for me," Roon explained. "If you're going to pretend to be a cattle rancher today, you should look like one."

Joe thanked him, put it on and glanced at her. "What do you think?"

In spite of her resolve to distance herself, Dani felt herself melting. "It looks like it belongs on you," she said, and meant it.

She loaded Remington and Winchester into

the Subaru, Joe climbed into the passenger seat and they headed out. Maybe a special agent with the DEA was a little overqualified for tracking down someone who'd shot four wild mustangs, but so be it. Dani was glad Joe was along for the ride and she was doubly glad he'd brought her to her senses about getting involved in another relationship too quickly. She hoped last night's chat convinced him that she wasn't a threat to the freedom he so obviously coveted.

When Jack had left Dani for another woman, she'd been determined not to feel vulnerable ever again, but her resolve had crumbled in Joe's presence. She had to protect herself. She couldn't—*wouldn't*—let herself get hooked on Joe Ferguson. She'd keep him at arm's length. She needed time to heal from the hurtful way her last relationship had ended.

She loved the mustangs because they were wild, because they were unbranded and belonged to no one. The same reasons that Joe had connected with them, admiring the photographs at her house in Helena. But she was pretty sure she couldn't love a man who shared those traits. Not even Joe Ferguson.

The drive to Josie and Kurt's place took over an hour. They debated swinging by the sheriff's office as they drove through town to check on any updates, but decided to stop on their way out of town instead. Joe was also against calling either the sheriff or his son ahead of time to announce their visit. "It's better not to," he simply said. Josie and Kurt Conroy lived just outside the city limits, in a pleasant homogenized suburb with small lawns neatly mowed and garages attached to pastel-colored, cookie-cutter houses.

"I can see why she kept her mare at her father's place," Dani said, pulling into the driveway just beyond the big gilt-lettered *Conroy* on the black mailbox. "I don't think anyone in this neighborhood would approve of her keeping a prized cutting horse in the front yard."

"Or the back," Joe said. "Josie's car's not here. Just that truck…"

Something in his voice alerted Dani, and she glanced at him as she cut the ignition. "What about the truck?"

"Nothing," Joe said. He opened his door. "Let's see if Kurt's home."

They knocked, but there was no response. "I can hear a TV inside, or a radio," Dani said after they'd knocked several times. "Let's check out back."

The backyard was the same size as the front yard, small and square with a cedar privacy fence defining the perimeter. The grass out back hadn't been mowed and the raised patio was littered with crumpled beer cans, cigarette butts and fast-food wrappers. The contrast between the neat front yard and the trashy backyard surprised Dani, but what surprised her more was the sight of the deputy sheriff sprawled in the lawn chair in a soiled T-shirt and jeans, an empty bottle of whiskey lying on its side near his dangling hand.

"Is he dead?" she whispered.

Joe walked up and bent close to check him over. "Kurt? Kurt Conroy?" He gave the deputy sheriff's shoulder a shake. There was no response. He straightened. "Dead drunk," he pronounced. "Now what?"

"We should call Sheriff Conroy and let him know. He could come over here and check on him. Someone should."

He tried the patio door and it opened. "Why don't you make him a pot of coffee? That might help."

"Seriously? You mean, go inside his kitchen?"

"Yeah," Joe said. "You know. Find the stove, a coffeepot, some coffee. Make it good and strong."

Dani flushed. "That's breaking and entering."

"That's being a Good Samaritan and keeping a deputy sheriff's reputation intact. It's either that or call an ambulance and make it a public matter." At that moment the deputy groaned, made another noise like a dry heave and shifted on the lounge chair. Dani backed away.

"I'll make the coffee," Joe said. "If he vomits, make sure he doesn't aspirate. Get him on the ground and roll him on his side."

The kitchen was a mess. The table was stacked with piles of unopened mail, the sink was full of unwashed dishes and more crumpled beer cans littered the counters. Two empty whiskey bottles crowned a brimming trash can. But Joe found the drip coffee machine, cleaned the moldy brew out of the carafe and filter, added fresh water and lots of coffee from a canister on the counter and started it brewing. Joe was just poking through the trash when Dani stuck her head around the kitchen door. "He's making more noises but he isn't waking up. What are you doing?"

"Thought I'd look around a little."

"Why?"

"Just a hunch. Did you notice the mud tires on that truck and the boots Kurt's wearing?"

"Joe, you need a search warrant to do this." She followed behind him while he opened the broom closet beside the refrigerator. "What if he comes in while you're snooping? Joe, really, come back outside before he wakes up."

Instead of retreating, he nodded inside the closet.

"Take a look at that," he said.

She peered inside. "So he has a rifle. I bet every man in Montana owns a hunting rifle."

"Not that caliber," Joe said. "That rifle takes a .300 Winchester Magnum."

"Come on," Dani urged, tugging his arm just as Kurt Conroy lurched through the door. His eyes were bloodshot and his features were ugly. "Who the hell are you?"

Dani stepped in front of Joe to head off a confrontation. "I'm a friend of Josie's. We came to talk to her about her horse, Moxie. Is she here?"

Kurt was weaving on his feet. Dani's words seemed to confuse him. He rubbed a hand over the bristle of beard on his jaw. He was a good-looking man but, just now, he looked like hell. His features hardened once he'd processed what Dani said.

"If you were a friend of Josie's, you'd know she wasn't here," he challenged.

"Do you know where she is?" Joe asked.

"She left me last week. I haven't talked to her since. I don't know where the hell she went and I don't care." Kurt was becoming more belligerent, but he was still drunk enough to be unsteady. "I don't care," he repeated.

"We fixed you some coffee. It's almost done," Dani said, gesturing toward the pot in an effort to defuse the situation.

"I don't want no goddamn coffee. Get out of my house. You have no right to be here. I don't have to call the cops, I *am* the law. I'll arrest you myself for breaking and entering and haul your asses off to jail. Now get out!"

"We're leaving," Dani said, edging toward the door. "Come on, Joe."

To her surprise, without a word Joe followed her back out onto the patio and around the side of the garage to her car. She backed out into the cul-de-sac and pulled away from the curb. "That was *crazy*!" she burst out when they were safely away. "Going into his house like that and searching through his closet! He's a deputy sheriff—we could be in big trouble. He could've shot us!"

"Maybe," Joe responded, gazing out the window at all the little cookie-cutter ranches in the development. "But I think we may have found our mustang killer."

JOE WAS ON a roll. So far everything he'd done had pissed Dani off, and this episode was no different. Five miles down the road and she was still harping on how outrageously illegal his behavior had been.

"Without a search warrant, none of what we saw is permissible in court—you should know that! And what makes you so sure he's the shooter?"

"He has the motive. Are you hungry?"

"Hungry? How could anyone be hungry after

something like that? I'm picturing the head-
lines in the newspaper if Kurt decides to press
charges."

"He doesn't even know who we are," Joe said.
"I heard there's a killer hamburger joint in this
town. I'll spring for lunch."

"Just because his wife left him, that's no reason to think he shot those mustangs."

"How about the fact that Josie's father told
him about how that mare'd gone off with Custer
just the day before she was shot? How about
those huge Redman boots Kurt was wearing
and the big mudder tires on his pickup truck?
How about the caliber of hunting rifle in his
bedroom closet, which just so happens to take
the same cartridges that were used to kill four
mustangs and one top-notch cutting horse? And
how about this?" Joe pulled a candy wrapper
from his pocket. "He eats the same candy bars
as the shooter. And this." On his palm rested
a cigarette butt that matched the one he'd retrieved at Gunflint Mountain. "I picked this up
off the back lawn."

"Great. You stole some of his trash. That'll
probably get us another five to ten."

"The name of the burger joint is the Burger
Dive. It's the town's top ranked hole-in-the-wall
diner. I checked it out on my phone. The re-
views are great."

"Is that all you can think about at a time like this? Hamburgers?"

"I'm starving, and we have just enough time to enjoy a nice lunch before seeing Shep Deakins's property," Joe said. "Seems like we should take advantage of one of Montana's best burgers, since we're in the vicinity."

"I think we should talk to the sheriff about Kurt right away," Dani said.

"Oh, I'm sure he'll be delighted to send his deputies out to his son's place with a search warrant." Joe studied his smartphone's screen. "Turn left at the next lights."

"If you really think Kurt's the shooter, Sheriff Conroy needs to know."

"Sheriff Conroy's retiring and his son's running for his job. A conviction and fine for shooting four mustangs and his wife's horse won't do anything for Kurt's political career. Comstock's the one to handle this investigation. Take your next right. The Burger Dive's up on the left about a block."

Ten minutes later they were seated in a small, lively restaurant tucked into the brick facade of an old building. The floors were red-and-white checkerboard tile, the big neon clock on the wall read high noon and the place was jamming. They ordered loaded burgers, fries and root beer. The service was quick, friendly and efficient, and the burgers were every bit as good as they'd been hyped up to be. They ate with gusto and when every last bit of burgers and fries had been devoured, they pushed back in their seats, pulled their mugs of root beer close and sighed with mutual appreciation.

"You were right," Dani said. "That was the best burger ever."

"The San Francisco fries weren't bad, either."

"Do you think Josie's in any danger from Kurt?" Dani asked.

Joe turned his mug back and forth between his palms. "She's probably still staying at her father's place. She could file a restraining order if she feels threatened. She may already have done so. I'll call Comstock. The warden will want to know what we found, and he can talk to Josie. They're old friends. What about the cattlemen's meeting? You still want to go?"

"Yes. I know you're convinced Kurt's our guy, but there may be other suspects, *and* I'd really like to know how these cattlemen feel about their leases and all the other animals that try to eat the grass and drink the water they're paying for. You still game?"

"I'm not sure I can pull off being a cowboy, but I'll do my best."

Dani gave him a slow, appreciative smile. "Oh, I think you make a very handsome cowboy, Special Agent Ferguson. Let's go check out that ranch."

"Are you seriously interested in Shep's place?"

"When my house in Helena sells, I'm hoping to find somewhere I can have horses—specifically Custer's mares. I want to rescue them and give them a safe home. So yes, I'm interested in Shep's place. I want to create a wild horse refuge. Mustangs need room to roam and nine hundred acres sounds just about right."

IT WAS EXACTLY thirty miles from the Burger Dive to the rutted dirt road that led to Shep Deakins's place. The real estate agent was already waiting at the end of the road, parked beside a rusty gray mailbox with no flag and a door that didn't look like it had ever closed and every plow truck had sideswiped it for the past five winters. They could just make out the faded name on the side—S. Deakins, hand painted in wobbly letters. For some reason the condition of the mailbox and the wobbly lettering struck Dani as very sad. Perhaps it was because Badger and Charlie had said Shep had died in this spot, holding a handful of unpaid bills.

The young woman who met them was dressed in a smart blue pantsuit and wore high heels with open toes. "The Deakins property is really rundown. Whoever buys this place will be doing so for the location. The house is a teardown," she warned as she got into her Volvo sedan before leading the way down the dirt road.

They followed the fancy sedan down a road that ended a third of a mile off the tarred road in front of a two-story dwelling with no window sash remaining in the windows and a porch that was littered with so much trash it was impossible to see the condition of the planking beneath.

"What a mess," Joe said as Dani parked beside the agent's car. "This dump could be listed as a Superfund site."

"Behave yourself," Dani said. "Remember, we're ranchers, shopping for a home base so we can pick up all those juicy grazing leases. Put your cowboy hat back on. When you're wearing that, you could fool even me." She unbuckled and climbed out, releasing the dogs from the back. They wagged circles around her as Dani stood and did a slow three-sixty, taking in the entire scope of the derelict property and junk-filled yard.

"As I said," the Realtor emphasized as she joined them, "the house would need to be demolished. It's the location you'd be buying. Look at that view!" She gestured to the mountains looming across the valley.

"The house has two separate front doors— that's very interesting," Dani said, studying the front of the weather-beaten building. "Why is that?"

"According to the history of the place, the man who built it was in love with a woman who wouldn't marry him unless he provided living quarters for her widowed mother. So he built his sweetheart a big house with two separate living quarters. Sadly, before he could finish it, his love married someone else. Shep Deakins bought it back in 1980 and lived here until he died. He was quite a character. If you notice, he put more attention into keeping the pole barn in good shape than he did the house. The barn and corrals are actually quite sound."

Dani walked slowly toward the house, kicking aside a bag of trash. Joe watched her, marveling at her composure. Most people would have run screaming from the place at first glimpse. "There's good water?" she asked the real estate agent.

"Oh, yes. That thick line of trees behind the house runs along the creek, and that creek drains out of the mountain range you see in the distance behind the house. It never runs dry. And there's a drilled well that serves the house."

"And I understand there are leases that go with this purchase?"

"Three or four. They'll all expire soon. But it's not necessary to purchase the grazing leases, unless you plan to utilize them. It's a good bit of land, around nine hundred acres."

"We'll need it all," Dani said. "We'll be running quite a few head of stock."

"Oh!" The woman looked startled. "I didn't realize... Are you ranchers?"

"Yes, rare breed beef cattle. Luings. Have you heard of them? Well, that's not surprising," Dani said when the woman shook her head. "They're of Scottish island stock, very hardy. Could we see the inside of the house?"

Luing cattle? Where'd she come up with that? Joe glanced at Dani but she paid no attention. She was focused on getting a look inside Shep Deakins's haunts.

The real estate agent gingerly lead the way up onto the porch. "The house has been ransacked by the local yahoos," she explained as she picked her way through the trash. "Many of the windows have been smashed. It's a wonder they haven't burned it down. It would probably be a blessing if they did. I'm honestly not sure it's safe to go inside."

"How old is it?" Dani asked, stepping over the threshold.

"According to my notes, it was built in the late 1800s."

"Wow," Dani said. "I'm surprised it's still standing. You don't have to come in with us. I know you're not dressed for it," she said to the agent. "We just want to take a quick peek."

The woman looked relieved. "All right, I'll wait by the car."

Joe had a hard time keeping up with Dani. She was down in the cellar in a heartbeat with a jackknife in one hand and a flashlight in the other, stabbing her knife into the sills. Then it was up into the attic, climbing over mountains of refuse, to stab at the roof beams and rafters. Then it was room by room, section by section.

"She's going to think you're about to make an offer on this place. She's probably already spending her commission," Joe said.

"Hmm…maybe so," Dani said, stabbing her knife blade into a windowsill. "Let's go take a look at the pole barn."

The pole barn and corrals were in good shape, as the Realtor had said. Apparently Shep had spared his animals the trash he himself had lived so comfortably with. The barn was tidy and clean.

She walked back out into the sunlight and wind and did another slow three-sixty. The real estate agent watched with bated breath as Dani looked down at the sheaf of listing papers and flipped through them one by one. "Well, there are a lot of 'unknowns' listed here. Unknown information on septic, on the well, on any contaminants from long-term ranching operations. And the property's a real dump. You're right, it needs to be demolished," Dani said slowly. "I've never seen so much trash and junk in one place. It'll be months before anything else can be built here, and who knows what toxic materials Shep Deakins might have dumped in the backyard, let alone what's leaked out of all those junk vehicles. Has a water test of the well been done?"

"No," the Realtor said.

"If the well water isn't potable, that would suggest long-term contamination. There's no point in even considering the purchase of the property if that's the case. How many acres?"

"Two hundred seventy deeded acres. The deeded land is well marked by fence lines and ranch roads, and as far as I know, Shep Deakins kept the fences on both the deeded and leased lands in good repair. As for the house itself, the town has volunteered to burn it as part of a training exercise, so the demolition shouldn't be an issue. Whoever's hired to haul all the junk away can deal with what's left of the structure."

"Hmm." Dani assumed a thoughtful stance, arms crossed, gazing out toward the mountain range with a slight frown. She turned to Joe. "I don't think it's worth anywhere near the asking price. What do you think?"

"You're the boss," Joe replied, hooking his

thumbs in his leather belt, assuming a cowboy slouch with his hat brim shading his face. "I know how much you love trashy houses and heritage cows."

Dani thought some more, taking her time. Finally she sighed. "I'd like to make an offer of eighty thousand under the seller's asking price, contingent upon the results of the water test. Right now, Joe and I would like to spend a little time walking over the land. Can you draw up the papers today and have them ready at your office for me to sign? I expect you'll need earnest money?"

The Realtor's tense expression dissolved in a smile of relief. "We'll need a deposit of five thousand dollars earnest money if your offer is accepted," she said. "My office is just a forty-minute drive from here. I'll be in touch with the seller this afternoon." She produced a business card from her pocket and handed it, along with the property listing papers, to Dani. "It's two p.m. now. I'll be there until five."

"YOU'RE CRAZY," JOE said after the Realtor had departed in her dust-covered sedan, brake lights flashing off and on as she cautiously navigated the rough ranch road.

Dani wrapped her arms around herself with

a rapturous sigh. "I'm going to buy this place. It's absolutely perfect."

Joe stared, slack jawed. "You're joking, right?"

"Look at that house. Just look at it! It's gorgeous, and the timbers are all sound as a dollar, thanks to that metal roof and a good rock foundation. Whoever built this place knew what they were doing. It might be full of junk and the windows might be busted, and for sure, it looks like a dump right now, but it's a beautiful building worthy of restoration, and I'm going to restore it. Did you even notice the hand-hewn log walls in the woodshed? I bet that woodshed was the original cabin before the house was built. Joe, this place is a historical treasure! I can't believe nobody's snapped it up. If the seller accepts my offer I'll be the happiest woman on earth, and if they don't, I'll just offer more." She reached for his hand. "Come on, I want to see the creek, and walk over the pastures. I want to picture this place with kids and dogs and mustangs." She tramped to the edge of the creek and stood in the shade of the big cottonwoods that lined the banks. "Look at this water, Joe, isn't it wonderful? It's deep enough to swim!"

"It's a long ways from Helena, Counselor," Joe said, trying to process Dani's infatuation with the place.

"I'm not planning to stay in Helena. I'll give my notice, sell my house and take a job in a Bozeman law firm. It'll be a forty-five-minute commute to work, but I'll be near Molly and Steven. I can babysit for them. I can watch your little niece or nephew grow up. How cool will that be?"

She started down the ranch road that paralleled the creek. Joe stopped and Dani took five more strides before realizing he wasn't there. She turned with a questioning look. Her dark eyes were shining with excitement and a questioning smile curved her lips. "You really do think I'm crazy, don't you?"

"Where'd you come up with the Luing cattle? Did you make that up?"

"I did my homework last night," she replied, her smile widening. "I researched rare Scottish breeds, figuring if we were going to play the part of a Scots/Irish cowboy ranch-shopping in Montana with a French/Scots mustang lover, we might want to play the part with our heritage breed cows. So no, I didn't make those cattle up. They're as real as we are."

The wind blew strands of dark hair that had escaped her braid back from her glowing face. Joe doubted he'd ever known a more vibrantly alive and strikingly beautiful woman, and without thinking he took three steps forward, cupped her face and kissed her. The kiss wasn't planned and it wasn't meant to be passionate, but it turned out to be both. Dani didn't shrink away. She kissed him back as hungrily as if she'd been starved for his touch, as if she'd been waiting for his kiss all her life. When they finally came up for air, her eyes were dazed, her face flushed and her breathing audible over the rustle of cottonwood leaves and the sound of the running creek. Joe smoothed the strands of hair from the sides of her face and traced the curve of her lower lip with his thumb.

"You're not crazy," he said, "but you scare me to death." And then he kissed her again, and after that second kiss, there was no turning back.

# CHAPTER FOURTEEN

THE PURCHASE AND sales agreement for Shep Deakins's ranch was signed at approximately 4:22 that afternoon. "I've already spoken to the seller," the Realtor informed them upon their arrival at her office, "and your offer's been accepted, pending the results of the water test, of course. If everything else goes smoothly, we could close in thirty days. Congratulations!" Dani wrote out a check for five thousand dollars as an earnest money deposit.

Joe escorted Dani out of the office and down the steps. She paused when she reached the bottom and waited while he picked a few stray pieces of grass from her braid. "Guess I didn't get it all," he said with a grin. She fished a green cottonwood leaf from inside her shirt and let it flutter to the sidewalk.

"No, you didn't, not by half," she said, flushing prettily and giving him a look that said she wasn't talking about grass and leaves in her hair and clothes. Joe's heartbeat quickened. After the hour they'd spent tangled up together on the banks of that creek, he wasn't sure what she meant but he knew what it was he wanted.

"Well, you're about to become the owner of a wild horse refuge," Joe said. "This calls for a celebration. I'll buy you a drink at that tavern just down the street. They probably serve food, too. We should eat something before going to the cattlemen's meeting. It could drag on for hours."

The tavern was dark inside, with old photos and dim wagon wheel light sconces on the walls. A bartender polished glasses, a few people sat at the bar and a group of what looked like high-school-age waitresses cleaned salt and pepper shakers and filled sugar bowls at one of the tables, getting ready for the evening rush. "Seat yourselves, I'll be right with you!" the older supervisor with the short bleached spikes called out. When they were seated, she left the group and came to their table wearing a name tag that said *Cindy*. "What can I getcha?" she said, notepad and pencil at the ready.

"I'd like a glass of La Posta," Dani said.

"Never heard of it."

"I'll just have a glass of your house red."

"Gotcha." Cindy scribbled on her notepad. "You?"

"Draft beer," Joe said. "Do you serve food?"

"Just breakfast, but it's real good and we

serve it all day long. We just started our new summer menu today. There's some real good stuff on it." She plucked two laminated one-page menus from the bar and handed each of them a copy. "I'll be back with your drinks in two shakes."

Joe tried to concentrate on the menu but all he could think about was the woman across the small table from him and how demure and proper she looked, sitting there with her head bent studiously over the menu. Had they really, just hours earlier, been tearing each other's clothes off beside that creek in a desperate rush to consummate an intimate act they both desperately wanted but equally feared? Had they really collapsed together onto the ground with all the romantic grace of two wrestlers trying to win a match? Had Dani really started laughing halfway through their wrestling match because she had a foot cramp? Had he really rolled over on a sharp rock with her on top of him and shouted a pain-filled curse into her ear, shifting her aside and saying, "Oh, God, I'm sorry!"

His performance had been an embarrassment. A joke. Worst ever. Was that what she had meant by that comment of hers—"not by half"? Was it because he hadn't measured up by half to her ex? He dropped his eyes to the menu, filled with a kind of sick despair. He'd wanted to impress her and he'd made a fool of himself instead.

Dani was being very quiet, studying the menu. Was she already regretting what they'd done? The awkwardness Joe felt began to build. He couldn't think of a thing to say and the silence between them became almost unbearable.

Cindy came back with their drinks and whipped out her notebook. "Have you decided?"

"I have a question, Cindy," Dani said in her most professional counselor tone of voice.

"Shoot!" Cindy responded briskly, pencil poised in midair.

"What are 'Breakfast Bubes'?"

"Huh?" Cindy snatched the menu from Dani's hand and studied it with a furrowed brow. "Oh, for cripes' sake!" she burst out, then stomped briskly along the bar to the kitchen door where she brandished the menu to the unseen cook. "Henry, we got Breakfast Bubes listed on the new menu! I wonder who made that typo!"

There was a chorus of giggles from the younger waitresses, who had picked up copies of the new menu and were scrutinizing it with delight.

"Breakfast Bubes! Look at that, only $1.99. What a bargain!" one hooted.

"Good going, Henry, that's your best typo *ever*!"

"This could become one of our hottest sellers! The guys'll love 'em!"

"Depends on the size of the order," another quipped. "Thirty-two double-A like yours? Not so great."

"My mother's a thirty-eight double-D. I don't know what happened to me."

"They might grow more if you eat a lot of parsley."

"That's enough, girls," Cindy snapped, marching back to their table. She handed the menu back to Dani. "That's supposed to read 'Breakfast *Cubes*,'" she said. "They're diced-up potatoes. I apologize for the typo. Henry's going to fix it, soon as he fixes the dishwasher, which hasn't run right in two years."

Dani hid behind her menu. Her shoulders were shaking. Behind her, the girls were now talking about men's feet as they filled the salt and pepper shakers. "Have you ever noticed how man feet are all big knobby knuckles and black hair?"

"Boy, you ain't kidding—ugliest things *ever*!"

"Clean those sugar bowls, girls!" Cindy snapped.

Dani made a choked noise as Joe handed his menu to Cindy. The awkward moment had been effectively erased by a menu typo and the young girls. He gave the waitress a big grin. "I'll have two eggs with a side of Breakfast Bubes, since this is probably the last time I'll ever be able to order a breakfast item like that for supper."

"Gotcha," Cindy said. "You want those eggs over easy or sunny-side up?"

THE CATTLEMEN'S MEETING began at 6:30 p.m. but Dani and Joe didn't leave the tavern until 6:15 p.m. Dani was feeling light-headed and euphoric after two glasses of house red and an hour of gazing at Joe across the tiny table as the tavern filled with patrons and jovial noise. She'd hardly touched her ham and eggs. All she could think about was the awkward tryst they'd shared beside the creek, and how sweet Joe had been, how tender. After that first searing kiss, she hadn't been sure what to expect, and the gun in a shoulder holster under his jacket had surprised her. But he was a cop, a federal drug enforcement agent with the Mob after him. Why wouldn't he be armed?

They hadn't exactly chosen the best of spots, swept up as they'd been in the heat of the moment, but he'd been so considerate afterward, helping her dress, picking the grass and leaves out of her hair, brushing off her clothes. Three times he'd asked her if she was okay and once he'd even asked, "Did I hurt you?"

*Hurt* her? The only thing that had hurt was how quick it had been, and yet, they'd had to get past that first dangerous place, past those first awkward moments carrying all the baggage from the past that they'd both brought into their relationship. Joe hadn't hurt her; he'd only whetted her appetite and now she wanted more. A whole lot more of a man she'd vowed not to get hooked on.

But she was caught, hook, line and sinker. It was pointless to pretend she didn't care about Joe when she was crazy about him. So much had happened in the past few days that she was dizzy from it all—meeting Joe, rescuing that orphaned foal, trying to find who shot the wild mustangs…and now she was about to become a real ranch owner. She'd have to walk the walk and talk the talk among these cattlemen, but one thing she knew for certain—she didn't want to walk that path alone.

She also knew she had to be careful. She didn't want to spook Joe, and nothing did that faster than a needy woman. She made a vow to herself that she'd never ask anything of him that he didn't willingly offer. She laced her arm through his as they walked into the old grange hall and took seats at the back, smiling and nodding at the curious faces that turned their way. Caleb wasn't there, which was unfortunate. His presence would have been welcome. Hershel

Bonner wasn't there, either, which was probably a good thing.

The meeting was called to order quickly by the chairman, who read the minutes of the last meeting. There was a much heated discussion about the federal government's latest attack on ranchers by trying to raise the price of the grazing leases. "I don't think it's going to happen," the chairman finally mediated. "The livestock lobby's too strong and we have politicians in key places. They've been trying to jack the rates for decades and haven't been able to do it yet, so I don't think we have anything to worry about. And now I'd like to bring up another subject along the same lines."

The chairman, a lean, gray-haired weatherbeaten man who looked like he could whip Clint Eastwood in a gunfight, picked up a piece of paper, put on his reading glasses, leaned on the podium and said, "We've all been watching what the BLM is doing about the wild horse problem. They realize the range is being destroyed by too many horses and they want to remove an additional forty thousand mustangs from our grazing lands, but the public is fighting them tooth and nail, and the BLM is giving in. I'd like to recap a letter that the Utah Cattlemen's Association sent to their senators and congressmen. It states good points that we should make our own, to put the pressure on the lobbyists and politicians. I'll read you the important points.

"First off, there's no need for additional wilderness areas or special protection of lands. Secondly, the *Endangered Species Act* needs a critical revision. Thirdly, the wild horse, wild burro and wildlife issues need to be resolved. Grazers continue to express concern that the resources cannot continue to be abused by wildlife and wild horses. The federal agencies need to recognize their overriding charter of protecting the rangeland resources and not continually give in to special interest groups that seek an increase of one species at the expense of the resources. The federal agencies must establish a functional system of management that is not always contested and stopped in the courts. Also, the federal government must recognize and respect that water rights are governed and protected under state water rights and laws."

He laid down the paper, removed his glasses and looked out over the crowded room. "There's more along those lines, but you get the gist. It's a good letter. I'll distribute copies to all of you after the meeting. Point is, we're losing control of our grazing rights to special interest groups, and it has to stop. We have to protect our public grazing lands from political posturing and ensure that we have the certainty we need to be able to manage our ranches for the benefit of our nation, or else we might end up with our public grazing leases being turned over to packs of wolves and herds of wild horses."

Dani felt a surge of anger and started to her feet, but a strong tug on her jacket plopped her back into her seat. She shot a sidelong glance at Joe, who looked as calm as if he was attending a Sunday afternoon church social. He rose to his feet. "Permission to speak?" he said.

"Granted," the chairman said, visibly surprised by the request. "I don't recognize you, son."

"My name's Joe Ferguson and my partner and I are guests here tonight. I don't know much about this ranching business, but my partner here's as local as they come, and she's looking at running some cattle in your neck of the woods. I'm confused about these grazing leases. If she holds grazing leases for her stock on public lands, do those leases apply to the water on those lands, as well? For instance, if a creek runs through the grazing lease, does the rancher have exclusive use of that water as it passes through that allotment?"

The chairman leaned one elbow on the podium. "Well, current regulations state that the right to use water on public lands for the purpose of livestock watering is regulated by the state in which the land is located, and here in Montana the use of the waters in our streams is declared to be a public use. Every citizen has the right to divert and use the water so long as they don't infringe upon the rights of another who had a prior right by appropriation. So, you can use the water for your livestock, as long as you're not taking it from someone who had a prior right to it. And when you're done, you have to restore the flow to the channel of the stream so other folks can use it. Does that help?"

"What about irrigating hay fields?"

"Same thing. You can use the water so long as you aren't robbing it from another rancher who had prior rights."

"How do you know if someone else has prior rights to a stream running through public grazing lands?"

"That information should be in your grazing leases."

"So if the creek runs dry because a rancher upstream has a prior right, and my animals suffer, do I have any recourse?"

"Yes. You can go to the state level and petition for fair water rights."

"You mentioned wild horses and their impact on grazing lands. Does a lease holder have the right to run them off the lease if they stray onto it?"

"That's why God made fences, son," the chairman said.

"And bullets," a man in the front row added, to a ripple of laughter.

"Just keep your fences in good repair and you shouldn't have any trouble," the chairman said. "We don't have much of a problem with mustangs in this part of Montana. Kids on four-wheelers are more of a nuisance."

"Thank you." Joe sat back down.

Back in Dani's car after the meeting adjourned, Dani was fuming over the comments that had been made. "And that comment about the bullets!" she burst out as she started the Subaru. "That was disgusting. You know what those people are? They're welfare ranchers, all of 'em. They use our public lands without paying diddly squat, running their cows all over, polluting the water sources, creating erosion and destroying the vegetation. We taxpayers subsidize their ranches to the tune of billions of dollars a year. Did you know that wild horses and burros have been squeezed into just twenty percent of the land allocated to them by the *Wild and Free-Roaming Horses and Burros Act* that was signed into law in 1971? Miners and frackers and welfare ranchers are pushing them to extinction! Those ranchers in that meeting are mooching off the American taxpayer while our wildlife and wilderness areas are being annihilated!" She pulled out onto the black road and accelerated. "Why didn't you let me speak up?"

"Too risky. They might've strung you up."

"Fifteen years ago, two percent of public land ranchers controlled *fifty* percent of permitted grazing acreage. And today that elite group of megarich owners has tightened its hold on federal grazing land even further through leases attached to those larger-than-life ranches they inherit or buy outright to use as tax write-offs?"

"It didn't look like many elite billionaires were in that meeting tonight."

"No doubt they had much more important things to be doing but they benefit from all that lobbying, believe me."

They left the outskirts of town. Up ahead a neon green motel sign flashed, bright even in the golden light of the early-summer evening. "Would you look at that," Joe marveled. "The Wagon Wheel Motel has vacancies."

He heard Dani blow out an exasperated breath, then she cut a quick glance in his direction. He wondered if she felt the sexual current running between them, but he didn't have to wonder for long. Her foot came off the accelerator as the neon sign grew bigger. It was a tacky-looking place with a little half-moon motor court, vinyl siding and green trim with fake shutters. Each motel unit had two little windows that looked out at the parking lot. Dani glanced at him again, then pulled into the gravel lot and parked in front of the little office with the big plastic wagon wheel mounted to the wall beside the door. Joe got out and went inside. A young kid sat behind the desk reading a newspaper. He got to his feet, pushing his glasses up his nose.

"I need a room," Joe said.

"Sixty-five bucks," the kid responded with a smirk, handing him a registration card. Two minutes later he was unlocking the door of unit six while Dani parked the Subaru in front of it. Four minutes later they were tearing their clothes off with the same furious haste they'd employed at Shep Deakins's place, until Dani stayed his hands with her own and they kissed with a hot, wet tangle of tongues that made his knees turn to water.

"Slow down," she murmured as they came up for breath. "Slow and easy, cowboy…"

This wasn't going to be another awkward wrestling match beside the creek with sharp rocks digging into his back. This was going to be the way it should be. The Wagon Wheel might not be the classiest hole-in-the-wall, but it had a bed and, at the moment, nothing else really mattered. She was unbuckling his belt when her cell phone rang. She moaned, arching against him for another passionate kiss.

"Don't answer it," he said when she pulled away on the fourth ring. Her phone was on the desk in her purse. She checked the caller ID. "It's Steven. He never calls me." She answered it. Joe flopped onto the bed with a frustrated moan.

"Hi, Steven, what's up?...No, Molly's not with us," he heard Dani say. "Yesterday she said she might visit Luther Makes Elk and might see us at the ranch when we got back. Did you call the Bow and Arrow?" Dani caught Joe's eye as he sat up, alerted by the tone of her voice. "Okay, okay...No, I get that part, Steven. Of course you're worried. You stay home in case she calls or shows up. We'll drive out to Luther's place and see when she left there. We'll call you from there. She hasn't been feeling well. Maybe you should call all the local hospitals, too, just in case...Try not to panic, Steven, I'm sure she's fine. She may have gotten off to a late start this morning and then lost track of time. Cell phone reception is lousy out there. We'll probably cross paths on our way to Luther's. I'll call you when we get there. It'll probably take us an hour or so. Let us know if you hear anything."

Dani slipped her phone back into her purse

and looked at Joe. Her face was grave. "Molly never showed up at the Bow and Arrow, and she's not home, either," she said. "Steven's pretty worried. Molly promised she'd be back home by six, and she's not answering her cell phone."

"She's probably still visiting with Luther Makes Elk and, like you said, she lost track of time and forgot to charge her cell or she's out of range," Joe said, already on his feet and fastening his belt. "We'll probably meet her on the road somewhere." But his stomach had twisted into a knot before they left the motel room and headed back to the Subaru. Joe knew his sister was always punctual. If she was going to be late, she would have found a way to contact Steven.

Molly was missing, and they had to find her before it was too late.

## CHAPTER FIFTEEN

DANI WAS ONLY too glad to let Joe drive. She was trying not to overreact, but her nerves were drawn taut as a fiddle string. Molly was pregnant and she hadn't been feeling well and now she was missing. She dialed and redialed Molly's number, text messaged her, left voice messages.

"She should have stayed home!" she burst out as Joe accelerated down the long empty stretch of road toward the Crow Indian Reservation. "Where could she be?" She dialed Pony's number on her cell. Pony answered on the second ring. Yes, Steven had called. No, Molly had not shown up at the Bow and Arrow. Caleb had driven into town to ask if anyone had seen her. Nobody had, so he was going to drive out toward the rez to retrace her path from Luther Makes Elk's place. He'd left half an hour ago. Pony gave her Caleb's cell phone number.

"The reception is spotty," Pony warned. "You might not be able to reach him."

Caleb didn't pick up when Dani dialed. She sent a text message, then stopped trying and cradled her phone in her lap, willing Steven to call and tell her Molly was home, but the miles passed and her phone didn't ring. She had a deep foreboding that something was really wrong.

"This shouldn't be happening," she said.

Joe was driving fast, faster than her Subaru had ever gone. His phone rang and he fished it out of his pocket. "Ferguson," he said. He was silent for a few moments and then Dani heard him say under his breath, "Oh, *shit*."

"What happened?" she cried out. "Is it Molly? Has something happened to her?"

Joe was shaking his head in response to Dani's outburst. "Are they doing an autopsy?" Another long silence. "Listen," he said to the caller. "Alison sent Ferg to a boarding school in Ledyard called Sedgewood Manor. Bring him in, Rico, and let me know when he's safe. Molly's just gone missing and this whole thing is starting to look really bad."

Dani felt a deep chill seep into her bones as Joe ended the call and set his phone on the console between them. "What?" she said through numb lips.

"That was Rico. My ex-wife was found dead in her apartment of an apparent heroin overdose this afternoon. The coroner's office is examining her but the results won't be released until tomorrow. It could be a coincidence. Alison never really shook her heroin habit."

"But you think it's more than that, don't you?" Dani pressed. "You don't think she died of a heroin overdose. You don't think Molly just stayed late with Luther Makes Elk. You think this is all connected, that Marconi's behind it. You think he took Molly, and you think your son is in danger, too."

Joe shook his head, concentrating on the road. "I don't know what to think, but I'm not taking any chances with my son."

"We should notify the police," Dani said.

"No. We'll wait until we know what's going on." He shot her a glance and Dani's chill intensified. Everything he felt and thought was in that brief glance, and none of it was good.

THE SUMMER TWILIGHT turned the distant mountain ranges violet and gold as they approached the reservation, but neither Joe nor Dani paid any attention to the beauty of the landscape they were traveling through. For miles they'd traveled in silence, each trapped inside a prison of dark thoughts.

"I shouldn't have come here," Dani heard Joe mutter. He wasn't talking to her; he was damning himself out loud.

"That's not true," Dani said quietly. "You can't blame yourself for any of this."

He didn't respond. It was as if she hadn't spoken. He'd shut her out as completely as if she wasn't sharing the vehicle with him. Dani shivered. The spring air was quite mild, but she'd never felt this kind of cold before. She ran different scenarios through her mind, of what might have happened to Molly. Molly had left Luther Makes Elk's shack and headed for the Bow and Arrow. Scenario 1: A cow had stepped out in front of her car and she'd gone into a ditch, hitting her head on the steering wheel and losing consciousness. Scenario 2: She'd left Luther's place and somehow gotten turned around on one of those rez roads and had run out of gas. She tried to call for help but her cell had no reception. She was probably walking along the road right now and they'd spot her at any moment. Scenario 3: Her friends in the area had sprung a surprise baby shower on her and she would have called Steven but her phone battery was dead.

But none of those scenarios were plausible. There was no Molly. No familiar car off the road in a ditch or out of gas. There were just endless miles of flat black road and a handful of slow-moving vehicles that Joe whipped past until finally they were turning onto the dirt road that led past Luther's place. It was just after nine p.m. when Joe pulled to a stop in front of the shack. Dani could see Luther sitting on the wall bench outside his shack and her car door was open before the vehicle even came to a stop. She covered the distance to the shack on knees that felt rubbery. Her mouth was dry. Luther acted as though he'd been expecting them. He was wearing his flat-topped black hat with the broad brim, and over his shoulders was draped the red-and-black-striped Pendleton blanket Steven had mentioned over the phone. Molly had been here!

"Luther," Dani said in a voice that sounded faint to her own ears. She dropped to her knees in front of him. "Nobody knows where Molly is. She was supposed to go to the Bow and Arrow but she never showed up, and Steven is very worried. When did she leave here?"

Luther watched Joe approach and nodded slowly in response to Dani's words. "She brought this blanket," he said, stroking the fine wool. "She came when she knew I was hungry and she brought food. She stayed a little while and then she left."

"Noontime, then?" Dani said. Her stomach churned with anxiety. Molly had been missing for hours. "Did she say where she was going?"

"She said you were trying to find who killed the wild horses and that she was worried about her brother Joseph," Luther said, looking at Joe. "She said she thought he might be in danger."

"What did you tell her?" Dani asked.

"I told her this was a good blanket, and it would be warm when winter came. I told her that her brother could take care of himself. You had a sweat lodge?"

Joe nodded. "Last night."

"Good. You will need to be strong. If I was strong I would not be sitting here. All good things come from the mother earth and we need to stay close to her. When you sit on the earth you think more clearly. If I was sitting on the earth I would see more things and the spirit would move through me like it used to, but I am old and my bones are weak. You are young and strong, but your biggest enemy is yourself. When you don't know what to do, be still and quiet. The spirit will talk to you if you wait and listen. Your courage will come when the doubts have gone from your head. Never forget there is great strength in silence."

Dani felt the sting of tears. She reached to grip Luther's twisted hand. "If you could hold good thoughts for her, Luther?"

Luther nodded, squeezed Dani's hand, then

removed the blanket from his shoulders. "Take this blanket with you. You will need it before the dawn," he said. "It gets cold up in the high places."

THEY DROVE AWAY from Luther Makes Elk's place and into the gathering darkness, heading toward the Bow and Arrow. Joe's head was full of the old man's words. He heard them over and over again like distant echoes from a deep abyss. He remembered his vision from the sweat lodge the night before. Molly, walking away from him, looking over her shoulder once and then moving farther away.

Dani sat with the wool blanket folded in her lap. The silence filled the space between them and Joe wondered what she was thinking. He wondered if the silence between them was the silence Luther had spoken of, because he didn't feel stronger for it. He felt helpless, paralyzed with fear, and when Dani's phone rang he thought his nerves would snap.

"Hi, Caleb," Dani said. She listened for several long moments, her head turned toward him and her brow furrowed. "Okay. We just left Luther's," she said in a voice that shook with emotion. "We're probably not far from you right now. Hold on a minute." She lowered the phone. "Caleb just found Molly's car," she choked out.

"He says it's parked on the shoulder of the main road, heading toward the Bow and Arrow. Her phone's on the center console and the keys are still in the ignition. He said he didn't touch anything. He didn't even open the door. He's waiting for us."

"Let me talk to him."

She handed him her cell. "Don't walk around the car," he said. "We'll need to look for evidence, footprints, signs of a struggle."

"Okay," Caleb said, his voice terse. "I'm sitting in my vehicle and my emergency flashers are on. I'll wait until you get here. Should I call the police?"

"Not yet. Not until we know if Marconi's involved. If he isn't, we call the cops. If he is, and we bring the cops in, he'll kill Molly. Something else you should know. My ex-wife just turned up dead of a drug overdose. Might be a coincidence, but my gut says Marconi's behind her death and Molly's disappearance. I hope I'm wrong. Sit tight. We'll be there soon." Joe handed Dani's phone back. "We'll find her," he said, and wished he felt as confident as he sounded.

Dani phoned Steven to tell him the latest development. Her voice betrayed her emotions and after she ended the call she started to cry. She stared out the side window, wiping the tears from her cheeks. "Steven told me he's coming to the Bow and Arrow. Now that he knows she's been taken, there's no point in him staying home."

"We'll find her, Dani," Joe said. "Molly's going to be okay." But he knew that if Marconi was behind this, the odds were against them.

BADGER HAD BEEN a part and parcel of the Montana landscape long enough to know when bad weather was brewing, and he predicted a heavy rain by morning. "Bet we get the first thunderstorms of spring tonight," he groused to Charlie, who was sitting beside him on the ranch house porch. "Nothin' like mountain thunderstorms. They'll flash flood the creeks and wash the passes clean of snow."

"Hope she ain't caught out in it," Charlie said mournfully.

"That gal? She's not lost and nobody's snatched her. You wait and see, all this crazy foofaraw'll be for nothin'. She's probably driving into her driveway right now and Steven's goin' out there to tell her what for. Women can behave might strange when they're in a family way."

"As if you know about such stuff," Charlie said, working a cramp out of his leg.

Jimmy and Roon stepped out onto the porch from the kitchen, where Ramalda was making her usual clatter, cleaning up and washing dishes. Lamplight spilled through the open door onto the worn planking and cast the boys' shadows far into the yard. They sat on the bench beside the two old codgers and shared a thoughtful silence that spanned two cultures and over six decades.

"What'll we do if Molly's been snatched by that gangster?" Jimmy said.

"Marconi?" Badger scratched his whiskers. "He wouldn't dare come out here. This place is too wild for them city folk from back east."

"You said yourself the wildest critters live in the city," Charlie countered. "What if he did snatch that pretty girl? We can't just sit here and do nothin'."

"Yeah," Jimmy said. "We have to do something."

"What exactly do you boys propose we do?" Badger said. His hip was bothering him worse by the day, and no matter how he shifted his weight on the bench, he couldn't ease the pain. Caleb had suggested more than once that he get a hip replacement. He'd even offered to pay for it. Imagine, going into a hospital like it was a garage and getting his hip replaced like it was a tie rod end or a ball joint. "Supposing, just supposing, this Marconi snatched that gal. What makes you think he'd be anywhere near here?"

"Molly was coming here," Roon said. "Marconi probably followed her, knowing she would lead him to her brother. If he thinks Joe's here, he might not be that far away."

"And if he's close by," Jimmy continued, "we just have to ambush him and rescue Molly."

Badger rubbed his whiskers and shifted his position. "And how do you propose to find him? This is a mighty big ranch."

Jimmy was silent, but Roon spoke up. "We know this land and he doesn't. We know how to be quiet when we travel. We know how to read signs, how to watch the animals and listen to what they tell us. If Marconi's anywhere around here, we can find him. He has Molly, but he *really* wants Joe. All we have to do is find him before he hurts either of them."

Badger sighed, listening to the brave words of youth. He remembered when he was young and thought no weight was too heavy to lift, no distance too far to travel, no horse too ornery to ride, but his fires had been banked long ago. "Marconi's a very dangerous man," he said carefully. "A cold-blooded killer. You boys stick real close to home if it turns out he's in the neighborhood."

"We are the Apsáalooke, children of the raven, and we are great warriors," Roon said.

"If Marconi is near here, we will find him. We won't let him hurt our friends."

BY THE TIME they saw the flashing lights in the road ahead, Dani had regained control of her emotions. Darkness had fallen, and made the situation all the more dire. Joe pulled over a good distance from Molly's car and cut the ignition. "Do you have a flashlight?"

"In the center console." Dani opened the compartment, rummaging for and producing an LED headlamp and a small flashlight.

"Stay put until I check things out," he said, pulling on the headlamp. "I don't suppose you have a pair of gloves?"

"I have a first-aid kit—there might be a pair in that." She pulled a compact kit from the glove compartment and unzipped it. "Here."

Joe pulled them on. "Just in case Marconi's not behind this, we'll need to get fingerprints." He reached to switch the headlamp on but his hand paused and he held her eyes with his. "Get into the driver's seat and stay inside the car. If anything happens, turn around, go back to town and call 911 while you're driving. Don't stop for anyone. Don't stop until you're outside the police station in Bozeman, surrounded by two dozen cops. Understand?"

Dani nodded, paralyzed with a kind of fear

she'd never experienced before. She watched Joe approach Molly's car, where he did a very slow walk-around, scanning for tracks, then dropping to the ground and sliding under to examine the underside of the car. He went around the vehicle three times, inspecting every minute detail, then he proceeded to Caleb's vehicle and switched the headlamp off while they talked through the driver's-side window. Dani's hands cramped and she realized she was clenching them together tightly. She tried to relax, tried to take deep breaths and quell the panic that was building inside of her. There was no traffic. There never was on this part of the road.

What were they talking about? She climbed into the driver's seat and rolled down the window. From this distance she barely heard the murmur of their voices, but suddenly she heard something else, and Joe did, too. The ringing of a cell phone inside Molly's car. Joe straightened and approached the car again. He switched the headlamp on, panned inside and then opened the driver's-side door cautiously. He leaned in and picked up the phone.

Dani watched as he listened to the caller. The headlights of the Subaru illuminated him like a target and she switched them off in a swift, impulsive movement. Joe glanced up and a moment later switched off his headlamp. He stood in darkness, still listening to the caller, then said two words, "All right," and put the phone back inside the car. He removed the keys from the ignition and walked toward the trunk.

Dani watched him. She felt a silent scream building inside her. The pressure in her lungs increased until she couldn't breathe. She wrenched the door open and jumped out. *"Joe!"*

"Get back in the car," he ordered, his voice curt. The trunk lifted open and the interior light came on. She ignored Joe's orders and rushed up to the trunk, half expecting to see her best friend stuffed inside, dead. But the only thing there was a lock of Molly's red hair.

Caleb approached the vehicle and Joe spoke to both of them. "That was Marconi," he said. "He said if we brought the cops in, he'd kill Molly. He wants to trade my sister for me, which is what I expected."

"He'll kill you," Dani said.

"He'll kill Molly if I don't do exactly what he says," Joe said. "Make no mistake, Marconi's in complete control here. He's calling the shots." He thought for a moment. "He knew we were at the car. Wherever he is, he's watching us." Joe lifted his eyes to the wall of mountains that cradled the darkness. "Somehow he got Molly to pull over and get out of her car. He took her without a chase, without a struggle. How? And how did he get up into those mountains high enough to be watching us right now when there are no drivable roads at that elevation?"

"My guess is, he has a chopper," Caleb said.

"Right," Joe said slowly. "He knows Molly will eventually lead him to me, so he stakes out the house. When she takes off down the long road this morning to bring Luther Makes Elk that blanket, he hijacks a pilot to fly him out here and nab her. We might want to find out if that pilot who flew us yesterday from Yellowstone Helotours has turned up missing."

"I'll make a call," Caleb said.

"So let's suppose Marconi hijacks this chopper and forces the pilot to land smack-dab in the middle of the road. Molly stops and gets out of her car because the chopper's blocking the road. Maybe she thinks we're in it, Dani and I, because we were up in a chopper yesterday. She knows that we knew she was coming out to the Bow and Arrow for a visit, and we spot her car and land in the road to intercept her. She stops, thinking it's us, and that's it—Marconi has her. He leaves her cell phone in the car and now has a way to communicate with us. He's holding her up in the mountains, someplace where you can land a chopper, get cell phone reception and see us all standing around her car."

Joe was speaking his thoughts out loud, slowly piecing the puzzle together.

"What else did he say?" Caleb said.

"He told me to take Molly's car, head due south on the dirt road outside Katy Junction and keep driving until he calls me again with further instructions. And he said to make sure I'm not followed and no cops are brought in or it's game over for Molly."

"If you do what he's asking," Dani said. "you won't get out of this alive. We have to call the police."

"That's the last thing we should do. This is my fight, Dani. I put you all in great danger by coming here."

"None of this is your fault, Joe. Let the FBI handle it!"

"She's right," Caleb said. "You can't give yourself up to that monster."

Joe stripped the gloves off his hands. "I don't know how else to get Molly back except to do exactly what he says. Marconi wants me. Period."

"Molly wouldn't want you to risk your life," Dani said. "And what about your son? He lost his mother today. He can't lose you, too."

"Don't sell me short," Joe said. "It's not over till it's over. The feds can put together quite the posse, but don't call them in until Molly's safe. Marconi plays hardball, and he plays for keeps."

"Joe, please don't go. Don't do this," Dani pleaded.

Joe shook Caleb's hand. "I'm sorry I brought this trouble on you." Then he turned to Dani. "Today should've ended differently for us, and I'm sorry it didn't," he said. "You're one helluva woman, Counselor, and you're going to make one helluva rancher." He looked like he wanted to say more, but he stopped, broke his gaze and turned toward Molly's car, keys in hand.

*"Wait!"* Dani returned to the Subaru, gathered up the red-and-black-striped wool blanket that Luther had given them and handed it to Joe. "Luther said it would be cold in the high places tonight." Then she pulled his head down and kissed him, hard. Tears stung her eyes and her throat closed up, making it hard to speak. "You come back to me, Joe Ferguson. I'll never forgive you if you don't."

As Joe drove Molly's car away from Dani and Caleb, he headed into the darkness, and the darkness became so thick he could find no way out of it. It filled him with despair. He kept Molly's cell on the console, and dialed Rico on his own phone. Rico answered on the third ring, his voice terse.

"We think we've found your son," Rico said.

"What do you mean, you *think*?" Joe snapped. "He's either at the school or he isn't."

"Not that simple. It's school break and the kids are all over the place—some stayed at the academy, others are with their parents. According to school officials, Ferg's with your parents and they went to the cape on vacation. They picked him up yesterday. We have a trace on their credit card and agents are going to the hotel as we speak. Hang on a second, there's another call coming in."

The headlights illuminated the dirt road he was supposed to turn down, and he swung Molly's car to the left just as Rico came back on the line. "Ferg's okay, we've got him," he said. "They're all okay, a little startled at being woken up at one a.m. We're going to assign two agents to them until this situation is resolved. Now fill me in. What's happening with Molly? Did you find her?" Rico listened while Joe spoke, then said, "Don't hand yourself over to Marconi. We'll get the feds out there to negotiate for Molly's release. We can stall for time, offer him a reduced sentence, amnesty if he gives us the whole cartel…"

"No," Joe said. "He said he'd kill her if the cops showed up. And you know he will, Rico. Give me time to get her out of there."

"You're making a big mistake."

"Promise me, Rico."

"Listen to me, you lamebrain idiot. As long as he's using Molly for bait to lure you in, she's safe. You give yourself up to Marconi and he'll kill her first, nice and slow, so you can watch, then he'll kill you, then he'll hide himself in Mexico for a while and have a good laugh at what a dumb cop you were. Don't play by his rules. We'll get a SWAT team and some snipers, a negotiator…"

"I don't even know where the hell Molly is. They took her out of here by chopper. Give me until noon tomorrow, Rico. Another twelve hours." The call was breaking up as he moved out of cell phone reception. "Then you can bring in the cavalry."

Rico said something but Joe couldn't make it out, and the call was lost. He drove another mile and then stopped where the dirt road pinched off into a brush-choked cattle trail. The headlights illuminated a jackrabbit on the side of the road, sitting up and staring into the headlights with a startled expression. Joe turned the car around, drove two miles back the way he'd come and then stopped again. Retrieving Molly's cell from the center console he redialed the last caller on her phone, Marconi. The phone rang and rang. Joe became aware of another sound and rolled down his window. He heard the deep *whop-whop-whop* of night air being beaten into submission by an approaching chopper, and a few moments later he saw the landing lights switch on, illuminating the rutted dirt road.

Joe ended the call and thought furiously about what Rico had said, that there would be no dramatic rescue of Molly unless he played by his own rules and got the hell out of here. He laid the phone down. Molly's car was a Mercedes sports coupe, small but built like a tank, and it had a powerful motor. He might be able to outrun the chopper, even over this rough road. He gripped the wheel and floored the accelerator just as Molly's phone rang. He slowed enough to grab it without crashing and answered it.

"Where're you going, Joe?" Marconi asked. "I was just about to hand over your sister."

"I don't even know if she's still alive," Joe said, not slowing down. "Let me talk to her."

"Oh, I'll do better than let you talk to her, Special Agent Ferguson. If you'd slow down a little and let us get ahead of you, I'll show her to you, and if you don't do exactly as I say, you can watch me throw her out of the chopper. What do you think—would she survive a drop of fifty feet or should we get a little higher?"

Joe hit the brakes and the chopper overshot

the car, turned and hovered in position a few moments before rotating sideways. The side door slid open. The Mercedes's headlights dimly illuminated the redheaded woman struggling between two men. Joe's heart constricted. "Okay," he said into the phone. "Don't hurt her. I'll do what you say. Just land the chopper and let her go."

For a few moments there was no response from Marconi as Joe watched his sister being dragged to the very edge of the open doorway. Joe threw the phone aside, cut the ignition and got out of the car. He walked toward the chopper a few steps, holding his arms out in surrender.

"Let her go, Marconi!" he raged, knowing they couldn't hear him over the chopper. "It's me you want!"

The chopper descended slowly until it was on the ground. Molly was jerked back inside and Marconi jumped out first, followed by one of his men, both illuminated in the car's headlights. With a pistol in his hand and a sneer on his face, Marconi's man approached Joe cautiously and patted him down. Took his Glock and cell phone, found his knife and his GPS tracer, and pocketed all of it. Marconi stood to one side, watching with an impassive expression.

"You've got me. Let Molly go," Joe said over the chopper wash.

"Now, why would I want to do that?" Marconi said. "Pilot told us a bad storm was coming and he can't fly us out till it passes. Your sister can provide me with some juicy entertainment tonight while you watch, and I'll kill you at dawn myself, execution-style, or maybe I'll throw you out of the chopper. I haven't decided."

"You son of a bitch. You told me you'd let her go."

"And you believed me. That's how stupid you are. After what you did to me, I'm going to make you suffer, and nothing will hurt you worse than watching what I do to your sister."

"You lay one finger on her and you die," Joe said. He was still looking at and talking to Marconi when he lunged at the man holding a gun on him. He moved so quickly the goon didn't have time to react. In three blinding moves fueled by fury and adrenaline he knocked the gun hand up, stepped in and delivered a kick to the groin that doubled the gunman over. Then with both fists clenched, he landed a blow to the back of his neck that dropped him to the ground as if he'd been poleaxed. The pistol fell and Joe lunged for it, scooping it off the ground, raising the weapon, aiming and squeezing the trigger in one motion and with one singular thought.

Marconi must die.

## CHAPTER SIXTEEN

WHEN THE SHOOTING STARTED, Molly forgot all about her terror, the awful paralyzing fear that had gripped her. All she saw was Marconi pulling a gun on her brother. She heard shots over the swooshing of the chopper blades, saw multiple muzzle flashes in the dark and then she saw them fall, both of them.

"Joseph!" she screamed, and the hand clamped painfully around her arm was nothing. She struggled furiously, wrenched free and jumped from the chopper, running toward her brother. *"Joseph!"*

Joseph was struggling up on one knee, still holding the pistol. Marconi was lying flat on his back. He wasn't moving but the big man on the ground was, and the one who'd had a hold of her in the chopper had jumped out and was in pursuit, while a third hovered in the open door, pistol drawn.

"Get in the car!" Joseph shouted to her as she raced toward him. "Get out of here!"

Molly bent when she reached him and tried

to help him. "Get up, Joseph! *Get up!*" But he was too slow. She grabbed the pistol from Joseph's hand for self-defense. The man on the ground was already on his feet and in her face, dazed but functioning. He slapped her hard and the pistol tumbled to the ground.

"Get 'em in the chopper!" one of them barked, scooping the pistol up. They lifted Marconi and carried him to the chopper, while the third jumped out of the chopper and grabbed Joseph, jerking him to his feet.

"No! Let him go!" Molly shrieked, attacking with her fists, but she was knocked down again. On her knees, she watched her brother being dragged away.

"Joseph!" she screamed.

"Molly, get out of here!" he repeated. "Get in the damned car and go!"

Molly raced to the car's open door and jumped behind the wheel, putting it into gear and driving toward the chopper. The two goons had stuffed Marconi into the helicopter and were now hauling her brother inside. "Joseph, get in the car!" She braked beside the chopper, got out, ran around, grabbed on to him. Grabbed his jacket. A blow to the head pushed her backward and she staggered against the car, the breath knocked out of her. The chopper's side door slid shut and almost immediately it lifted into the air. Molly crumpled to the ground, sobbing.

The chopper rotated as it rose into the dark, and just as it began to fly away, the storm cut loose. First came a powerful gust of wind that tipped the chopper up on one side, then came the torrential downpour, the thunder and lightning. For a few moments she could still see the chopper, the dark bulk of it, the light blinking on the tail, the beam of light streaming from its nose, and then the sight and sound of it were swallowed by the fury of the mountain storm.

She sat sobbing until she had the strength to pull herself to her feet again, then she got inside the car. She was shaking so hard her teeth were chattering. Water dripped from her hair and clothing. She tasted blood on her lower lip. "Oh, Joseph…" she wept. Minutes or hours later, while the storm still rocked her car, her phone rang, rousing her from her shock. She snatched it up. "*Help us, help us, please help us! They have Joseph! He's been shot and we need help!*" she screamed into the cell, not knowing or caring who the caller was.

"*Molly!*"

"*Steven!* Where are you? Please help, *please help*. They've taken Joseph. They landed in the chopper and took him!"

"Molly, where are you?"

"I'm here, I'm here, *I'm here*! On a dirt road—I don't know where. Please help, Steven, please help! They have Joseph!"

STEVEN WAS SITTING in his Wagoneer on the road to the Bow and Arrow, phone in his hand, surrounded by a darkness his headlights didn't begin to penetrate. The rain was coming down in buckets, creating a deafening roar on the roof of the vehicle. The hand that held his phone was shaking. When Molly had answered his call instead of Joe, he'd almost driven right off the road into a ditch the shock had been so great. *Molly!* She had to be sitting in her car. The same car Joe had driven off in, following the kidnapper's instructions. Joe had found her and rescued her and now she had her own phone back and was pleading for help to save her brother.

They had Joseph, but she was safe! Molly was safe! She couldn't tell him where she was, but he knew someone that could. He held the phone to his ear, struggling to connect with her. "Molly," he said in a voice that broke, so great was his relief that she was alive. "Listen to me. Stay right there. I'm coming to get you. I'll be there soon. Just stay inside your car and lock the doors. I'll call you back in a couple minutes."

Then he made two calls, the first to Pony, the other to Sheriff Conroy.

MAPS WERE SPREAD over the kitchen table at the Bow and Arrow, and all the adults were bent over them, except for Ramalda, who was making another pot of coffee. Caleb, Pony, Dani, Badger, Charlie, Jessie and Guthrie. Roon and Jimmy were the only boys in the kitchen, and nobody was paying any attention to them. Jimmy was working on his goat cheese because it made him feel better to stay busy. He was upset that Molly was missing but determined to make a good batch of goat cheese for when she was found. Roon was standing on the edge of the ring of light around the table, silently listening to everything that was being said.

"This is where we found her car," Caleb said, pointing to a spot on the map. "Not five miles from here, just before you reach the ranch road."

"That's more'n five miles," Badger said, bending closer and tracing the map with one gnarled finger.

"Joe was told to take that dirt road just this side of Katy Junction," Dani said. "I think we should go after him. Call the feds, the state police and the local sheriff, and go after him. We can't wait until noon tomorrow. We need to do something right now, before he's killed!"

"The road you're talking about is here," Jessie said, tracing with her finger. "It gets rougher and climbs up into the foothills. Local ranchers used to use it to access the high pastures. I don't think it's drivable for very far, but if that's where he went, that's where Molly's car will be. And I agree with Dani. We can't wait and do nothing. We need to call in the cavalry."

"If they were traveling by chopper they could be anywhere in these mountains," Caleb said. "We need to contact the authorities, you're right about that. If there's a chopper flying around out there, it had to have come from somewhere. I couldn't get an answer from Yellowstone Helotours, just their answering machine."

Pony's cell rang and she answered it, spoke briefly, listened for several long moments and said, "Steven, it's the road this side of Katy Junction, the only one that leads up into the foothills. We'll contact the authorities and head out there ourselves to meet you, too." She ended the call. "Steven's almost to Katy Junction. He just called Molly's phone thinking he might get Joe, but Molly answered. She's all right. She's been released." Before everyone could break into cheers, Pony quickly added, "She told him they had Joe, he'd been shot, they took him in a chopper and she couldn't tell Steven where she was. He's going to call Sheriff Conroy and tell him what's happening, and then he's going to drive down that dirt road, find Molly and bring her here."

"I have to do something," Dani said abruptly.

"You stay put," Caleb said. "It's a helluva storm brewing. Wait here for the sheriff, we'll go meet Steven and bring Molly back here. Might be an hour before Conroy gets here in this storm. He'll notify the state police, and they'll alert the feds."

"I'll get the rifle from my truck," Guthrie said.

"I have one, too," Badger said. "I'll fetch it along, just in case." A flash of lightning and a low rumble of thunder made Badger pause while following Guthrie out the kitchen door. "Here it comes, just like I said," Badger commented. "First thunderstorm of the year, and it couldn't be worse timing."

Jimmy watched the men leave the kitchen and felt a frisson of fear and excitement run through him. He finished mixing the chives into the chèvre and began portioning it into recycled yogurt containers, ending up with two quarts of fresh chèvre. Dani had paid no attention to his efforts. She was still standing at the table, staring down at the map, her face very pale. The encouraging words spoken by Pony and Jessie had had no effect on her.

"I can't stand waiting around and doing nothing," she said, as if talking to the map. "I can't stand not knowing if Joe's dead or alive. I just can't."

Jimmy carried the yogurt containers over to the table. "I finished the goat cheese, Dani. It came out good."

She looked up at him with a blank expression, then forced a smile. "That's good, Jimmy."

"You want to try some?"

She shook her head. "Not right now, but thanks."

Roon chose that moment to depart. Without a word to anyone he walked out the kitchen door. Jimmy turned and followed on his heels.

"You boys try to get some sleep," Pony's voice said after them into the darkness. "Molly will not need an audience when she gets here, and we will not know anything about Joe until morning."

Jimmy had to half run to keep up with Roon's big strides as he crossed the yard. "Whatever you're thinking about doing, count me in," he said.

"No," Roon replied, not looking at him.

"If you don't let me come along, I'll tell Badger and Pony that you're up to something."

Roon stopped and rounded on him. "You heard Pony. It's late. Go to bed."

"You know where they took Joe, don't you?" Jimmy said, his heart beating fast.

"You would, too, if you'd have been paying attention instead of making your stupid goat cheese." Roon continued on toward the school building with Jimmy close behind. The other boys were still up, sitting on the floor around another large geological survey map they'd pulled out of the school library.

"Roon knows where they are," Jimmy announced as soon they came through the door. His words electrified the other boys. They jumped up and demanded to know everything. They gathered around Roon, who, at their vocal insistence, reluctantly laid the big map out on a table. He picked up a yellow highlighter and bent over the map.

"This is where Molly's car was found, and way over here is the nearest cell phone tower, the only one that serves this area, and it's spotty service." He made two X-marks on the map. "The cell phone signal was strong enough by Molly's car so that Joe was able to receive a phone call from the kidnapper on Molly's phone, which was left in her car by the kidnapper. We know all the dead zones in this area where our phones won't work. There are lots of them and we've found them all, over the past year."

The boys nodded in agreement and bent closer.

"Here," Ralph said, pointing.

"I can't get any signal here," said Jimmy.

They pored over the map, pointing out dead zones. For every area that was a designated dead zone, Roon filled in a big yellow circle.

"We can eliminate all those places," he said. "Now, where can you be up in these mountains and see that section of black road where Molly's car was abandoned? Where could you be where you'd spot Caleb's emergency flashers and the headlights from two cars? Where could you go and have room enough to park a chopper and still get good cell phone reception?"

The boys studied the map intently. "Here," they all said simultaneously, stabbing their fingers in the same spot.

"Right near the old line camp," Roon concurred. "Bet you anything that chopper is sitting up in that high meadow by the line camp, and that's where Joe is. They can't fly in this weather. They'd have to put down in the same spot where they'd been watching the road."

"So, we're going up there?" Ralph said. "What'll we do when we get there?"

"Rescue Joe, stupid," Jimmy replied.

"How?"

"We'll have to come up with a plan," Roon said.

Another crack of thunder made them look up. "Should we leave now or after the storm?"

"We'll go to bed just like any other night. Pony'll check on us in another hour or so. At three a.m., we'll meet in the horse barn."

"We're *riding* up there?"

"We could take the four-wheelers, but horses are quiet and they can go where four-wheelers can't. There'll still be snow up there, in places that the four-wheelers couldn't get through. If we leave by three, we'll be there at first light. We'll tether the horses and walk the last of it and then scope things out," Roon said. "We don't know how many are up there, but we can assume they all have guns."

"And we *don't*," Jimmy pointed out.

"We have one," Roon corrected. "An air rifle that shoots buffalo tranquilizers."

The boys stared at him in awe. "Won't that kill 'em?" Jimmy said.

"I'll adjust the dosage and preload ten darts. They'll get staggering dopey drunk and fall down. That's how it works with the buffalo and longhorn cattle."

"Okay, so you shoot the first Mob guy, he hollers and screams and all the others grab their guns and shoot us," Jimmy said. "That's stupid!"

"You could try poisoning them with your goat cheese if you think that would work better," Roon countered. Jimmy flushed at the snickers. "The rest of you will have to stay hidden and figure out ways to lure them away from the group one at a time until I can get a dart into them."

"Out of earshot so nobody else can hear them holler when they get darted? Far enough so the drug affects them before they can make it back to the group?" Ralph said. "Jimmy's right. That's a stupid plan."

"You have a better one?" Roon asked.

The boys looked at each other. "No," they said in a subdued chorus.

"Then we'll meet in the barn at three. Anyone who doesn't want to go doesn't have to. If you come up with any ideas of how to distract them, we can brainstorm on the ride up the mountain. Jimmy, maybe you could bring your bow and arrows, just in case. You're a pretty good shot."

Nobody snickered at Roon's comment this time. This was for real, and it was dangerous. Roon looked at each of them in turn and it seemed to Jimmy that they all stood a little taller that night. They weren't boys anymore.

BADGER AND CHARLIE sat in the backseat of the Suburban as Caleb sped down the ranch road ahead of the thunderstorm. "Roon's up to something," Badger commented after a particularly bright flash of lightning lit the sky.

"Yep," Charlie agreed. "The way he was standing in the kitchen, studying that map, listening to everything we said, he's plotting. Don't blame him a bit. Sitting around waiting for a miracle to happen seems like a poor way to get Joe back. And Joe's got himself hurt again, which makes matters more urgent. He's turning into a regular human colander. What time's it now?"

"About ten minutes later than when you last asked," Badger said, bracing himself against the bumps in the road. "Close to midnight. We might get to the cutoff before Steven does, the rate we're traveling."

"If we don't crash first," Charlie said. "Don't know why you bothered to bring that old rifle. You couldn't hit the broad side of a barn with it when you were young."

"I've had a few years to improve my aim."

"You've had a lot more than a few years to slow down to a crawl."

"Being quick doesn't matter near as much as being steady," Badger said. "Coolness and a steady nerve will always beat quick. Take yer time and you'll only need to pull the trigger once."

"If you don't die of old age first," Charlie said. "Going up against the Mob, I'd rather have a gatling gun, myself."

"The cutoff's just up ahead," Badger said as

a bolt of lightning streaked sideways across the valley. Caleb slowed and turned off onto the dirt road.

"There're fresh tire tracks but I can't tell if there's one set or two and it's about to start pouring any second now," Caleb said. He drove as quick as he could until he spotted taillights up ahead. He hit the brakes hard. "That's Steven's car," he said. They pulled up behind it and everyone piled out, grabbing their weapons, but the weapons weren't needed. Steven had walked ahead of his car and was standing beside Molly's Mercedes. Molly was in his arms. They clung tightly to each other, oblivious to the storm. To the rain that started pouring down just as they arrived. To the crashing thunder and brilliant flashes of lightning. To the gusts of wind that lashed the searchers as they approached.

"They're gone," Steven said while they stood in the full fury of the storm. "They got who they came for and they're gone." His voice was calm, Badger thought, for a man whose fiancée had been kidnapped and whose future brother-in-law was probably dead, or as good as.

Steven was the calm in the eye of the storm.

AFTER THE MEN LEFT, Dani collapsed into a chair at the kitchen table and buried her face in her hands, overwhelmed. She wanted to cry, to release all the pent-up tension, but the tears wouldn't come. She was paralyzed. She felt a hand on her shoulder and Pony spoke gently in her ear.

"Come and sit by the fire with us," she said. "Bring your dogs in. We will wait together."

Pony had started a fire in the living room and Jessie was there, too. They sat together in the flickering light of the flames while the thunderstorm lashed the ranch house. They shared hot toddies that Ramalda had made and wondered what was happening out in the darkness and the rain. Dani closed her hands around the warm mug and tried to think positive thoughts, but it was impossible. Marconi had released Molly and taken Joe, and from what Molly had told Steven, Joe had been shot. As if he hadn't been hurt enough by this heartless mobster! What had possessed Joe to become a drug enforcement agent? Why would anyone want to spend their days dealing with criminals like Marconi? Did he like the excitement? Did he think he was making a difference? If he survived this nightmare, would he want to go back to that job?

And why was she even thinking thoughts of the future, when Joe might already be dead?

Pony placed another log in the fireplace. Dani tried to swallow a small sip of the hot toddy. It smelled of apple-pie spices and honey, but the

whiskey fumes made her eyes water and the
small swallow burned going down. She stared
into the flames until they shimmered through
a veil of tears.

The storm was fierce. The flashes of lightning, the thunder that shook the old ranch house,
the torrential rains that drummed on the roof almost obliterated the sound of the vehicles driving into the yard, but the cow dogs and her own
two goldens raised their heads from their paws
and pricked their ears. They jumped up as one
entity and moved to the door. Dani pushed past
them and ran out into the deluge to where Steven had parked. Molly sat in the passenger seat
and Dani wrenched open the passenger-side
door. Her tears were lost in the rain and it no
longer mattered that she tried to be strong and
brave because at that moment she was neither,
as Molly reached for her and choked out the
words, "They took Joseph!" Dani could only
sob in response.

Steven helped them both into the house, and
once inside, Pony whisked Molly upstairs to get
her into dry clothes, leaving the blanket that had
been draped around Molly's shoulders in a heap
on the kitchen floor. Dani picked it up. It was
the red-and-black-striped wool blanket Luther
Makes Elk had given them, her and Joe, when
they'd left his place. The same blanket Molly

had given Luther Makes Elk just that morning. It was wet and smelled of wool and she held it in her arms as if somehow it could connect her to Joe and keep him safe. She took it back into the living room and sat with it in her lap, her two dogs at her feet, staring into the flames. She felt numb all over as she listened to Steven answer questions, listened to the conversations around her and waited for Molly to come back downstairs. But in her mind she was already out in the stormy night, up on the mountain, searching for Joe.

THE CHOPPER PILOT barely made it back to the clearing on the mountain before all hell broke loose. The heavens opened up, the rain and hail came down and a strong gust of wind nearly flipped the chopper as he was touching down. Marconi's men were too busy arguing amongst themselves to pay much attention to the rough flight or how close they'd come to crashing. Half wanted to keep flying north to the border before the feds arrived, the other half wanted to land until the storm passed. It was the pilot who finally ended the argument by saying, "Gentlemen, we either land right now or we crash, so unless one of you decides to shoot me, I'm landing this bird."

From what Joe could make out, none of Marconi's men had any grasp of how badly Marconi had been hurt. Joe had aimed for the heart and, if he'd come anywhere close, Marconi might be dead. Nobody was paying much attention to him *or* Joe. They'd hastily bound Joe's hands behind him with duct tape but that was all. Joe had clenched his fists tight when they bound him, and he could feel a slight play in the wrapping of the tape.

Now they were safely on the ground, engine shut down, chopper blade slowing, violent winds buffeting the big machine as the lightning flashed and hail hammered against the chopper's metal skin. One of them slid the door open; another jumped out and made a run into the wall of rain and darkness. The pilot was escorted off at gunpoint by a third man, the one Joe had tackled. A few minutes later the first man returned and helped the other gunman carry Marconi off.

Joe was halfway out the chopper door, intending to make a run for it, when the man who'd taken the pilot returned. He held a flashlight, shining it in his eyes, and waved his pistol back and forth in a menacing fashion. "I wouldn't try that if I were you. The only reason you're still alive is because Marconi wants to kill you himself."

Joe was prodded at gunpoint through the

pouring rain and shoved inside a small log cabin. Someone had lit an oil lamp at the table and the soft glow illuminated the chopper pilot, seated at the table, brim of his baseball cap dripping water. In the lamplight, the recognition between them was instant. It was Nash, the same pilot who'd flown them to look for Custer's mares the day before, the pilot who flew for Yellowstone Helotours. No wonder Molly had stopped her car and gotten out when she spotted the chopper. She probably thought he and Dani were on board searching for more clues as to who killed the wild mustangs.

Joe was shoved down in another chair at the table. Marconi had been deposited on a lower bunk on the far wall and two of his goons were huddled over him.

"Is he dead?" Joe heard one of them say over the wild thunderstorm raging outside.

"Dead men don't bleed, you idiot," the other replied.

"We gotta stop the bleeding. What'll we do if he dies?"

"Same as we always planned to do—get the hell out of here before the feds catch us."

"What about the money Marconi promised us?"

"You kidding? If we get out of this mess alive

we'll be lucky. Get me something to stuff in the wound—a dish rag, an old sock, anything!"

While they fussed over Marconi, the third gunman, the one whose weapon Joe had used to shoot Marconi, sat down at the table. He pulled a flask out of his pocket and laid his pistol down to uncap it. He took a long swallow, screwed the cap back on and slipped the flask back inside his jacket. Then he picked up his pistol, aimed it casually at Joe and smiled an ugly smile.

"One way or another, this night isn't going to end well for you," he promised.

# CHAPTER SEVENTEEN

ROON WAS WIDE-AWAKE. All of the boys were. Pony checked on them at one a.m. and they all feigned sleep, but they lay awake through the storm. They heard the return of Caleb's Suburban and Steven's vehicle, and then a little later, the arrival of the sheriff's car. They were filled with adrenaline at the thought of what was to come. By two a.m. the sheriff's car had left, presumably to rally his troops and return at dawn since nothing could be done in the dark. By three a.m. the heavy line storms had tapered off in intensity and Roon rose, told the boys to get ready but remain in the building while he crept down to the barn. The air rifle and tranquilizer were kept in the locked cabinet in the tack room, but he knew where the key was. Jessie had told him the last time he'd had to fetch it for her when they were heading out to work on a longhorn cow that had hoof rot.

The darts were in the cabinet, as well, and he wore his headlamp while he filled the darts with the tranquilizer. He used one-quarter the dosage they would use for an adult buffalo. He figured that amount would have considerable effect on a two-hundred-pound human. But he wasn't concerned about side effects—these were dangerous men. They had taken Steven's woman and now they had her brother, and they deserved no mercy.

He had just finished loading the last syringe when he heard the barn door open and close. He shut off his headlamp and stood in the dark, holding the rifle and slipping the darts inside the book pack he'd brought. Soft footsteps and the beam of a flashlight passed the door of the tack room and continued on to the stall that held the orphaned foal and the mare that was fostering it. He heard a woman's voice. Dani. She was speaking softly, first to the mare and then the foal. She was telling the foal how handsome and brave Custer, the band stallion, had been. How he had kept them safe and watched over them, how she had known him for years and how his life and the life of his little band of mares had changed her own life forever. Roon wished she would hurry up and go back to bed. Instead, he heard strange noises and realized that Dani was crying, sobbing. He opened the tack room door quietly and peeked out. She was crumpled in a ball outside the stall, arms on her knees and head buried in her arms, shoulders heaving.

This wasn't good. Roon set the air rifle and pack down and crept out of the tack room to the door of the barn. He opened and closed it loudly. Dani raised her head and saw him walking toward the stall. She quickly wiped her cheeks and struggled to her feet.

"Roon. What are you doing up? It's three a.m.," she said.

"I always check on the barn at three a.m.," Roon said. "It is the weakest hour, when the young and the sick sometimes drift away." He looked into the stall. "Not this time, though. She is strong, and getting stronger by the day. But you are weak. You should get some rest before the dawn."

Dani nodded. "I was just heading back," she said. "Thank you for all you've done, Roon. Saving that foal is the one good thing that's happened in the past few days."

"There will be others," Roon said.

"I hope so," she said, but there was a look of hopelessness about her. She probably thought she would never see Joe again, but she was wrong about that. "Good night, Roon," she said, and left the barn carrying her flashlight. Roon waited until he was sure she was back at the house before pulling his phone out of his pocket and contacting the boys.

It's time, he messaged.

DANI CLIMBED THE steps to the porch with great weariness. She sat on the wall bench and looked out at the night. The rain and strong wind had mostly passed, and the storm was a distant rumble moving eastward, over the mountains. In the morning the ranch would be crawling with federal agents and local police. Right now, all was quiet, just the drip of rainwater off the eaves. She could have gone back to her room but she would have only lain in bed awake, waiting for dawn.

She went inside. Everyone had gone to bed to get what rest they could, but the coffee in the pot was still hot. She poured herself another cup and carried it back out to the porch along with the wool blanket Ramalda had hung behind the kitchen stove to dry. She sat with the blanket over her shoulders and the mug cradled in her hands. The minutes turned into an hour, and then a hoarse whisper came out of the dark and roused her from her meditation.

Badger's voice, trying to be quiet.

"I can't get my boot on, dang it. My sock's all folded up in the toe!"

"Hush up, you'll wake the dead," Charlie whispered back. "It's gonna be light soon. We have to make tracks before everybody rolls out of bed. Thought you said you wouldn't fall asleep."

"You weren't no better at staying awake, and now we might've lost 'em."

Dani sat up, straining to see in the murky darkness. It sounded like the men were coming out of the old cook shack they bunked in, but why were they wandering around at this time of night? And where were they going? She set her cold mug of coffee aside and rose to her feet, gathering the blanket around her like a cloak. She could hear them walking toward the barn, still whispering hoarsely.

She followed them, and when she entered the barn there was a light on at the far end where the tack room was. There were noises from within and then Badger and Charlie emerged, carrying saddles and bridles. They stopped short when they saw her. "Wherever you're going, I'm coming with you," she said.

"You can't," Badger replied. "Ain't safe."

"If you don't let me go with you, I'll wake everybody up," Dani threatened.

"These here are snuffy horses we'll be riding," Charlie said. "Mustangs dropped off by the BLM for the boys to gentle. You could get pitched off pretty easy, and where we're going, it's almost a vertical trail. A tough ride for an experienced hand."

"Saddle me a horse," Dani demanded.

Badger glared at her. "No time to argue. Saddle her a horse, Charlie." To Dani he said, "It'll be whatever Charlie's rope catches first. These horses can be dauncy," he warned. "The boys took all the broke ones."

"The boys are gone?"

"We figure they're riding up to the line camp and they got an hour's jump on us."

"So that's why Roon was out in the barn," Dani said.

"They must figure that chopper's up near the line camp and they've headed up to rescue who-ever needs rescuing. We'll have to ride fast to catch up."

"I won't slow you down, I promise."

Badger nodded. "Grab a saddle and bridle and follow us to the back paddock."

Ten minutes later Charlie had roped three of the snorting, stampeding horses they'd startled into wakefulness and he and Badger were sad-dling them. Badger had a rifle and he slid it into a saddle scabbard. Charlie was unarmed. When Dani figured out which horse was to be hers, she used the leather straps behind the saddle to securely fasten the rolled-up blanket. The mus-tang shied in circles around Badger as she tied it on, but she followed the horse around until the job was done. She wasn't leaving Luther Makes Elk's blanket behind.

"We'll lead 'em out a way, to where the trail

heads up toward the pass," Badger said, handing her the reins to the bay horse, who looked very excited about the prospect of a predawn ride.

"What's his name?" she asked.

"Damned if I know," Badger growled. "We just got this new batch in last week."

Dani attempted to give the horse a tentative pat on the neck and he flung his head up in alarm and shied away from her. "Easy," she said, then followed the two men out of the corral, her horse dancing at the end of the reins. They walked a fair distance before Badger said it was time to mount up. Dani stopped her horse, who stepped nervously around her, snorting and tossing his head.

"You think he's going to buck me off?" she asked as they prepared to mount their horses.

"He does look hostile," Badger replied.

Badger pulled his own horse's head around tight toward him when he stabbed his boot into the stirrup and his horse jumped forward, causing him to lose his balance and stumble backward with a curse. It took him three tries and a big struggle, complete with some painful moaning and cursing, to get his leg over the saddle. Dani observed this and decided if Badger could ride a wild mustang with all that arthritis pain and a bad hip, she could dang well do it, too.

But it wasn't lost on her that if Charlie hadn't come over and held her horse while she awkwardly hoisted herself into the saddle, she would never have gotten aboard. "Just keep this mustang reined in tight. Don't let him have his head. This horse wants to run," Charlie told her before letting go of the reins. "He'll get tired out quick enough once we get goin'. The trail gets real steep in a mile or so. If you can stay in the saddle for that long, you'll have 'er licked. Just follow after Badger. I'll be right behind you."

Without further talk, they were off. Dani's horse was a bunched-up ball of energy underneath her, and it only took five steps before she realized it would be a miracle if she stayed on this horse for even the next five steps. She felt a pang of real fear and then she thought about Joe, and she grit her teeth and took firm hold of the reins. "You're not going to get rid of me so easy," she murmured softly into the nervous flicker of her horse's ears. "Just be a good boy, okay? This is my very first horseback ride."

Her horse didn't buck or jump sideways, but he pranced off as if on tightly coiled springs, snorting at every step, and Dani knew she was riding a potential rocket that could easily blast her to the moon. She caught up to Badger at once, and thankfully the trail closed in and steepened, so there was nothing her horse could do except charge up to Badger's horse and then follow behind. The trail that she'd thought was steep in the beginning was flat in comparison to what lay ahead. Within fifteen minutes she'd dropped the tightly clenched reins and was holding on to the saddle horn with all her strength as her horse lunged upward. She hoped the saddle didn't slide off because if it did she was a goner.

"Yer doin' jest fine," she heard Charlie reassure her, but she was reasonably sure he was lying.

ROON HELD HIS hand up to stop the boys behind him. They reined in their tired horses and let them take a breather while he looked through the fringe of trees at the edge of the meadow. The whole time they'd been climbing up to the line camp he'd been racking his brain for a way to cause an effective diversion, but nothing came to mind. And now, here it was, right in front of him. It was a miracle, sent by White Buffalo Woman and Luther Makes Elk.

"Buffalo," he said. "Two o'clock. I count eight."

Jimmy kicked his horse up alongside, craning to see. "Pony says buffalo are scared of people on horseback."

"That's right," Roon said. "That's why we use the four-wheelers to move them around, but we can use their fear of horses to our advantage.

We'll move the buffalo ahead of us, toward the cabin. We'll stay behind them and get as close as we can. We have to do this quick, because as soon as it gets light, they'll fly that chopper out of here."

Martin stood in his stirrups, peering into the murk. "Can you see the helicopter?"

"No," Roon said. "But it's there, and so are they. I smell wood smoke." He looked behind at the other boys. "Keep your phones in your pants pockets, but make sure the ringers are off. We'll communicate by text message."

"Traditional Crow warrior tactics." Jimmy snickered nervously, adjusting the sling around his shoulder that held his bow and quiver of arrows.

"Beats smoke signals," Ralph said.

"Do we have a plan yet?"

"We do now. Those buffalo were sent to help us," Roon said. "I'm going to get around them and find a good spot on the other side of the creek from the cabin. Give me ten minutes to get into position. I'll text you once I'm in place. Then start the buffalo moving. Get them running, if you can, but don't make any human noise. Don't give yourselves away. The noise'll bring one or two or maybe even all of Marconi's men outside to see what's coming. I'll shoot them with the tranquilizer darts as they exit."

"What if they start shooting at us?"

"Be like the deer, don't give them a target," Roon said. "Once the buffalo start running toward the cabin, get off your horses and hide in the woods. Split up. Become invisible and crafty like the coyote. These are city slickers—they don't know what's out here, so every little noise will sound like a big scary grizzly to them. If everything falls apart, hide in the woods, keep out of sight and make your way back to the ranch." He looked at all of them, each in turn. "We can do this," he said. "We *will* do this. We are the children of the raven. We are warriors."

Roon nudged his horse forward, holding the air rifle crosswise in front of him. The boys watched him ride off.

"Be careful," Jimmy called after him in his thin, reedy voice, but Roon didn't pause or look back.

## CHAPTER EIGHTEEN

DANI WAS AT the limit of her endurance, and still the trail climbed. The horses lunged upward. They were plowing through patches of snow, deep patches that other horses and riders had already struggled through, breaking trail and making passage easier for them. It was light enough now so she could see the color of Badger's faded denim jacket and the time-worn shabbiness of it. He hadn't looked back once to make sure she was still there, but then, he'd made it pretty plain that he hadn't wanted her along. He was worried about the boys, and she understood that. She felt it, too. Fear for the boys, and for Joe.

She clung to the saddle horn with all her strength and alternately wrapped her arms around the sweaty neck of her horse when it seemed he was clawing his way vertically into the sky. She praised him when she could, which wasn't nearly often enough for the heroic effort he was making. Every muscle in her body was shaking when they finally crested the trail and

Badger reined in his horse and raised his hand, halting them abruptly.

"Listen. Hear that?" he said.

All Dani heard was the deep, gasping breaths of three lathered-up and winded horses and the loud pounding of her own heart, but Charlie, behind her, said, "Yep. That's buffalo, and they're running hard."

Badger pulled his rifle from the scabbard and jacked a round into the chamber. The sharp sound made all three horses jump. He looked back at her for the first time. "You wait here," he said, steely-eyed.

"But—"

*"Wait here,"* he repeated, his voice like a whiplash. Dani knew better than to argue. She nodded, dry mouthed with fear. She knew death was riding on this dawn.

Charlie nudged his horse around hers. "We don't have much time to waste if we're goin' to help them boys," he said.

Badger drew a deep breath and blew it out in disgust. "Damn that Roon. He always was a wild one, wild as these horses," he said. "Well, come on. We best get to doing what needs to be done."

Two old men, Dani thought as she watched them ride into the early light. Two brave old men. But what could they possibly do to thwart a bunch of professional killers? What could those boys do? She had to hold her horse back tightly to keep him from following Charlie and Badger as they rode toward the meadow's edge. She could hear it then, finally. The low rumbling sound of distant thunder. So that's what running buffalo sounded like, she thought.

Like a thunderstorm at dawn's first light.

ROON KNEW HE had to get close to the cabin porch in order for the air rifle to be effective. He couldn't shoot from a hundred yards. He left his horse back in the woods and crept toward the edge of the mountain stream, searching for something to hide behind that would give him an unobstructed view of the cabin door. He found the perfect spot, a tree that had fallen half into the creek at an angle, and he hunkered down behind the big trunk and began laying the medicated darts in a row on the ground within easy reach. He'd have to reload quickly, and his aim would need to be true. He wouldn't get a second chance. He'd tranquilized half a dozen buffalo and longhorn steers for Jessie over the past year while helping her with the vet work, but shooting a man with a tranquilizer dart would be a first for him.

When Molly had been brought to the ranch after being rescued, he'd eavesdropped on the conversations in the kitchen and learned there were four gunmen in the chopper—Marconi and three of his goons. He knew the chopper pilot wasn't one of them because they'd hijacked the chopper, so altogether, counting Joe, there were six people crammed inside that little line camp. If the chopper pilot came out and prepared to fire up the chopper, he'd have to tranquilize him, too. That possibility worried Roon, because he wasn't sure the dose in the darts was safe for humans.

He picked up the rifle, loaded the first dart into the chamber and retrieved his cell phone from his jacket pocket. It was still dark enough that the little screen on his phone seemed alarmingly bright when he typed in his text message to the boys and hit the Send button. Then he tucked the phone back in his pocket, laid the barrel of the air rifle across the top of the log to steady it and drew a deep, slow breath to calm his nerves. The next few minutes would be critical. He heard the first birdsong fill the morning air and the sky to the east began to glow a clear, pale yellow.

Then he heard the buffalo.

NASH HAD BEEN in some tight spots before but none quite as dire as this. From the moment those four city slickers had hired him for a so-called private tour of Yellowstone, his normally mundane and borderline boring day had been turned upside down, but once airborne there was no turning back. First Nash was ordered to cruise around south of Bozeman, checking out the ranch lands and scenery and paying abnormally close attention to the community of Gallatin Gateway. It seemed like he'd been flying in pointless circles for over an hour before Marconi, in the copilot's seat, had spotted a distinctive red Mercedes sports coupe leaving Gallatin Gateway and speeding east. He'd let out a victorious whoop, said, "Finally!" then pulled a pistol out of his jacket, aimed it at Nash and said, "Follow that car."

Not hard to do on the road that headed toward Katy Junction. The Mercedes was the only vehicle on it. Getting around in front of the car had proved a little more difficult because the driver had to be topping ninety miles an hour, but the Helotours chopper was pretty quick, and when Nash set it down in the middle of the road, the driver of the Mercedes had plenty of time to stop. Plenty of time to turn around and speed off again, too, but she didn't. Only later did Nash learn that Molly Ferguson had thought Ben Comstock was on board the chopper, and maybe her brother Joe and best friend, Dani.

That's why she'd stopped so willingly, gotten out of her car and approached the chopper.

Snatching her was effortless. All Marconi did was jump out, walk a few steps toward her, wave that damned pistol and say, "Molly Ferguson? You better come with us if you want to see your brother alive again."

Marconi had taken Molly's cell phone from her, entered her number into his own phone and put Molly's back inside the red Mercedes. Then he'd gotten back on the helicopter and ordered Nash to find a place to land where he could stake out the car using a pair of the Helotours binoculars. The old line camp at the Bow and Arrow, high on the mountainside, turned out to be the perfect location and the meadow made for a safe landing area. The wait for Molly Ferguson's abandoned car to be discovered just before dark seemed endless, and Nash was held at gunpoint the entire time. Oddly, they hadn't searched him. Inside his jeans pocket were his car keys and a small Swiss Army knife.

That jackknife was what he was thinking about now, sitting at the table with the gunman and Joe Ferguson and listening to the last of the thunderstorm receding into the distance. He was thinking about his knife and how easily it would cut the duct tape that was binding Ferguson's wrists. Ferguson had been shot in the arm and had been bleeding slow but steady as the overnight hours passed, but the arm wasn't broken and he'd kept working his wrists against the duct tape when Marconi's man wasn't paying attention. Nash wasn't sure how effective Ferguson's efforts were, but he did know the odds of escape were against them.

What would happen if Marconi died? Would Marconi's men just shoot Ferguson and then force him to fly them out in the chopper? The minutes dragged like hours as dawn approached. The storm passed, the winds died, the rain stopped and a thick oppressive silence filled the cabin, broken only by the intermittent thrashing and moaning of the man on the bunk and the slow drip of Ferguson's blood onto the cabin floor. Nash sat as unmoving as Ferguson, both reluctant to draw attention to themselves, both hoping for a chance to escape. Marconi's three men had been sharing occasional sips from a flask but none showed any signs of falling asleep. As dawn crept closer, both captives knew their time was running out.

The gunman seated at the table suddenly jerked upright, raising his pistol.

"Listen," he said, his eyes darting around. "Did you hear that?"

"Bear, probably," Nash responded in his laconic voice. "There's a big boar grizzly that hangs out on this mountain. Killed one of Jessie Weaver's mares a year or so back. Grizzlies move around a lot in spring. Probably smells the blood and he's looking for a good meal."

The gunman glanced nervously to where Marconi lay, with the other two men seated in chairs beside the bunk. "He dead yet?"

"No, I'm not dead yet, you dumb bastard," Marconi choked out, surprising all of them. "Get that chopper fired up. We have to get out of here before daylight. Help me up, you fools, and get Ferguson in there first. I want to be the one to push him out when we're airborne. If it's the last thing I ever do, I want to watch him die."

While the two goons assisted Marconi, the gunman at the table pushed out of his chair and stood. "I hear something," he repeated. "It's not thunder. Something big, coming toward the cabin."

"Better go see if it's that big grizzly," Nash suggested. "Fire a few shots—you might be able to scare him off long enough so's we can make it to the chopper without being eaten alive." As the gunman moved toward the door, Nash reached into his pocket, slipped out his jackknife, flipped open the blade and caught Joe's eye. Joe read the message loud and clear.

*It's now or never.*

DANI WAS COLD. Steam rose from her horse's lathered shoulders and flanks. She felt the rapid spring of his rib cage between her calves as the mustang regained his breath after the steep climb. He was quiet at the moment, but she had a feeling the calm wouldn't last. As soon as he recovered, he'd be wondering where his friends went and wanting to catch up. She unlaced the wool blanket from the back of the saddle, un-rolled it and tied two of the ends around her shoulders, making a cape that she arranged over the horse's rump, so that they both might ben-efit from its warmth.

The muted thunder of the running buffalo was fading. She wondered how far Badger and Charlie had already traveled. It was still murky dark but there was a glow in the eastern sky. Morning was near.

Her horse snorted and tossed his head while taking two quick steps sideways. "Easy," she soothed. "Whoa now, easy." But the brush of the wool blanket against his flank as he moved was enough to make him snort again in alarm and jump around in a big circle. "Easy, boy, whoa," she soothed as she held the reins in one hand and attempted to untie the tight knot in the blanket with the other. The mustang was about to explode, but Dani couldn't get the knot undone and didn't dare try to pull the blanket off over her head. Should she dismount?

"Whoa, easy..." she repeated, giving up on the knot and grabbing the reins in both hands, pulling him in a big circle. He halted abruptly, threw his head back, drew a huge lungful of air and shrieked at the top of his lungs. It was a full-voiced scream of panic at being left behind by his equine companions. In spite of Dani's tight death grip on the reins he took off like he'd been catapulted from the back of an aircraft carrier, moving in the direction Charlie and Badger had gone. In three great lunges he was traveling at warp speed, his hoofbeats sounding like machine gun fire as he sprinted down the meadow at a full gallop.

*"Geronimo!"* Dani cried out impulsively, inadvertently naming the mustang in that one wild moment, then she leaned over his withers, pressing herself against his neck, holding on tight to the reins and hoping he didn't fall or they'd both be killed. Luther's red-and-black-striped blanket floated out behind them like a pennant, the landscape blurred past and the wind stung tears from her eyes and tore the breath from her lungs. "Hang on, Joe!" she cried into the mustang's flattened-back ears as she herself hung on for dear life, hoping beyond all hope that Joe was still alive.

THE GUNMAN HAD just stepped out of the cabin when he heard the terrible, unearthly scream from across the meadow and stopped dead in his tracks, peering nervously into the murky light. He took three quick steps, jumped off the end of the porch and rounded the corner of the cabin to look toward the source of the sounds, pistol at the ready. Whatever was coming toward him was starting to shake the ground. He was scanning for a target when something struck him hard in the neck. He staggered, whirled around and slapped his hand to the side of his neck, tearing out a very large dart. He flung it to the ground with a high-pitched scream as panicked as the one he'd just heard in the distance, then turned and plunged back toward the cabin. He charged up the last three steps and kicked the door inward just as two men charged out.

INSIDE THE CABIN, all hell had broken loose. The men trying to help Marconi outside abandoned him when both prisoners jumped up simultaneously from the table and bolted for the door. Nash slashed the tape binding Ferguson's wrists and at the same moment jerked the cabin door inward just as it was kicked from outside. A bullet whipped past Joe's head from behind and hit the incoming gunman just as Nash tackled him. They fell together, blocking the doorway in a tangled heap. Joe spun and charged Marconi's man before he could fire again, hoping to give Nash time to escape. He rammed him hard enough to knock him down, but the second gunman gave him a sharp rap with the butt of his weapon that sent Joe crashing to the floor. He lay stunned, fighting for breath and thinking all was lost until he heard the whine of a helicopter engine starting up.

"You idiots!" he heard Marconi rage. "Where's my gun? Put it in my hand, give it to me! Stop the pilot! He can't leave without us!"

ROON SWIFTLY FED another dart into the air gun and slid the barrel up over the log, squinting through the sites. The first man had barely made it back to the cabin when the door opened inward and another man bolted out and collided with him just as a shot rang out. Both men fell but the second man got up and sprinted toward the chopper, gaining the safety of it before Roon could squeeze off a shot. Was it the pilot? He didn't know. The man on the porch was rolling around, holding his shoulder and cursing. He'd dropped the pistol, and Roon knew he was feeling the combined effects of the tranquilizer and the bullet. Roon heard the chopper's engine starting up. Another gunman burst out the cabin door at a dead run and Roon aimed and squeezed the trigger. This time the dart hit lower in the body. The man broke stride, pulled the dart out and flung it aside with a wild cry, then fired his pistol blindly into the woods before seemingly realizing that the man in the chopper was about to leave without him. He continued toward it and tried to open the side door.

"Stop!" the gunman shouted. "Shut it down or I'll shoot!"

Roon ejected the air cartridge and fed a third dart into the rifle. The sedative wasn't going to work fast enough. The chopper pilot was about to get plugged, but just as the gunman raised the pistol and moved to the front of the chopper, the buffalo came. The ground trembled beneath the pounding of their sharp black hooves and their mighty weight as they approached. The gunman dove beneath the chopper as the small herd swerved past the cabin and kept going toward the old Native American trace that led to the upper range.

Now what? All Roon could do was wait, and hope that tranquilizer worked fast.

BADGER CAUGHT UP with Jimmy just as the buffalo passed the cabin. Jimmy was about to dart from the cover of the woods and run to where he knew Roon was hiding behind the blow down along the creek. He gripped a bow in one hand and had a quiver of arrows slung over a shoulder. When he spotted Badger he looked relieved.

"Roon's behind that log up there by the creek—see him?" Jimmy said, loud enough for Badger to hear him over the chopper. "He shot two men with tranquilizer darts, the ones Jessie uses for the buffalo. One of them's lying on the porch and the other's under the chopper, but Joe's still in the cabin and we don't know how many more there are."

"All right, son," Badger said, squeezing the boy's shoulder. "You stay right here, you hear me? Right here. You see any of the other boys, you keep them in the woods out of sight. Wait till I tell you it's safe, and if you don't hear me say that, don't come out. Stay in the woods and make your way back to the ranch. Understand?" Jimmy nodded vigorously. "These are dangerous men. They'll kill you just as quick as look at you. Don't even think about trying to shoot them with one of your arrows."

He left Jimmy crouched in the safety of the woods and skirted the edge of the clearing. When he was near Roon, the boy looked over his shoulder right at him. Badger made a down gesture with his hand and Roon nodded. Badger pointed to the cabin and then to his eyes. Roon nodded again. *Watch the cabin. Stay put. Understood.*

Badger moved cautiously past Roon's hiding place and upstream about fifty yards, which put him slightly above the cabin and behind the chopper. He was trying to sneak up on the man crouching under the chopper. He had just hunkered down to get the drop on the guy when the cabin door opened and a third gunman bolted out.

WEAK AND DIZZY, still dazed by the blow to his head, Joe rolled over, pushed himself into a sitting position against the wall and found himself staring into the muzzle of Marconi's pistol from just six feet away. Marconi was being braced up by his one remaining gunman, but it was a losing battle. His knees were buckling and the pistol in Marconi's hands shook badly as he tried to aim it at Joe. He leaned one hand on the table and shrugged off his goon. "Get out there, you stupid bastard, and stop the chopper from leaving," he snarled. When the gunman hastily departed, Marconi focused on Joe.

"I'll see you dead before I die," he vowed. "You've been a thorn in my side for years. *Years!* I would have knocked you off a long time ago but Alison begged me not to, not because she loved you, but because she said Ferg needed a legitimate father." Marconi gripped the back of the chair with one hand, while the other struggled to keep the pistol pointed at Joe. "A legitimate father!" he repeated with an ugly laugh that turned into a cough that brought blood to his lips. "Alison said you knew about us. She told me the thought of the two of us being together drove you crazy. You couldn't stand the fact that it was me she loved. That's why nailing me became such an obsession with you, not because I broke all your stupid laws, but because I stole your woman long before you met and married her. Even if you had managed to bag me, it wouldn't have changed the fact that you were never the one she wanted!"

For years, Joe had been trying to bring Marconi down for all the crimes he'd committed—heading up the drug cartel, the weapon smuggling and sex trafficking—but Marconi was right. None of that held a candle to the hatred Joe felt toward him for the affair he'd had with Alison. Joe could only stare at this deranged, wild-eyed, heinous criminal and wait for him to pull the trigger while the turbulent and loveless years of his marriage with Alison, from grandiose wedding day to ugly divorce, burned like wildfire through his mind. Adrenaline flowed through him. He wanted to kill Marconi so badly that he was starting to shake.

"You dumb Irish cop," Marconi sneered. "She was my mole, Ferguson. Your wife was my mole! She told me everything the DEA was up to. *Everything!* All those years she was snitching on you, and you didn't even know it!"

Joe struggled to focus his eyes and rally his strength. "If that's true, if she was so loyal to you, then why'd you kill her?"

Marconi's expression changed from blind fury to blank shock. He wove on his feet and the weight of the weapon in his hand pulled his arm down to his side. *"What?"*

"Alison died of a heroin overdose yesterday. I figured you had your goons kill her just to get to me."

"You're lying." Marconi tried to raise the pistol but his hand was shaking too badly.

Marconi staggered back two steps and collapsed into a chair at the table. "You're lying," he repeated, stunned. "She was just with me in Mexico. I saw her four days ago." The pistol clattered from his hand onto the tabletop. He was staring at the wall but wasn't seeing it. "She was fine then. She told me where I could find you. She told me your sister was getting married, where she lived. We were going to meet back in Mexico once I took care of you..."

Joe heard a soft scraping noise on the cabin roof and kept his eyes on Marconi. "She's dead,

Marconi. And it wasn't just me she snitched on. I learned a lot about you, too. How do you think I managed to crash your little party and shoot you full of holes?"

This was a lie. Alison had left him long before that fateful night.

"Alison would never betray me."

"No? Then how did the feds know where you were hiding out in Mexico?"

"You're a liar!" Marconi lunged to his feet, grabbing for the pistol. Joe pushed off the wall and staggered upright, reaching deep inside of himself for the strength to defeat his hated foe. He knew the odds were against him, but as he launched himself at Marconi, he felt no fear.

He was going to die fighting.

# CHAPTER NINETEEN

BADGER SAW THE third gunman bolt down the cabin steps and head for the chopper at a dead run. He stepped out from behind the chopper and raised his rifle. "Hold it right there!" he shouted over the whine of the engine and the thumping of the chopper blades, trying to keep his eyes on both men at once. "Drop the gun or I'll shoot!"

The gunman under the chopper heard him, rolled over and fumbled for his pistol at the same time the third gunman skidded to a stop, still holding his weapon. Badger stepped away from the helicopter in a manner that allowed him to keep both men in his sights, and at that moment the chopper lifted off the ground. It rose quickly, wasting no time, and took off toward the pass, barely skimming the treetops. The gunman under the chopper was having trouble finding his pistol and Badger stepped forward to kick it away, but his hip gave out and he stumbled, going down hard on one knee. The other gunman made his move, crouching and bringing his weapon to bear on Badger, but before he could pull the trigger he jumped forward with a loud squall, looking behind him in disbelief.

"I've been shot!" he cried out in horror. "I've been shot! There's an arrow sticking in my ass!"

"There'll be another one right quick if you don't do as I say," Badger growled, struggling to his feet. "Drop the gun, mister." He thumbed the hammer of his rifle back. It made a nice loud sound, clicking into position. The gunman froze, then let his pistol fall to the ground. "Kick it away from you. That's right. Now lie down on the ground, facedown, arms out. Do it. *Now!*" Badger wondered if his voice sounded as old as his years, and guessed it probably did, but the man didn't hesitate. He carefully laid himself facedown, arrow sticking out of his ass.

Charlie was working his way up to the cabin from the other side where the lean-to for the horses was attached. Badger waited until he saw the silhouette of Charlie's battered Stetson moving above the roofline of the cabin. He held his breath, glad he wasn't the one trying to step soft and silent on that cabin roof. He and Charlie were too old to be creeping around like scouts, but thanks to the loud altercation coming from within the cabin, Charlie pulled it off. Badger watched as Charlie dropped two ignited sulfur sticks down the chimney and lofted his jacket over the top of the metal stovepipe, effectively stopping the flow of the acrid smoke up the chimney. Then Charlie's hat disappeared from sight.

It didn't take long at all for the sulfurous fumes to back up inside the small cabin. There was coughing from inside and Badger heard Charlie's gravelly voice shout from the far side of the cabin, "We got you surrounded. Come out now with your hands in the air and nobody'll get kilt!"

WHEN THE SULFUR fumes started to fill the air, Joe was locked in a death grip with Marconi, struggling for control of the pistol Marconi held. The Mob boss was weakening, but so was Joe. Neither man spoke. Their energy and efforts were focused solely on the destruction of the other. The table and chairs had been overturned in their violent struggles, and Joe tripped over a chair and shoved Marconi hard against the cabin wall, in more of an off-balance stagger than an intentional body block. His grip was slipping on Marconi's bloody wrist and they were both breathing raggedly. Joe had done a lot of street fighting as a kid and he knew every dirty trick in the book, but so did Marconi. When Marconi pivoted away from the wall, together they staggered over another overturned chair and collapsed to the floor. Marconi landed on top, driving the breath from Joe's struggling lungs.

The pistol went flying but neither man had the strength to lunge for it. Marconi's hands closed around Joe's throat. Joe tried to knife his knee into him, throw him off, but he couldn't. Marconi's hands squeezed, and Joe hit him hard as he could in the chest, where he was certain his bullet had gone. Marconi's grip weakened. Joe hit him again but there was no strength behind the blows. He tried to gouge Marconi's eyes out. Lights began to flash in his own eyes and darkness bled into his world, but then Marconi started coughing. Blood sprayed Joe's face as Marconi's grip weakened more. With a convulsive movement and the last of his strength, Joe threw Marconi off him, scrambling on hands and knees toward the pistol as the room filled with choking fumes. As he picked up the pistol, his one thought was to kill Marconi. Shoot him. But he couldn't even see him. Couldn't breathe. He made it to his feet as he reached the doorway and stumbled onto the porch, tripping blindly over one of Marconi's unconscious gunmen and falling off the narrow porch to land facedown in the dirt.

While Joe struggled to regain his breath, he saw a blur of movement out of the corner of his eye. An old cowboy carrying a revolver that hailed from *Gunsmoke* days came from around the back of the lean-to, trotted up the cabin steps and ducked through the door. Charlie. He wasn't inside for long. He came back out, coughing his lungs up, and when he could speak he knelt beside Joe, rested his hand on Joe's shoulder and said, "It's over, son. Marconi's inside, and I'm pretty sure he's dead."

ROON WAS ALREADY on his feet, crossing the high creek water to join them. He checked immediately on the gunman who was lying on the porch, unmoving. "I used too much tranquilizer," he said to Badger, who held his rifle on the man lying spread-eagle and facedown on the ground. "I was afraid I might've killed him, but he's still breathing."

"Too bad," Badger said. "The other one is, too."

The man at Badger's feet with the arrow in his rear craned his head to look around as the boys gathered in a group around Roon. "They're just a bunch of kids!" he said in disbelief.

"Not all of 'em," Badger growled, brandishing his rifle, "but those kids were plenty man enough to take you down." He nodded to Jimmy, who had appeared, still gripping his bow. "Good shot, son."

Charlie helped Joe off the ground and got him settled on the wall bench before walking toward Badger.

"You bring them ties?" Badger prodded him.

"Yep." Charlie pulled them from his jacket pocket and had commenced fastening the industrial zip ties around the wrists of Marconi's three men and cinching them up tight when the staccato drumming of a horse's hooves coming closer at a rapid pace gave him pause.

They all looked toward the sound as a bay mustang came into sight, running hard. When the horse spotted the group outside the cabin, he sat back on his haunches and came to an abrupt stop. Head flung up, nostrils flaring and flanks heaving, he blew like a deer, a sound that seemed to activate movement on his back. Even as the black-and-red-striped woolen banner settled regally over the horse's rump, it rose up over his withers and they realized there was a rider crouched beneath the blanket. Clinging to the saddle, pale of face with eyes as wild and wide-open as the horse she'd ridden in on, Dani Jardine had arrived.

THE LINE CAMP was nearly half a mile from where Dani and Geronimo had started their wild run, and the distance took no time at all to travel. Dani had zero control over the mustang; all she could do was press herself against his neck and hold on with all the strength she had left. Through a fast motion blur she saw the weather-bleached log cabin by the edge of a creek and a group of men and boys gathering outside. She saw Badger holding a rifle on a man lying prostrate on the ground, and then another man, also on the ground, being patted down by Charlie. Roon stood on the porch holding a rifle. When Geronimo hit the brakes, she nearly flew over his shoulder like a human projectile. The only thing that kept her in the saddle was her death grip on the horn.

She sat up slowly in the momentary stillness following the mustang's abrupt stop, breathless and dazed, registering the scene she'd just ridden into the middle of. Whatever had happened, had happened not long before she'd arrived, but it was over, and she didn't see Joe among the standing. She'd tried to prepare herself for this eventuality, but couldn't accept it. She flung herself out of the saddle, shrugging the blanket off her shoulders as her feet hit the ground. "Joe!" she cried out as she ran toward the cabin, toward the very end of everything that might have been.

At that moment, Badger gestured with his rifle and she saw Joe sitting on the wall bench. She read the ordeal he'd been through in the cuts and bruises and blood on his face, in the dark blood saturating his jacket and the burning look in his dark eyes.

But he was alive! Joe was alive!

Dani didn't remember crossing the distance between them but somehow she was beside him, packing the big folded-up bandanna that Badger handed her against his wound to staunch the bleeding. "He'll be all right—he's tougher'n a range-bred mustang," she heard Badger say. "Just keep the pressure on that wound till the bleeding stops." Her fingers were wet and sticky with Joe's blood. He appeared to be in shock. Dani felt the terrible dry-mouthed fear building inside of her again. One of the boys silently handed her Luther's red-and-black-striped wool blanket and she wrapped it around Joe's shoulders, then he reached his good arm out and pulled her down next to him on the bench. He didn't speak. He didn't need to. He just pulled her close.

Dani kept pressure on the wound for a long time while the group by the cabin averted their eyes and went on quietly with all the things that needed doing to secure Marconi's men. She didn't realize she was crying until Badger handed her another bandanna. "Help's on its way," he said gruffly.

She pulled herself together, for Joe's sake. It

felt like a lifetime had passed since she'd first laid eyes on Molly's brother, yet it had been only days. So much had happened in so short a time. First the mustangs, then Marconi taking Molly and now this. She leaned against Joe and wasn't ashamed of the tears that ran down her cheeks.

THE RISING SUN turned the sky to the east a bright, polished gold. Roon pulled his cell phone out of his jacket pocket and called Pony, who'd been trying to reach him repeatedly for the past hour. He listened for a moment to her rush of frantic words, and then reassured her. "We're all right. We're up at the line camp," he said. "Everyone's okay. Joe's okay. The boys are okay. Badger and Charlie are okay. Dani's here, too, and she's fine. Marconi's dead, and all three of his men are tied up. The Yellowstone Helotours chopper was here, too, but Nash got away and flew it out of here." He listened to her rapid-fire talk awhile longer before she ended the call. Roon slipped the phone back into his pocket and passed his somber gaze around the group.

"That was Pony," he said. "She says the feds, the sheriff, the deputy sheriffs, the Billings and Bozeman police, the warden, the state police, two ambulances, four EMTs and a twelve-member

SWAT team traveling in an armored troop carrier have arrived at the ranch over the past hour. She said the Yellowstone helicopter just landed in the yard and Nash told them what was going on up here. She says they're sending Nash back with a team to secure the prisoners and he'll fly Joe directly to the hospital. Oh, and she says that we're all in real big trouble."

JOE OPENED HIS eyes and stared up at a familiar pattern of acoustic ceiling tiles and thought for one awful moment that he was back in the Providence hospital.

Then he heard his sister's voice.

"Joseph? Joseph, can you hear me?" He turned his head and Molly bent near. Her face was so pale he could count every freckle over the bridge of her nose. "You're in the hospital in Bozeman. The surgeons just fixed up your arm," she told him. "Everything went okay. No bones were broken. You lost a lot of blood, but you're going to be just fine. Mom and Dad are flying out as soon as they can, and they're bringing Fergie with them."

"Ferg?"

Molly nodded. "Yes. He really wanted to come. He misses you, Joseph, and now that Alison's gone, he needs to be with his father." Molly touched his hand. "I'm sorry about Alison."

Joe remembered Marconi's taunting words

back at the line camp, those last few horrible moments of blind fury before he'd tackled Marconi and knocked him to the floor. He'd wanted to tear that evil man apart with his bare hands, and would have, except he'd run out of strength. How could he ever erase Marconi's hateful words from his mind, along with the certain knowledge that Alison had betrayed him, and the sickening suspicion that Ferg might be Marconi's son?

"Everything's going to be all right, Joseph," Molly reassured him.

He felt like he was drifting through a thick fog that was growing darker by the moment. "Dani?"

"She's been here all day. She's waiting right outside. They won't let anyone but immediate family into the recovery room. I tried to get her to go back to our place for some sleep but she won't leave. Just rest, Joseph. You'll see her soon."

Dani was the only person he'd ever told that Ferg wasn't his real son. But nobody could ever know that Ferg might be Marconi's son. It was a secret he'd take to his grave.

# CHAPTER TWENTY

THREE DAYS LATER, Joe was waiting in the hospital lobby when Dani arrived to pick him up. His arm was in a sling and he was pacing impatiently. She swept through the main entrance like a cool Montana breeze and flashed a smile that lit up his world. Her clothing was attorney chic, a classic dark skirt suit with a pale pink blouse and conservative heels that accentuated a pair of very beautiful legs. Her entrance mesmerized everyone in the lobby. She walked right up to him and kissed him on the mouth, and all at once he felt like everything would be okay.

"Hey, cowboy," she said. "Your text came as a complete surprise but it was perfect timing. So they're discharging you early?"

"It was either that or I was going to leave without their permission."

"But you're okay, really and truly?"

"Never better, now that you're here."

She smiled again and took his hand. "My car's out front. Let's go."

"How'd your job interview go this morning?"

he asked as she pulled out of the hospital parking lot.

"It didn't. I drove all the way down here and then called them and canceled. I explained that I appreciated the opportunity to interview for a position but I had too much on my plate right now, and they understood. Yesterday I gave my notice at the law firm in Helena and told them I'd work out whatever time period they needed me to. They came back with an offer to set me up in a satellite office down here and even mentioned a raise in pay. Something for me to think about, for sure."

"I don't blame them for wanting to keep you. What's the news on Shep Deakins's ranch?"

"The results of the water test were good. By the end of June I'll be a ranch owner. Then I'll have to figure out how to go about renewing the leases."

"You'll need all that land for your wild horse refuge," Joe commented.

"Nine hundred acres is just about right," Dani agreed with a smile. "Geronimo's going to be my very first horse once I adopt him. Roon told me I was the first person to ever actually ride him. He said all they'd done was get him used to the saddle and bridle. I was his first rider and he was my very first horseback ride, straight up that mountainside. Hard to believe, really, and somehow we both survived the experience. Anyhow, he's one of the BLM mustangs that's up for adoption. The boys and Pony are planning to round up Custer's last four mares as soon as the snow melts from the pass and move them to the Bow and Arrow temporarily. Pony's given me first dibs on them, once the boys have worked with them a little so they're safe to handle. And she also said that if I wanted her, Custer's daughter was mine to keep. Roon was the one who insisted on that."

"So you'll have a herd of six mustangs right off the bat. Are wild horses still considered mustangs once they've been tamed?"

"That's a question for Jessie—she's the mustang expert." Dani had stopped for a red light. She looked at Joe pensively. "Molly told me Roon and Jimmy could be in some trouble for shooting Marconi's men with tranquilizer darts and arrows. Apparently all three have filed suits against the boys for reckless endangerment."

Joe uttered a short laugh. "That's choice, coming from three kidnappers, drug dealers, sex traffickers and hired assassins."

"Molly said she'd be their attorney if it ever goes before a jury."

"Then they have nothing to fear." Joe stared out the side window as the light changed and Dani proceeded through the intersection.

"Molly's moved her wedding up by two weeks," Dani said. "She probably already told you. Since it's such a small wedding, all she had to do was call a handful of people and tell them the date's been changed because her parents are flying out with your son. When're they arriving?"

"Tomorrow. They're flying into Helena. Molly and I are driving up to meet them."

"That's great. I bet you can't wait to see Ferg."

Joe shifted in his seat and stared broodily out the side window. "Yeah."

Dani cast him a quick sidelong glance. "He's probably still grieving his mother. It'll be good for him to spend time with you."

Joe was so twisted up inside he couldn't respond. The poison Marconi had planted in him was killing him more effectively than any bullet ever could have, but what good would telling Dani do? He had to keep this to himself, learn to live with it.

Dani was outside the town now, driving toward Gallatin Gateway, toward Molly and Steven's house. She cast him a questioning glance, put her signal light on as they approached a scenic turnout, pulled off the road, put the Subaru in Park and cut the engine. She turned in her seat and fixed him with a level gaze. "What is it? What's wrong? Talk to me, Joe."

He shook his head. "Nothing's wrong."

"You've been carrying the world on your shoulders ever since your showdown with Marconi. Tell me what's bothering you."

He looked into her eyes and was instantly trapped. She deserved to know the truth. He looked away from her, out across the distance to the mountain range that walled off the horizon. "Marconi said some things to me before he died. Some heavy things," he began slowly. "Alison was in love with another man before she met me. I knew that, and right after we were married she told me she was pregnant with that man's son. And when I saw the photos of her and Marconi in those gossip rags, I knew they were seeing each other. I should have guessed the rest, put two and two together.

"Marconi meant something to Alison—she saw him just a few days before she died. Apparently she flew to Mexico, to be with him when he was getting patched up from the bullet I put in him. She loved him. And while she was there, she told him where I was. She never loved me. I suspected that on day one of our honeymoon. She married me to save her career and provide her child with a legitimate father. For the next five years she was Marconi's lover and mole. Which makes me the world's biggest fool—and I can live with that, I guess. But it never occurred to me that Marconi might be the father of her child, too."

Dani's dark eyes widened as his words struck home. She sat back in her seat, expelling a big breath. "Wow. So *that's* why you've been so withdrawn." She looked at him again for a long, somber moment. Joe felt the power of her gaze, and suddenly it felt like a thousand pounds of dead weight was being lifted from his shoulders. He could breathe again and the pain was gone.

He wasn't alone anymore.

She reached for his hand. "Listen to me. Marconi's vendetta with you was personal. The things he said to you up on the mountain may or may not have been true. He could have said those things just to hurt you, to twist a knife into you, to destroy you. But either way, his reign is over and his men are all dead or in jail. He can't hurt you anymore. You have to pick up the pieces of your life and move on."

Joe shook his head. "I don't know if I can."

"Of course you can. You have to. You'll go to the airport tomorrow, meet your parents, hug your son and get on with your life." She tightened her grip on his fingers. "Come back with me to Helena, Joe. Spend the night at my place. I'll go with you to the airport tomorrow, and I'll stick around for as long as you need me to."

Joe nodded. There were a thousand things he wanted to say to her, starting with "thank you," but he couldn't manage a single word. Dani just squeezed his hand gently and said, "It's going to be all right, Joe. Everything's going to be fine."

# CHAPTER TWENTY-ONE

DANI DREW THE needle through the delicate fabric and tightened the thread just enough to draw the seam tight. "I'm not used to sewing by hand," she said, frowning a little as she concentrated on the task. "I've been spoiled by my very sophisticated sewing machine, which is set up in a room specifically for sewing, and yet here I am, the day before your wedding, sitting on a bench outside the kitchen at the Bow and Arrow, surrounded by wild horses, buffalo, dairy goats, cow dogs, kids and ranch hands, slaving away on your wedding gown."

"Don't think that I don't appreciate your efforts. A few days ago, I didn't think I'd ever see Joseph alive again, let alone that I'd live long enough myself to get married to Steven." Molly sighed, gathering the loose folds of her wedding dress over her knees to keep the fabric off the worn porch planks. "And now, look at us, sitting here, just like none of it ever happened. My parents are doing the tourist thing in Bozeman and Fergie's down at the corrals having the time of his life with Joseph. I've never seen a happier kid. That hat Roon gave him is the cutest thing. He looks like a pint-size cowboy."

"Being here's good for him. All the activity with the other boys takes his mind off his mother," Dani said, drawing the thread through the fabric again. This sewing task called for tiny stitches, hundreds of them, but it was therapeutic. If only she could stitch her own life together as neatly as Molly's wedding gown. "We'll need to have another fitting today, as soon as I'm done altering this seam."

"Okay," Molly said. "Though I haven't eaten much the past two weeks."

"Babies don't stop growing just because the mother's lost her appetite from being kidnapped and having morning sickness." Dani squinted critically at the tiny row of stitches.

"Steven's returning the blanket to Luther Makes Elk when he picks him up tomorrow to bring him here for the wedding. I'm looking forward to the big barbecue and dancing into the night. Everyone needs to party after what we've been through," Molly said. She sighed again and gazed toward the corrals. "Joseph's been so quiet. That's not like him. I know he's been through so much, but Marconi's dead. He should be relieved that it's over, but something's still bothering him."

"Give him time, Molly," Dani said. "It's been a rough week."

"Is he going back east after the wedding?"

"I don't know."

"You haven't talked about it?"

"No." Tiny stitches, neatly done, one after the other. She concentrated on the task.

"Ask him to stay, Dani. Tell him he needs to raise his son out here, where he can breathe fresh air and ride horses."

"It's his decision. You know that."

Molly made a frustrated sound. "It's obvious you're crazy about each other. You're buying a ranch and you need a partner. You don't want to tackle that project alone. And Joseph needs to settle down, get a boring job and stop getting shot at. Fergie needs a full-time father and he adores Joseph. Joseph has to stay. It would be foolish for him to go back east. *You* have to tell him that. That's what he needs to hear right now. It's probably what's bothering him—he doesn't know what direction to go in."

"I suppose this is legal advice that you'll be charging me for?"

"I just want you and Joseph to be happy," Molly said. "Here he comes. Tell him how you feel," she urged. "He's a man, and men can be so thick-headed. They need to be prodded, especially the ones like Joseph."

Dani shifted her gaze to watch the man and the boy walking toward her and felt a sudden, painful wrench to her heartstrings that brought the sting of tears to her eyes. She was remembering the night Joe had spent with her in Helena, how she'd fixed him supper and how they'd sat late into the night, talking through all the traumas of the past week until Joe had fallen asleep on the couch, his arm around her shoulders.

Then the next day, how Ferg had spotted Joe at the airport gate, how he'd cried out, "Daddy!" as he pulled away from Joe's parents, running toward his father with his little arms outstretched. How Joe had swept him up into a big bear hug. And most of all, she remembered the look on Joe's face as he held his son in his arms, all the doubts he'd harbored banished forever by the love he felt for that little boy. She looked back down at the sewing and concentrated hard, blinking to clear her vision. She didn't look up again until he was standing at the foot of the porch steps.

"Walk with me," he said.

Molly gathered the gown from Dani and stood. "C'mon, Fergie," she said to the adorable little boy wearing a felt Stetson that was a bit too large for him. "Come hang out with your aunt Molly. I'll show you the prettiest little filly down in the barn—it's Dani's horse. Just let me put this gown inside and we'll go down and see her. She's a tiny thing, all legs and ears and big eyes, cuter than a speckled pup, so Badger says. Dani helped her all the way down the mountain, can you imagine? We're all trying to come up with the perfect name for her, maybe you can help. C'mon."

"Daddy?" Ferg said.

"It's okay, Ferg. Go with Molly."

Ferg followed Molly inside the kitchen, and when the screen door banged shut after them, Dani met Joe's eyes. She rose to her feet and took his extended hand as she descended the steps.

Hand in hand they walked toward the creek in the hazy diaphanous light of a late-spring afternoon. He led her down beside the creek and they sat on a bench hewn from one big log, listening to the rushing water. Joe bent his head and examined the way their fingers intertwined. "I wanted to thank you for everything you've done for me these past few days. For taking me home with you after I got out of the hospital, for making me feel like everything would be okay and for sticking around when I picked Ferg up at the airport.

"You were right," he said. "No matter what's happened, Ferg's still my son and he always will be. When he was a baby I changed his diapers, fed him, burped him, sat up nights with him when he was sick. I knew all along he wasn't my biological kid, but I loved him as if he was. I was there when he took his first step, right into my arms. *Daddy* was his first word. I stuck it out with Alison for five years because I loved that kid." He looked at her. "I still do, and I always will."

Dani smiled. "He lights up like a Christmas tree when you're around, and I know just how he feels. This has been one crazy week, Joe Ferguson, and I wouldn't want to repeat it, but I'll be sorry when you leave." She felt sick with longing and didn't want to make a fool of herself, but maybe Molly was right. Maybe she just needed to say how she felt.

"Funny you should mention leaving," Joe said. "I got two calls this morning. First was from my boss back in Providence. Wanted me to know he was recommending me for promotion. Said I'd be getting a pay raise."

Dani felt her hopes for the future plummet into a dark abyss. She forced a smile. "That's great news. Congratulations, Joe, you deserve it."

"I told him thanks, but I didn't think I'd be going back east."

Dani's heart skipped a beat. Had she heard him right?

"Right after that chat with my boss, Sheriff Conroy called. Told me Kurt had unexpectedly quit as deputy sheriff and taken a job at a used-car dealership."

"Did you mention our visit to Kurt and Josie's place?"

"No, I thought discretion was the better part of valor. I did call Ben Comstock and filled him in. I thought it was best to stay out of the whole mess, but I'm pretty sure Kurt's our shooter. Trying to get back at Josie for leaving him. Comstock said he would talk to both Josie and Kurt, and he was going to follow up with Sheriff Conroy. Let him handle it from here."

"I think that's a good idea," Dani said.

"Anyhow, Conroy told me I am overqualified for the deputy sheriff's position, the pay is lousy, the hours long and there is a lot of territory to cover, but if I sign on with his department, there's a chance I could pick up his job when he retires in the fall."

Dani stared, incredulous. "You mean, he called to offer you a *job*? Are you thinking of taking it?"

"Yeah, actually, I am. See, I was told if you stayed out here long enough to wear out a pair of shoes, you'd never want to leave, and this morning I noticed the stitching in my left shoe was blown. That was a sure sign. The other thing is, Ferg wants to be a cowboy when he grows up, and this is where all the cowboy action is," Joe said. "But those aren't the only reasons. I want to see what you do with Shep's ranch. I want to watch you create your mustang refuge. I don't know what the future holds, but I want to be a part of your life, Dani. I'm not a rancher or a cowboy, but I can learn."

Dani looked at him straight on. "What about wanting to stay unbranded? Untamed like those wild mustangs? What about wanting your freedom?"

Joe looked down at their intertwined fingers again. "While I was driving out here with Ferg they played a song on the radio by the Eagles. 'Desperado.' I was listening to the lyrics and thinking they paralleled my life. Maybe it's time I came down from my fences and opened the gate."

Dani could scarcely breathe. "You're sure?"

"Sure as I've ever been," he said. "I don't want to go through life alone. And I want to help you out with Shep's place. I'm used to lousy pay and long hours, and once my arm heals a little more, I can haul a lot of junk and help you clean up the place. Just don't ask me to ride those wild horses of yours! And if there ever comes a time when you don't want me hanging around anymore, just say so."

Dani didn't answer, but her actions left no doubt in Joe's mind that she definitely wanted him to stick around. When they finally came up for air, he gently smoothed her hair back from her face. "I've been crazy about you since the first time I saw you."

"I was so afraid you didn't feel the same way," Dani said.

"We have about three hours until Ramalda rings the dinner bell."

"Three whole hours. Whatever shall we do?"

"I can think of a few things."

"What about your arm?"

"My arm wasn't one of the things I was thinking about," Joe said. He took her hand and they rose to their feet. "C'mon. Let's take a walk and see if we can find something wild."

# *EPILOGUE*

"STOP YOUR FIDGETING, Molly, I'm almost done," Dani pleaded as her fingers deftly fastened the endless row of pearl buttons that ascended Molly's back from waist to shoulder blades. "And hold your breath. Please don't breathe."

"Easy for you to say," Molly said. "This dress is way too tight. I'll never make it through the ceremony without fainting."

"I told you we should have had another fitting yesterday."

"You disappeared with Joseph," Molly returned. "You almost missed supper you were gone so long. Where'd you go, by the way?"

"Hold your arms up a little more. Higher… Okay, that's good. Two more buttons and I'm done. There!" Dani stepped back.

"You're glowing," Molly said. "You've been glowing since last night."

"Turn around slowly," Dani ordered, giving the gown a critical appraisal as Molly followed orders. Through the open window came the sounds of a Bow and Arrow gathering. People talking, dogs barking, a horse whinnying. A car door slammed and Dani glanced out the window. "Luther Makes Elk just arrived with Steven. Don't you dare look! If Steven sees you before the ceremony, it's bad luck."

"Is he wearing the black tuxedo?"

"Yes."

"Is he handsome?"

"How could that man of yours be anything other than handsome?"

Molly closed her eyes and heaved a deep sigh, rapturous enough to create a ripping noise in the back of the gown. Tiny pearl buttons scattered over the floor like buckshot. She froze, eyes wide-open. "Did I just…?"

"Yes, you did," Dani said.

Molly looked over her shoulder into the door-length mirror with an expression of horror. *"Oh, no!"*

"I *told* you not to breathe."

"Do something. I can't get married with my gown hanging wide-open in the back!"

Dani leaned her palms on the window ledge and looked down at the gathering. The caterers had set up their barbecue in the traditional spot; a three-piece country-western band was out of sight below her on the porch but she could hear them tuning their guitars in preparation for their strummed version of the "Wedding

March." She saw the entire population of Katy Junction, approximately thirty people, gathered in small groups, socializing. She saw the boys standing with Charlie and Badger, young and old fidgeting visibly in their best clothing. She saw Joe, with his parents and Ferg, talking to Pony and Caleb. Joe spotted her leaning out the window. He nodded and grinned. She grinned back, blushing furiously. She spotted Steven, the bridegroom, handsome in his tuxedo, and Luther Makes Elk standing at his side, dressed in his ceremonial attire with the folded red-and-black wool blanket draped over his arm.

"Something borrowed…" Dani said softly to herself. She moved away from the window and toward the door. "Wait here, I'll be right back," she said to Molly.

She raced down the back stairs into the kitchen, where Ramalda was scrubbing the counters and grumbling about not having anything to do because the caterers had put her out of a job. Pushing out the kitchen door with a squeak and a bang, she dodged past the plucking and strumming band members and trotted down the porch steps to where Steven and Luther Makes Elk solemnly watched her approach. She came to a stop in front of them, a little out of breath. "Molly's almost ready, but there's a small problem."

Luther nodded his head and held out the blanket. "I thought she might need this."

Dani accepted it with a grateful nod. "Thank you."

Back upstairs in the bedroom she draped the blanket over Molly's shoulders, then picked up the bridal bouquet of wildflowers that Pony had made and placed it in Molly's hands. "You look beautiful," she said as the band started playing what sounded like a mariachi wedding march.

"Tell me what happened between you and Joseph yesterday."

Dani shook her head. "Today's your day, Molly, and Steven's waiting."

"Give me a hint."

"Okay, just one. Joe's not going back east. He and Ferg are staying. I'll tell you the rest after the ceremony. Right now it's time for you to marry the man you adore."

Molly flung her arms around Dani with a cry of delight, oblivious to the sound of ripping fabric as the ruched panel Dani had worked so hard on the day before gave way. "I *knew* the two of you were made for each other! And I'm so glad Joseph's staying. This is the best wedding present ever. Thank you!"

There was a tap at the door. Molly's father poked his head in and gave his daughter a proud, paternal smile. "Sorry to intrude, but the maid of honor's being requested to make her appearance," he said to Dani. To his daughter he said, "It's time." If he noticed the red-and-black-striped blanket draped, cape-like, over his daughter's wedding gown, the pearl buttons scattered on the floor or the tears streaking his daughter's carefully applied makeup, he gave no sign. Dani swiftly repaired Molly's face, adjusted her gown, straightened the blanket over her shoulders, then edged around him and descended the kitchen stairs in a breathless rush, coming face-to-face with Joe on the bottom step.

"I was just coming to get you," he said.

Dani stepped into his embrace with a smile. "You got me, cowboy. I'm all yours."

\* \* \* \* \*

# Get 2 Free Books,
## Plus 2 Free Gifts—
### just for trying the Reader Service!

HRLP17R2

# Get 2 Free Books,
## Plus 2 Free Gifts—
### just for trying the Reader Service!

### HOMETOWN HEARTS ♥

**YES!** Please send me **The Hometown Hearts Collection** in Larger Print. This collection begins with 3 FREE books and 2 FREE gifts in the first shipment. Along with my 3 free books, I'll also get the next 4 books from the Hometown Hearts Collection, in LARGER PRINT, which I may either return and owe nothing, or keep for the low price of $4.99 U.S./ $5.89 CDN each plus $2.99 for shipping and handling per shipment*. If I decide to continue, about once a month for 8 months I will get 6 or 7 more books, but will only need to pay for 4. That means 2 or 3 books in every shipment will be FREE! If I decide to keep the entire collection, I'll have paid for only 32 books because 19 books are FREE! I understand that accepting the 3 free books and gifts places me under no obligation to buy anything. I can always return a shipment and cancel at any time. My free books and gifts are mine to keep no matter what I decide.

262 HCN 3432 462 HCN 3432

| Name | (PLEASE PRINT) | |
|------|----------------|--|
| Address | | Apt. # |
| City | State/Prov. | Zip/Postal Code |

Signature (if under 18, a parent or guardian must sign)

### Mail to the **Reader Service:**

**IN U.S.A.:** P.O. Box 1867, Buffalo, NY. 14240-1867
**IN CANADA:** P.O. Box 609, Fort Erie, Ontario L2A 5X3

* Terms and prices subject to change without notice. Prices do not include applicable taxes. Sales tax applicable in NY. Canadian residents will be charged applicable taxes. This offer is limited to one order per household. All orders subject to approval. Credit or debit balances in a customer's account(s) may be offset by any other outstanding balance owed by or to the customer. Please allow 4 to 6 weeks for delivery. Offer available while quantities last. Offer not available to Quebec residents.

> **Your Privacy**—The Reader Service is committed to protecting your privacy. Our Privacy Policy is available online at www.ReaderService.com or upon request from the Reader Service.
>
> We make a portion of our mailing list available to reputable third parties that offer products we believe may interest you. If you prefer that we not exchange your name with third parties, or if you wish to clarify or modify your communication preferences, please visit us at www.ReaderService.com/consumerschoice or write to us at Reader Service Preference Service, P.O. Box 9062, Buffalo, NY. 14240-9062. Include your complete name and address.